# Dreams

(Dream•Research•Employing•Astral• Manipulation•Strategy)

## By

## Mike Walsh

Deep Indigo Books
Published by Indigo Sea Press
Winston-Salem

Deep Indigo Books
Indigo Sea Press
PO Box 26701
Winston-Salem, NC 27114

First Deep Indigo Books edition published
May, 2020
Deep Indigo Books, Moon Sailor and all production design are trademarks of Indigo Sea Press, used under license.

For information regarding bulk purchases of this book, digital purchase and special discounts, please contact the publisher at indigoseapress@gmail.com

Manufactured in the United States of America
ISBN 978-1-63066-504-3

"We are such stuff as
dreams are made on..."
—*William Shakespeare*

"No one ever dies in a dream."
—*Jenni Butler, protagonist*

"They do now!"
—*Elymas, the demon*

# Chapter One

Jenni Butler was crashing at her younger sister's house in Queens, a borough in New York City, until she found an apartment in Manhattan. At the moment, she had no place to live. After seven years in a failing marriage, she had finally left her husband, Ed, and abruptly quit what many considered a dream life in Connecticut. She accepted her sister's offer to stay with her until she relocated.

Jenni, four years older than Lottie, who had two young-ones asleep upstairs, was in her mid-thirties and childless. The ladies were watching television while waiting in the foyer for Lottie's husband to pull his car out of the garage. This evening he was prepared to drive Jenni into Manhattan's Upper East Side to keep an appointment to view an apartment. For the past week Jenni had been searching for an apartment to fit her budget.

The ongoing search was a dreamless nightmare. Jenni had moved out of an upscale community in a suburban town in Connecticut. Because of her pending divorce, she had changed a seven-year sheltered lifestyle for one that does not indulge such luxury. A small New York City apartment was vastly different from a four bedroom colonial with four thousand square feet of living space. Besides which, renting an East Side apartment on the income she earned was pushing her limit.

Bill Chambers sounded the SUV's horn from the driveway.

"Lottie," Jenni said, "you don't have to do this. Bill doesn't have to drive me into the city. I can take the subway."

"We've been over this," said Lottie. "You have to meet the building manager at eight. By the time you've finished seeing the apartment and catch the train back here it'll be after ten. It's no trouble for Bill to drive you into the city."

"But I've imposed enough on you guys already," Jenni said. "Letting me stay here at your place until I locate. You've been too gracious."

Jenni climbed into the SUV next to Bill Chambers.

"Seat belt on," Bill said. "I'd have to give you a ticket if you didn't," he quipped.

1

"Once a cop, always a cop," said Lottie, standing in the doorway, chuckling softly.

Jenni, she thought, was an enigma. Trouble seemed to follow her. Things were never simple or well defined for her sister. Her problems existed for a long time. Because the two girls had been very close while growing up, they shared intimacies that transcended being mere siblings. Yet the two were very different people. While Jenni suffered and agonized through various phases of her life, Lottie was more concerned with the next boy she dated.

Oddly, their differences did not affect their companionship nor impair their ability to relate to one another on practically every level. Their rapport was borne of a mutual understanding of each other's goals and a respect for each one's needs. Now Jenni was totally immersed in her personal tribulations.

It came as a shock to Lottie that Jenni had come to a parting with her husband. Lottie had considered Ed Butler a perfect "catch." He seemed the ideal husband, a good provider, handsome, a man on the way up in business with apparently no limitations. Lottie wondered if the young Jenni, the girl who always seemed to be beyond the reality that surrounded her, had interfered with the harmony of her marriage. Lottie wondered if Ed Butler was completely at fault.

Jenni nurtured a secret side to her personality, part of her that had always managed to escape Lottie's comprehension, a part she kept all to herself. Jenni was a dreamer. Daydreams, illusions, fantasies. Lottie couldn't understand Jenni's need to escape her reality. Why was the imagined world so much better than the real one? Jenni was obsessed with the idea that the ability to dream could alter one's life.

Scary, Lottie remembered. Jenni had frightened her a few times when they were younger. Once, in particular, when she and Jenni had been studying together, Jenni had slipped into a trance. She stared blankly past her. Lottie waited quietly for Jenni to return to her, when she had the strangest sensation that she could visualize Jenni's thoughts. She was seeing Jenni's daydream in her own mind. She screamed and woke Jenni.

Yes, she thought, Jenni was definitely an enigma.

It took Bill Chambers only thirty-five minutes to reach their destination, a fourteen-story red brick building near the Fifty-Ninth

Street Bridge. As they turned onto the targeted street Jenni tried to pick out the apartment she sought, knowing it was on the sixth floor. She grimaced, thinking her effort tonight might be futile. She could hardly afford the rent on this place without her share of assets from the sale of the Connecticut house she owned with her ex. Her salary as an editorial assistant on a weekly women's magazine wouldn't increase enough in the near future to swing this place. No, she could not cut it on her salary alone. The money had to come from Ed.

Although divorce was her initiative, uncertainty overwhelmed her. Independence did not seem as ideal as it had before. Escaping the alienation of life with Ed had seemed the only goal that mattered. Now she wondered if she had merely created a new set of obstacles to overcome.

Bill Chambers left Jenni in front of the building's entrance. "Do you want me to keep you company?" he asked her.

"No. I'll be fine," she said, exuding confidence.

"All right, then. I'll drive around until I find a parking space. I'll give you about half an hour. Okay?"

"Sounds good."

Jenni rang the night manager's bell as her brother-in-law's SUV went down the street. A middle-aged, portly man in a rumpled blue suit admitted her through the outer entrance.

"It's on the sixth floor," he informed her.

She followed him to the apartment. It was exactly what she had in mind. She wanted to sign a lease immediately. The electricity was off in the apartment but there was still enough light coming through the windows to see the layout. As she suspected, both the living room and bedroom windows looked out to a view of the East River.

I'll take it, she muttered to herself.

"Did you say something?" asked the building manager.

"No."

"Well, then, what do you think?"

"I like it very much. But I'll have to get back to you."

In the lobby he handed her his card. "Call me right away. This place won't last."

"Thank you," Jenni said, hiding the disappointment she felt with a weak smile.

She watched the manager go back to his lobby office, as she turned and exited the building, hoping Bill Chambers wasn't parked too far away. It had taken her no more than a half hour.

As she stepped to the sidewalk what she saw hit her like a sudden mule kick to the stomach.

* * *

Bill Chambers decided to circle the block since there were no parking spaces on the street. On his third pass through the surrounding streets he found a spot two blocks away.

He parked and walked back. As he turned the corner, an incredible and dangerous circumstance exploded before his eyes near the building Jenni Butler was visiting. A man, clothed in a dark suit, came from the shadows, raised a pistol and opened fire at a man and woman walking towards him. It happened in an instant.

"What the hell!" Chambers swore. He reacted instinctively, drew the off-duty .38 caliber piece he carried in a holster at the small of his back and moved swiftly forward. He saw the crime was in full view, even though he was half a block away. At the precise moment that he burst forward he saw Jenni Butler come out of the building entrance and walk into the murder scene. She screamed and ducked back into the building entryway. The murderer saw her and whipped off a fast shot.

Bill Chambers increased his pace.

A taxicab, driving by, stopped suddenly. The cabby jumped out wielding a wrench, screaming at the assassin as Bill closed on them. The gunman dropped the cabbie with a single shot.

Bill Chambers anticipated the gunman's actions and ducked between two parked cars just as a shot fired at him slammed into the windshield of the car behind him. He peeked out, saw the assassin turn to run, and drew down on him, returning gunfire. Have to be careful, Chambers thought. Innocent people might come into the line of fire on a city street. The gunman started to run. Chambers followed, sprinting toward the action. The murderer cut through the parked cars and across traffic as Chambers got to the fallen victims. He stepped past them and turned to the building entrance. Jenni stood up when she saw him.

"Stay there," Bill Chambers commanded. "You'll be safe."

He went back to the fallen bodies and checked them for signs of life. Too late. All three victims were dead. He then turned and sprinted in the direction the killer had gone, his gun in his right hand held down, pointed at the street. Within a block he knew that the killer had escaped.

# Chapter Two

He was a dangerous and deadly man. His name was Johnnie Limbo.

He had killed before and always covered himself, error-free. Tonight, though, he made a serious mistake.

He behaved more like an amateur than the professional murderer he was. He had staked out his target for two days, studying the man's habits, and decided to hit him at night, near the apartment house in Manhattan where he lived. It was a mistake.

Limbo was the perfect assassin. He lacked conscience and killed with absolute disdain. He did not take chances and considered killing merely a business function. He was a loner who trusted no one and never had to face betrayal. Limbo was born into a family of utter turmoil and never knew the father who ran off or the mother who faded from his life when he was a child. Consigned to an orphanage and trapped in "Limbo," his nickname fit.

A man without conscience, he learned early on to commit any act of violence when it suited him. The contracts came from all over the country, organized crime, legitimate businesses, government agencies. He lived alone in an upscale apartment in Manhattan. The right people always knew how to get in touch with him through a series of complicated, cryptic steps. He was paid well and invested his money. He had come a long way from the penniless urchin of his youth.

Still in his early thirties, he had already dispatched over two-dozen human lives on contract. His appearance of apparent innocence was a facade that concealed this diabolical murderer.

This night he waited in the dark for the target to return home from an engagement. The man would be alone. Limbo would step up to the victim, drop him instantly and slip away into the night.

But something went wrong.

For one thing, the target had a woman with him. Limbo could not wait. The opportunity and setting were perfect. He had been paid to eliminate this man within a time frame and only two days remained on the contract. It had to be now. He resolved instantly to kill them both.

He stepped out of his hiding place and blocked the sidewalk where they were walking. There was no one else near them. In his peripheral view he saw a couple turning the corner of the street, but they were too far away to identify him.

Now or never. From a shoulder holster he lifted the Walther PK automatic he had fitted with a silencer, leveled it at the horrified couple and fired one shot at each of them. He aimed directly at the chest area. The silencer spurted twice and the couple fell to the concrete. On contact, the hollow-point bullets burst their hearts apart. He stood over them and unloaded another shot into each brain.

Then he heard the scream.

He turned to see an attractive young woman standing by the apartment house entryway. She must have just come out of the front door. She was staring straight at him, screaming. He could see her face as well as she saw his in the entrance light.

She turned, reacting quickly, and ducked back into the apartment house. He fired off a quick shot that chipped the brick wall where she had been standing and started after her.

Got to kill her quick, he thought. She can identify me. My face will be sealed in her memory. Got to kill her.

But a taxicab was coming up the street at the moment that he had fired at her. Farther down the street, he spotted one man running toward him. For an instant, he was tempted to plunge into the building and find her, but thought better of it. He didn't have time to hunt for her. He had made his quota of mistakes for one day. The cab and the oncoming figure were getting closer. He turned to run down the street away from the scene.

Got to move out, he thought. A few turns down a few streets and he would be safe. It was easy to get lost in Manhattan.

Suddenly the taxicab screeched to a halt alongside him. The cabby leaped out of the driver's side holding a wrench in his hand.

"Hey you!" he called to Limbo. "Hold it there!"

The cabby ran around the front of his vehicle and cut Limbo off. He was a big man, tall as Limbo, but broader and much heavier. And there was that guy closing on him from the other end of the street, now wielding a gun. Must be a cop, he thought.

"Where the hell do you think you're going?" the cabby yelled.

Limbo calmly fired a shot into the man's chest, dropping him instantly. Then he turned and snapped a shot at the man with the gun. The running man ducked behind a car. Limbo holstered the Walther and bolted away. As he passed the entrance to the building, he briefly turned and looked back in that direction. There she was, the woman who saw the killings, crouched in a corner of the vestibule, partially concealed by a large potted plant, and locked out by the main interior entry doors. This time he saw her face clearly. Short brown hair, wide round eyes, heart shaped face.

He reached for his pistol. Kill her now, his mind roared. But a gunshot cracked the air. The man behind him had fired a shot, missing Limbo, reminding him that he had no time. He moved swiftly, bolted through parked cars, crossed the street and ran.

Later, when he got a safe distance away, he stopped in a small, crowded bar and quickly downed two scotches. The girl's face stuck in his mind. Witness. She was a witness. Never had such a thing happened to him. Certainly, she would remember his face as he remembered her image so perfectly. He must silence her. He would pick his time, but eventually he would find her.

\* \* \*

Two years ago, Limbo got into a bar-fight while heavily imbibing and was thrown into a lockup in lower Manhattan. Before he was booked, he was miraculously set free by a mysterious man named Elymas who simply appeared one night in the holding cell. It was the strangest event ever to have occurred in Limbo's abnormal life. The cell somehow became unlocked and both men simply walked out unseen in the face of all the guards they passed. Other incarcerated men in the large cell never noticed that Limbo had left.

When asked about the fact that they had merely walked out of prison without being noticed, Elymas, the strange, enigmatic man who freed him, told him that they moved ahead of the guards' perception of them by minutes. Although not certain of what that meant, Limbo went with him and became his hireling. His mentor controlled him both mentally and physically. He did what he was told, killing, brutalizing. He felt safe with Elymas until a rueful day in Maine, two years ago, when Elymas disappeared abruptly, not to return. It was then Limbo reverted to form once again, surviving on his previous independent ability, killing on contract.

\* \* \*

Weeks later, even while he was buried in the embraces of a high-priced call girl Limbo had a sense of being observed. Something seemed wrong. All day long, he felt someone was watching him. He left the girl, caught a cab back to his apartment. He decided to get out of town. Immediately. Pack some clothes and catch an Amtrak to Chicago. He always liked the windy city. He could get lost for a while. Just in case.

He never made it to his apartment. Two men, both wearing dark blue suits, looking like average business executives, caught him coming out of the cab. They took him from each side, pinning his arms. Before he could get the hidden Beretta out of its holster, he felt a needle sink into his arm.

"What the fuck...?" was all he could manage to say before he lost consciousness.

\* \* \*

When he awoke, Limbo was in a white room on a white bed. There was nothing else in the room but a chair. The light from the ceiling was a bare bulb that burned his eyes. He got up groggily and tried the door. It was locked. He sat in the chair and rubbed his eyes. His head hurt. He had been drugged. He felt for the Beretta. It was gone.

He realized immediately the men who took him were professionals. This was not the work of bunglers. Someone *had* been following him. Police? FBI? He couldn't guess. Friends or relatives of someone he had knocked off? Could be.

After a while the door opened and the same two men who had grabbed him entered the room. Another man, slim, short gray hair, came in behind them. They stepped aside and let him pass.

"I'm Clayton Bancock," the gray-haired man said to Limbo. "We've detained you for a short period of time. You'll be staying here with us."

"Why?" Limbo said. "What the hell is going on? Who are you?"

"You'll be working for us."

A sarcastic grin cracked Limbo's face. "I guess I know who you are, then," he snickered. "I probably already work for you."

"You'll work in a different way," Bancock said somberly. "You are going to be involved in a new experiment."

"Like what?"

"You'll know soon enough. It will take a while to get you ready."

"What if I say no? I'm good at what I do. I don't like changing my methods."

"You'll cooperate with us, Limbo, or you'll go over. We can lay a dozen murders at your feet. Some states will want to burn you. Let's just pick one. What about your girlfriend, Gloria? We know you killed her."

"If I go down so will you," Limbo threatened.

"Don't delude yourself. Who would you name as an accomplice?"

Limbo pondered the question for a moment. "What the hell do you want of me?" he questioned. "There are plenty of others you can get."

"Your time has just about run out, Limbo. The FBI is on to you. Your life expectancy is limited. You'll do what we tell you and there's nothing you can do about it."

"You're FBI? CIA?" Limbo guessed.

"Just make yourself comfortable," Bancock said bluntly. "Don't give us trouble and you will enjoy your stay."

"Here? This room?" Limbo looked around the spare room. "In this place?"

"No. We've got much better accommodations."

Limbo was brought to a room where he was immediately tested. A team of pseudo-scientists worked on him with flash cards, assessing his cognitive powers. He was tested for remote viewing, telekinesis, and precognition. Who or what did they think he was? Even though he believed his efforts had failed, he apparently passed their tests.

He was taken again to a small room and a tiny metallic object no larger than a grain of rice was implanted in his head. When he awoke he felt the area on his skull where there was a small bandage behind his left ear. Something planted in his skull, his brain? For what purpose? Who were they and what good was he to them?

Limbo was placed in a private apartment on the fourth floor of the facility. He was given clean clothes; a light-blue outfit that resembled an orderly's uniform and a pair of slippers. He felt he was either a patient or a prisoner.

He was told to obey all commands without dispute. Limbo was no fool. He did what they told him. He assumed that a secret arm of the CIA or some other government agency held him. Knowing how they worked, he knew his life was not sacrosanct. If he did not escape he was going to die in this building.

He was informed that his planned function was to participate in an experiment involving sleep. He was to receive commands while he slept which involved complete acceptance in his subconscious. Something happened to Limbo when he was hooked to the monitoring systems in the "sleep" lab. Something strange. He felt sudden ebullience, a sense of magnificent euphoria. Cold electrodes were connected to his chest, arms, fingers and an IV unit fed serum into his bloodstream. At first he didn't like what was happening. He didn't know what was expected of him other than sleep.

Confined to his lodging, his universe limited to the boundaries of plaster walls, TV shows and a limited selection of reading material, his mind wandered. He thought immediately of the girl with whom he was obsessed. Eventually, she was going to testify against him. Limbo thought constantly about her. In his mind, she remained a threat. She had eluded him. She remained the one recurring torment that dominated his thoughts. Someday she would recognize him and identify him.

He could still see her face as clearly as he had the night of the murders. He thought of her so often he had burned the image of her in his mind. His subconscious knew her well. He began to dream of her. If he could put the pieces together, he might be able to find her.

# Chapter Three

**One Year Later**

The sight of him overwhelmed Jenni Butler. His extreme good looks were deceitful. He seemed unreal, with movie-star dazzle. The blond hair, streaking back from a widow's peak, complemented an Adonis nose over the stern lip and square, strong chin. High cheekbones framed a face that she could not hope to duplicate in her wildest fantasy. The deep eyes burned into her psyche.

She saw him on the Madison Avenue bus. From her seat near the center of the crowded vehicle, she felt his probing stare demanding her attention, overpowering her and forcing a confrontation. She turned and their eyes met and held for a brief instant.

She watched him leave the bus. As he entered an office building, he turned and glanced again in her direction, as if he knew he was being watched. Caught staring, she quickly turned away, avoiding his piercing eyes.

Yes, he certainly was God-awful good looking. She imagined immediately having him in her bed. The bonding would be perfect. He was in his early thirties, she presumed, probably close to her own age, and her own slim attractiveness would enhance their coupling.

She was so much a slave to the fantasy she almost passed her stop. She jumped up quickly and ran to the rear door just before it closed, heading to her office. Her imaginings of the man on the bus seduced her and her day disappeared in a seeming instant.

That night she and a friend, Toni, entered a club called *The End* in the "Meat-Packing District" in lower Manhattan. It exploded in sound and light, a kaleidoscope of colors and noise. The crush of people was overwhelming. The girls pushed their way to the bar. Drinks in hand, they moved to the least crowded corner.

All around them the place pulsed with human energy. The strobe lights and lasers exaggerated the movements of the dancers, making them flicker like apparitions in garish color within a silent film. Jenni watched the dancers on the floor, transfixed by their movements and the driving beat from the quadraphonic sound system.

And suddenly she saw him, the man from the bus. The divine one. Dancing. In the middle of the floor. But he wasn't dancing. He stood there stiffly as the horde whirled around him.

She stood up quickly, trying to get a better view.

A guy came out of the crowd and moved in close to the girls. He took Toni's arm and together they disappeared into the crowd. Jenni flashed a smile at her departing friend. It didn't take long for her turn to come. As she watched Toni depart, she turned and walked right into him, the good-looking blond guy from the bus.

Her heart leaped into her throat.

The music started again. Awkwardly surveying each other, neither speaking nor moving, both knew this was meant to be.

They danced and the crowd of writhing bodies around her disappeared. She had ascended to a new high and surrendered herself to this glorious stranger. The world suddenly became a dizzying affair as she spun to the beat of the music aptly led by his confident movements. Would he leave when the dance ended? Off to greener pastures and better pickings? The moment passed as the music ended. He would turn and go. But no ... he was walking with her across the dance floor. She had to go with him. She was impelled to obey.

At the bar they sipped their drinks.

"I saw you on the bus this morning," he said.

"Yes. I remember." How could she not remember? His face was all too familiar.

"It seems I know you. We were destined to meet, you know."

"I know," she replied. She must be dreaming. He could not be saying these things.

"My place or yours?" he said with a confidence that implied acceptance was a foregone conclusion.

"Mine," she answered without thinking. Why her place, she wondered. Was she reluctant to go to his place?

They pushed through the crowd toward the exit. The trip to Jenni's apartment was a blur. Suddenly they were there as if no distance existed between the club and this ultimate rendezvous. Her attention was focused on this man. She couldn't remember the journey at all.

His lovemaking proved to be all she imagined. He knew the territory. She gave herself over to him totally and he took her to depths of pleasure she had only dreamed of. He devoured her. She was limp and exhausted when he finished. She lay naked on her bed, her body still tingling. She watched his every move. He put on his pants and stood at the double window that looked out over a courtyard in the rear of the building. He threw both windows open and stood, staring out at the night.

He turned and came back across the room to her, moving smoothly, unfaltering. What more can he do, she wondered, suddenly excited again. He paused for a moment, standing over her, looking down at her nakedness. He scooped her up in his arms and carried her across the room.

What is he doing? Where is he taking me? What can he do that he hasn't already done?

"What are you doing?" she asked, her voice suddenly laced with anxiety.

He carried her quickly to the open windows, paused for an instant, balancing himself.

It was then that panic took over. She looked into his eyes. And suddenly she knew. Reality kicked in. She recognized him.

"It's you!" she cried. "Oh God! You killed those people!" Why had she not recognized him immediately? What was happening?

"*Now* you know me," he said calmly and threw her out into the night.

She screamed. Fear raged through her body, clutched at her throat. I'm falling! I'll be killed!

The air raced around her naked body as she plummeted to the concrete, three floors below.

# Chapter Four

Jenni Butler was jolted into consciousness. She awoke with a fright that stunned her. A scream stuck in her throat. She sucked air in terrified gasps. Had she screamed?

God! She thought, was it a dream?

She was awake and unhurt, on her hands and knees though, looking down at the floor next to her bed and completely naked.

She raised her head and looked around. The familiar surroundings looked undisturbed. The windows were closed. There was no one in her bedroom but her.

Suddenly there was a loud banging on the door.

"Jenni!" a female voice rang out. It was Toni, her neighbor from the next apartment. "What the hell is going on? What happened?" Toni cried. "Are you all right?"

"Yes, I'm okay," Jenni responded breathlessly. She found her pajamas on the bed and quickly threw them on. She opened the door and let Toni in.

"What happened," Toni asked. "I heard you screaming."

"Bad dream," Jenni said.

"A dream? Must have been a beauty."

"It's hard to explain. Just a scary dream."

"You're scaring the hell out of *me*, Jenni, you know. You sure it's okay?"

"Yes, Toni. I'm fine. Please, go back to bed. Get some sleep."

"You sure?" Toni asked.

"Yes." Jenni smiled weakly. Then she smiled, the images fresh in her mind. "You were in this dream, Toni," she said.

"God. I hope I wasn't the one who frightened you."

"No," Jenni said. "It was a pleasant dream up until the end. I dreamt we went to a club together and we each matched up with hot guys. You stayed in the club. I came back here."

"For sex I hope," Toni quipped, smiling.

"Well, yes, at first." Jenni became somber. "But then he got rough, lifted me in his arms and...you won't believe this...he threw me out the window."

"Good lord, Jenni!"

"It was the bastard who killed those people I told you about. This is the strange part though...I didn't realize it was him until it was too late. Like a mental block. I lost control of the dream."

"But, Jenni," Toni said, "you're not saying you actually controlled the dream."

"I'm not sure. Damn, Toni, it was so real. I feel the same fear I felt when he fired his gun at me last year. It grips like ice in your veins. Damn him. I started with a simple fantasy tonight and slipped into a nightmare."

Toni frowned at Jenni's explanation. "Is it getting worse, Jenni?" she asked.

The "it" Toni referred to was dreaming, Jenni knew. Jenni was a lucid dreamer, capable of creating and manipulating dreams to her own design; aware of entering a dream and proceeding through it with the knowledge that she *was* dreaming. During the months since she befriended Toni, she had hinted of her ability to create a dream, set the mood and scene and manipulate it to her will. But she knew once again by Toni's tractable expression that she still didn't accept the concept.

"This one was worse," she answered.

"Will you be all right?" Toni asked. "Can I do anything to help?"

"No. I'll be fine," Jenni assured her neighbor. "I've just got to relax."

"You're sure?"

"Yes." She appreciated Toni's offer and was pleased to have the company of her newfound friend. "Go back to sleep, please."

Toni gently closed the door behind her. Back in her own bedroom, her current, half-naked boyfriend, Harry Conners, who waited by the bed, said. "What the hell went on? Is everything okay?"

"Yeah. She's cool now." Toni put her finger to her lips. "It's that stupid thing again. You know...I told you."

"About dreaming?" Harry said.

Slipping into bed together, Toni whispered. "Yeah, dreams. She has this crazy idea that she can create a dream."

"Yeah, sure," Harry mocked. "Sometimes I think about something before I fall asleep and maybe I'll dream about it. But I can't actually create it."

16

*Dreams*

"It's not that simplistic, Harry," Toni said. "She really believes she can create a dream. Says she does it all the time. She claims she can plan a dream, go to sleep and manipulate it as she moves through it. It's like she writes a script in her mind and makes it happen in her subconscious."

"That's impossible," Harry said with pretentious conviction. "Can't be done."

"Shh. Keep it down. That's what I think too," Toni asserted. "But I don't argue with Jenni. She's a good person. She worked her way through college as a waitress. Went to Boston or someplace. She just has issues. She married this guy who screws around on the side. I'm telling you she's got problems; the divorce she's going through, her new life after she left her husband, her job. She saw some guy murder two people right in front of her. Lots of stuff. And she uses dreams to escape her problems."

"Strange. Really strange," Harry said. "She has problems all right. But...creating her own personal nightmares? That's scary shit. I still say it can't be done. You can't take over when you're dreaming. Out of the question."

"Well, you can't tell Jenni that. To her dreams are as much a part of her life as breathing."

"Sounds like she's playing with disaster. She's going down a slippery road," Harry affirmed. "So what happened tonight?"

"Apparently she had a nightmare. A dream that, she's says, got out of hand. She dreamed a guy killed her."

"Son of a bitch," said Harry Conners.

"Threw her out the window into the courtyard."

"Christ!"

"Here's the strange part," Toni said. "She claims I was in the dream with her. And the two of us went out to a club."

"Maybe it was you who scared her," Harry quipped. "Hell. I wouldn't call it a nightmare with you in the dream."

Toni smiled and rolled over on him, smothering him with kisses.

\* \* \*

What happened? Jenni was still puzzled. It *was* a dream, a nightmare. But one of the most realistic she had ever had. The sense of falling to her death was too believable for even her subconscious

17

mind to accept. She was jolted awake before impact. Didn't she read somewhere that you never die in your own dreams?

She got back into bed, propped up her pillows, reached over to the table beside her bed, and snapped on the lamp. Still shivering from the experience, she sat in bed and contemplated her plight. She stared at a long thin plaster crack in the ceiling that should be repaired. It reminded her that city life was more perplexing in many ways than living a sheltered existence in the large house in Connecticut. The image loomed in her mind in startling contrast to her present environment. The sumptuous master bedroom there alone was the size of this entire apartment. She gave up so much, she pondered, to attain independence and an uncertain future. The few years in Connecticut, away from her Manhattan job had lowered her awareness of change.

It had taken over a month to find an apartment she could presently afford. It was a walkup third floor rear in a hundred-year-old brownstone near Second Avenue in the mid-twenties; a small studio affair with a sleeping alcove that looked out onto a courtyard. A sliver of sky was barely visible over the roof of the building next door.

Jenni went to the double window and looked at the courtyard below. She shuddered at the frightful image she retained of falling to her death. How strange, she thought, that she didn't recognize the assassin in her dream until it was too late.

# Chapter Five

Since the shock of witnessing a multiple murder, Jenni assumed that this assassin, a constant bane in her life, who might be stalking her, was buried in her subconscious. He had appeared in other of her dreams. This was the first time, though, he had touched her, and sexually to boot. If these were her subconscious thoughts, why was he suddenly a repressed sexual predator? Did she actually desire the unusual, the thrilling encounter? If there were true meanings to dreams, she dreaded what the symbolism here might be.

Troubled by the frightening dream she had last night, the lingering threat of a murderer whom she could identify hung out there like a trap ready to spring. At the time of the murders, she had been summoned by police to run through hundreds of suspect mug shots but there was no match.

It was only a dream, she repeated to herself, only a dream.

Yet there were times when dreams were as much a part of her life as reality itself.

Dreams had fueled her life as pure escapism during periods of sexual frustration. She had used dreams as a potent vehicle to achieve the ultimate sexual adventure, her mood dictating the scenario. At times, she had even achieved orgasm in her sleep.

Since her rift with Ed and the return to work, her dreams had become more nightmares than the fantasies used as sexual tools before her marriage. Her fears and frustrations had brought her to the point of seeking answers through psychological therapy. Thus began her sessions with Carl Spendler, a psychotherapist, who guided her through each trauma. Her entry into his world had been an awakening.

"Let me ask you this, Jenni," Dr. Spendler had asked on one of her first visits, "When did you first realize you had this capability to create dreams to your will?"

"Since I was a young girl. About ten years old, I guess," Jenni had answered. "It started early on in grammar school."

"When did you take this faculty seriously?" the psychotherapist had asked.

"I guess when I was a teenager. My parents were strict, highly disciplined. I grew up in a religious household. My parents enrolled me in Catholic schools."

"You resented that?"

"Yes, I resented it. I rebelled against an endless barrage of negative commands: 'don't do this...don't say that...don't think that.' I discovered my only escape was through my own mind, my ability to daydream. I created moments of relief. I found I could easily convert consciousness into an unconscious state and pursue fantasies in a dreamlike trance. And I could return in an instant."

"During class?"

"Yes, even there. My teachers never suspected that I had mentally left many of the classes while they were speaking. I had perfected an ability to daydream so that I could hear the teacher while I drifted into my world of make-believe with my eyes wide open. It worked as well with my parents. I could be involved in a conversation with them and drift without them realizing what I'd done."

Carl Spendler made notes in the file.

"I suppose all this sounds strange to you," Jenni said.

"No, not at all. Please continue."

"It started as daydreaming," Jenni explained. "But these were not just ordinary daydreams the way people expect them to be. Mine were different. I could escape into a daydream, actually live it, feel it as reality and still consciously remain aware of my surroundings. It was like living in two worlds at the same time. I found that, at night, I could take a planned daydream into sleep and control it as a dream. I could manipulate it to my will."

"Lucid dreaming," Spendler stated. "It's been done."

"Yes, I've heard that term," Jenni said. "What is it exactly?"

"Well, it's been interpreted as having a clear understanding of one's dream," Spendler explained. "Let's say it would be having full use of one's mental faculties during a dream; realizing you are in a dream and have it under control. Most dreams are a study of one's self in depth. It's not only possible to drag one's conscious memories into dreams but also a dreamer can provide the environment for the dream. It is as easy for some people to program a dream as it is for others to awake at the same time every day without the use of an alarm clock."

"Do the people we meet in dreams have meanings?" Jenni

asked, attempting to introduce the images of the assassin.

Spendler rose from his seat and stood by his desk. He looked directly into Jenni's eyes.

"Perhaps," he said. "There are many interpretations of the meanings of dreams. The subconscious part of the mind is composed of opposing forces, much like everything in life, containing a good and evil nature. The emergence of the evil side produces nightmares and dreams that are tempered with a fetish for destruction. The dark side of the subconscious need not be programmed. It emerges by itself."

"Why is that?" Jenni asked.

"Well," Spendler explained, "it seems the mind travels to levels of passion which, at times, may actually reach a spiritual plane many mystics believe exists in the world of sleep. Once there, the mind is able to tap into other spirits traveling on that same plane. Extrasensory perception, clairvoyance, precognition and powers of the psychic find their way into the minds of many through dreams. There are people who can foresee the future, have visions of disasters, can predict events happening to others about which they have no knowledge but which manifest through dreams. The mind never sleeps. When the physical body falls into slumber, the mind, it is believed, merely ascends to a different level of consciousness. What really exists on that level? No one really knows."

Jenni nodded, acknowledging the explanation. "Perhaps that's what I am able to do, travel on some unknown level."

Spendler paused, glanced at his notes, and continued on a different tack.

"After you married, did you use dreams as a means to escape the reality of your life?"

"Not for a few years? It was only after Ed turned cold on me that I resumed slipping into my fantasies. When I found he was cheating on me I let the sexual fantasies take over."

She thought of her soon-to be-ex-husband, Ed. When they first met, she was an editorial assistant on a national magazine, while Ed was a young salesman who had just sold the magazine a network computer system. When they married Jenni was twenty-seven and Ed was a few years older. He was a passionate enough man at first, she thought. Not really a sexual being but romantic enough in the usual bent.

21

Their split-up had been escalating. It was since they moved into the Connecticut house that their sex life took a distant second place to Ed's goals in business. Success and image had always been Ed's primary motivation. Jenni gave up her editorial job at the magazine after five years into their marriage when they moved to Connecticut. At that time, she argued with Ed on his demands to leave her job and become a stay-at-home wife. He was adamant about her resigning. After all, he proclaimed, he made more than enough for them to live well.

"I can't have a working wife when I'm cruising for the top," he had proclaimed. "How the hell would that look to the boys upstairs?" Never mind how it seemed to her.

"I don't care what 'the boys upstairs' think," Jenni had countered. "Besides which, we have no children. What am I going to do at home?"

"I don't know," Ed vehemently retorted. "You're in publishing. Write a book."

That was the initiation of the rift in the marriage. Now Ed demanded possession of the house until the divorce was concluded, part of his image, he said. After all, she had walked out on him.

"Go if you must," he had told her. "You can clear out, but I keep the house." Somewhere along the way, she felt she too had become one of Ed's possessions, a trophy wife, as simple as that.

The symptoms of the cheating husband fell into place during her "stay-at-home" period. Ed spent too much time away from home, too many late nights at the office, too many apologies. It was the nature of his work, he claimed. Her suspicions were confirmed at a pool party at the Connecticut house in their final year of living together. Ed was in the midst of closing a substantial deal with a potential customer. He had invited company executives and the prospective client along with their families.

She noticed that night at poolside, there were many people who should not have been at the gathering. She saw Ed's secretary, Miriam, across the pool, standing alone. She was a tall attractive brunette with just the right body type to qualify as "eye candy." Jenni noticed that the girl was staring at Ed, who was with two men, for what seemed an inadvertently long time. It appeared to Jenni that Ed had rendered her spellbound.

Was she imagining it?

# Dreams

Since she suspected Ed of having an affair with his secretary, she had to prove to herself that it was not true, that it was probably her vivid imagination that was distorting her marital problems. So she spied on Ed. She came down to New York City on a weekday afternoon. Ed was staying overnight in town on that particular occasion. Conferences, he maintained.

Jenni took the train into the city, got to Ed's office building at four and waited across the street in the lobby of another building watching for either Ed or Miriam to appear. At five-fifteen, she spotted her leaving the building in the midst of traffic. Jenni followed her at a safe distance as the girl walked through the crowded streets heading east. Twenty minutes later Miriam turned into a small apartment building on Second Avenue. Jenni ducked into a coffee shop across the street. From there, she could watch the building where Miriam lived. She waited. After an hour, Ed showed up. He got out of a cab in front of the building and ducked inside.

Jenni left the coffee shop and went into the building after Ed. She found Miriam's apartment number and pushed through the glass doors into the lobby as someone was coming out. She found the apartment and rang the bell. The door swung open and Miriam stood there, her mouth agape.

"Mrs. Butler!" she exclaimed, loud enough for Ed to hear inside the apartment.

"Tell him to come here," Jenni said calmly.

The woman closed the door and when it again opened, Ed Butler was standing there. He looked at her sheepishly.

"Jenni, let me explain...the workload..." he said, but she cut him off. She balled her right hand into a fist and threw a perfect right hook from Brooklyn that caught him flush on the left cheek. Ed staggered back into the room, a look of astonishment on his face.

That had happened over a year ago but to Jenni it seemed like last week.

When she decided to end the marriage, she left Connecticut for Manhattan. First, get a job and then an apartment. It took a few weeks before she connected. She got a position on *Lady*, a magazine for women, as an editorial assistant. She was back to where she had been years ago. The job might have been the same but the salary was a bit higher than it was then.

While bunking in with her sister, Lottie Chambers, she had

found the small apartment in which she now lived. During this time, she cleared out her checking account in Connecticut, transferring money to a Manhattan branch. Just after renting the apartment, as she left a furniture store near Delancy Street where she purchased some basics, she suddenly felt like crying. Instead, she sucked it up and called Ed on her cell phone.

"Jenni!" he cried when he heard her voice "Where are you? I've been worried sick. Why did you leave? I thought we could work things out."

"You know damn well, Ed."

Silence on his end of the call.

"How long has it been going on?" Jenni said.

"Listen, Jenni, I love you. You know that." His voice noticeably quivered.

"I do?" she questioned.

"Please, don't do this. Come back. We'll talk about it."

"Like hell I will. We're finished, Ed. Your affair with Miriam was the last indignity. There's no way back."

"Please, Jenni," Ed had pleaded. "I'll make it up to you. The thing with Miriam, it was nothing. It didn't mean anything. I need you."

"You're only making it worse," Jenni said, trying desperately to control the rage she felt. "If you had fallen madly in love with her, I might possibly understand. Things like that happen. But to tell me it meant nothing to you...don't you realize what you are saying? You demean our marriage even more."

"You can't do this to me," Ed cried. "You can't just leave me."

"Oh, yes I can. And I have. I found out about Miriam. But, tell me, Ed, how many others were there?"

No answer.

"You've answered me, Ed, by your silence. In the meantime, I want some of the furniture from the house. Just a couple of pieces I need."

"What things?"

"I'll make a list. And I need some money."

"Jenni," Ed's voice mellowed. "Where are you?"

"In Manhattan."

"Are you all right?"

"Yes. I've got a job. And an apartment."

*Dreams*

"I'm truly sorry about this," he said, sounding somehow sincere. "I really didn't want us to end up like this."

"Of course you didn't, Ed. You just didn't plan on being caught."

* * *

Jenni Butler could hardly contain her emotion to explain her recent ordeal to Carl Spendler.

She felt comfortable with the psychotherapist who emanated confidence. A tall man, he stood a full head over her and was, to her, an icon. In the times she had been to his office, she trusted him and admired his honesty.

"All right then, Jenni," Spendler said calmly. "Let's get started. Tell me what is troubling you." He had granted Jenni time to see him because she sounded urgent. This was only her third visit and he limited her to a half hour since she was now cutting into other patients' time.

"He's in my dreams again," Jenni said, excitedly. "It's the same man. He's back. He tried to kill me. In this dream he threw me out of the window in my apartment."

"How did he come to be in your apartment?" Spendler asked, not exhibiting excitement at all.

At first, Jenni was reluctant to answer but she realized the pieces had to fit for the therapist to make sense of her dreams.

"I started a planned dream," she said, thinking perhaps this sounded ridiculous. "I initiated a sexual scenario. I think I may have drawn him into my fantasy."

"Can you explain?" Spendler said.

"I created a setting I liked. A dance club in Manhattan. I placed a lover in it. I had the outcome fixed in my mind before I drifted into sleep." Should she eliminate the details, she thought? She might reveal intimate facts no one should know.

"Go on."

"I lost control almost at the beginning. Normally when I plan a dream I am aware of what is to happen and my mind reacts to the circumstances. But this latest one wasn't the same," Jenni continued. "It was pure reality to me. In this instance, I was not aware that I was dreaming. And never before was I threatened so

25

directly. In the past the blond assassin had stalked me, but only briefly from a distance. In this dream he not only threatened my life but he entered my sexual fantasy."

"Why do you think you lost control this time?"

"I don't know. Maybe because in this dream he was my lover but I didn't recognize him as such until the end."

"Is the role of this person as a lover entirely new for you?" Spendler asked. "Has he ever appeared in that capacity before?"

"Never!" Jenni was aghast at the suggestion. "He pursued me in other dreams. But he never touched me. Dear God, does it mean he's near? That he's found me?"

"Not necessarily, Jenni. The subconscious is its own entity. It is more dominant than the conscious mind. It stores everything the human mind absorbs. It will not judge the difference between reality and dreams. On the other hand, the conscious mind reacts to the activities of wakefulness and only borrows from the subconscious. The conscious mind separates truth from lies. The subconscious does not distinguish the difference. When you enter a dream the subconscious comes into play where both truths and fictions will react to your dream.

"And buried there is the lurking murderer whom you witnessed kill people. He is in your subconscious as a threat. That he has again emerged may be due to your divorce becoming final."

"My divorce! What has that got to do with a nightmare?"

"Remember, you have been through a period of great upheaval in your life in the past year," Spendler continued. "In a dream, envisioning your own death can indicate that you are subconsciously dealing with change. It's the end of your former life and the beginning of the new one. That the assassin is the instrument of your death is natural. You have identified him as a life challenging threat to you. You cannot wipe away that image in an instant, as you well know."

Jenni pondered Spendler's explanation for a moment, then said, "But it's like he had found his way into my dream and has taken over. I was not planning the outcome. He was."

"The role of this man as a lover in your dreams, through your sexual fantasies, I believe, is a substitute," he said.

"How? Substitute for what?"

"When you first came to me you related you had sexual

fantasies about men other than your husband," Spendler said.

"Yes," she answered reluctantly.

"It was never with this man though?"

"Hell no!"

Spendler opened Jenni's file and browsed for a moment before he continued. "Now that Ed is no longer with you it appears you have substituted fantasies with an element of risk. And you have equated the man who represents ultimate danger as the anonymous body in your dreams."

"Am I crazy? Why would I do that?"

"As you say, you haven't fantasized about him deliberately. Your subconscious is doing it for you...in symbols. It's what he represents that matters in your dreams."

"And what is it that he represents, Dr. Spendler?"

"In a word, fear."

Jenni fell silent, not knowing if this explanation qualified as a solution. Fear is exactly what she felt. It sounds all too simple, she thought.

* * *

Carl Spendler, parapsychologist turned psychotherapist, loved Manhattan. It endured as one of the most unique places in the world. For him there was nothing like it. He delighted in the magnificent Manhattan skyline. He felt at home in the environment of skyscrapers. Man's monuments to achievement, he often thought. God made mountains while man made skyscrapers. May it ever be so.

He smiled across the dinner table at his current gal-pal, Jillian. They were dining at one of his favorite neighborhood restaurants, located near Columbus Avenue only a few blocks from his West Side brownstone. It was quaint, quiet and tucked away in the street-accessed basement of a one-hundred-year-old townhouse. There was a sense of familiarity here that he embraced, like a welcoming home-away-from-home. Dark wood paneling surrounded a working brick fireplace that was the central attraction of the main room. The couple, though, chose to dine in the rear garden since the weather allowed. Jillian smiled at him over martinis.

Jillian was younger than Spendler by over a dozen years; he

was in his mid-forties. The distinctive difference between them was exaggerated both by his age and height. He towered over Jillian by a full head topped by a harvest of slate-gray hair. Spendler ran almost every day through the paths of Central Park to stay trim. Although he was in excellent physical condition, he could not hide the fact that he appeared to be a middle-aged businessman with a younger mistress.

Spendler and Jillian had connected two years ago as he ran through Central Park almost every morning. As he came out of the park, he made a habit of glancing up at Jillian's third floor apartment window. Her apartment faced front and it seemed to Spendler that she watched his return many mornings as he passed in front of her building. When finally he waved to her, she closed her Venetian blind in a sudden seeming act of rejection. He then dismissed the assumption that she had been flirting with him.

A month passed before he saw her again, during which time he never again glanced toward her window. One day she stopped him in the local supermarket. She deliberately ran her cart into his.

"So what happened?" she had asked. "You never look my way anymore. Did I grow horns or something?"

Spendler was surprised by her pluck. "Was that about the time I thought you brushed me off?" he said. "I waved to you and you shut your blind one morning. I figured you wanted no part of me. So I gave up."

"I must have shut the blind without thinking and ran to the phone," she quickly replied.

Spendler thought the excuse was lame but possible. "I wouldn't have guessed that," he said.

"There's no reason why we can't pick up where we left off, is there?" she eagerly asked.

"None that I can think of."

"Then why don't we do something to make up for the lost month?" she offered.

"Dinner tonight?" asked Spendler.

They became an item. Since his divorce Spendler had a number of relationships with women but during that period, only one commitment, sort of...to Jillian. But he admitted to himself the commitment was purely sexual in nature. The divorce was the result of his strange life, tracking "occult" occurrences around the world, which strained his marriage to a breaking point. Spendler had one daughter from his marriage, whom he saw as often as possible. Nowadays, he earned his substantial income primarily from royalties on his bestselling books about the paranormal and from speaking engagements, mostly at universities.

He had begun his career as a parapsychologist by either debunking the paranormal or finding proof of its actuality. In recent years, though, he had assumed the role of psychotherapist. He began an impetus into dream therapy as a result of his long-time involvement in dealing with occult events. He had grown reluctant to chase ghosts around the world and he found a new interest in the relationship of dreams, particularly nightmares linked to the paranormal. It didn't take long to establish a practice that brought him sufficient clientele to nurture his inquisitive mind. His reputation, already established, broadened to even new horizons.

Spendler lived on the west side of Central Park and spent most of his time at the brownstone house he loved, writing or preparing speeches. He should really be there right now, he thought, working on a dissertation he was to give at New York University. The subject was the reality of evil manifesting itself into physical form, if it was possible for a demon from the netherworld to appear within mankind as a trial. A subject inspired by the presence of Elymas, the demon, with whom he had confronted in his own life. Demons, he knew, *did* exist in reality, far more than humanity was aware.

Now, at dinner, he thought of the undaunted task of relating his opinion to Jillian, a woman who shared his bed, bringing him the sexual satisfaction he craved but lacking in the compatibility of cerebral dissertation.

He began to unscramble his thoughts, perhaps broaching the subject of ingrained evil in all mankind to Jillian when he noticed that the slight movement of her eyes had been mentally distracted for an instant. She was looking past him at something other than him.

There was no doubt that her eyes were straying. Apparently, Spendler thought, this is not going to work. The expression on her beautiful face told him to keep his boring opinions to himself and confine their relationship to the bedroom.

And the meal was excellent topping off an evening of abundant physical pleasantries without the preponderance of intellectual effort.

# Chapter Six

Jenni Butler spun through the revolving glass doors and plunged into the lobby of the building in which she worked in mid-Manhattan. It pulsed with the activity of the morning rush hour. She left the elevator at the fourteenth-floor offices of *Lady*, a magazine run by women for women. She hurried to her desk in a partitioned cubicle and immediately plunged into her workload. As an editor, she was hassled by the constant pressure of unending deadlines.

Even though she would have to brace Edna Rothmann, her immediate superior, Jenni preferred the challenge of facing a female executive rather than a male. She recalled her initial session with Rothmann, who had been her boss since she had started with *Lady* almost a year ago. She sensed that she was going to get the job after only one meeting.

Rothmann was all business. She was tall, her body more angles than curves. Her short, mousy brown hair was brushed back from a stark white face devoid of makeup. She wore a somber, gray suit. She gave Jenni the impression of a woman who wanted to be thought of as a man. There was nothing soft about her.

"Do you think being away from a magazine environment for a few years will hurt your ability to work?" Rothmann had asked.

Jenni assured her that she would indeed get into the swing of things right away, that necessity dictated her adjustment. Rothmann pondered her for a long time, her eyes rapidly moving over the length of her body. Jenni thought she was being mentally stripped.

"Normally it's against my principles to hire women who preferred being housewives rather than staying in business. I hope you're not one of those who is just bored and looking for change."

She told Rothmann about her pending divorce. It seemed to be the deciding factor that made the difference. Rothmann hired her.

"We'll take a chance with you, Butler. You had a good work record. I assume it will continue the same. You'll join us, then," the senior editor said. "Welcome aboard *Lady*. You know that we're one family here." She held out her hand to Jenni who marveled at the strength of Rothmann's handshake. Just like a man.

Now, this morning, the word had come that Rothmann wanted to see her right away. Jenni feared the worst. She couldn't lose her job now. She had to go on making a living.

Her head ached. She felt rundown. She knew she must look as terrible as she felt. She needed rest, the trouble-free sleep of forgetfulness. The blond murderer was still haunting her subconscious and he would not vanish.

She dreaded the meeting with Rothmann.

Jenni was admitted to Rothmann's office that was flooded with a blizzard of papers. The editor sat erect before her desk. She gestured for Jenni to be seated while she finished her phone call. A full two minutes passed before she turned her attention to Jenni.

"I'm sorry, Butler," she said. "You know what this job is like. I just wanted a few minutes of your time."

Jenni had taken a position opposite her in a chair that had to be cleared of file folders. She said nothing.

"Is anything wrong, Butler?" Edna Rothmann said, getting to the point immediately. "Personally, I mean. You know, I am worried about you. You're starting to scare me." Jenni suspected her physical appearance had already revealed her mental strain.

"I'm sorry I give that impression," Jenni said.

Rothmann persisted. "Jenni, my dear, half the time you seem restless and out of it. I've noticed a change in your work lately. Little mistakes. Things you should never have let slip by. It's not like you. And you've been taking time off lately. More than normal."

"It's just..." Jenni fished for an answer. She couldn't tell her boss about the murderer who dominated her dreams. She wanted to talk about it to someone but certainly not the senior editor. She couldn't guess what Rothmann's reaction might be to the truth. She might think her absolutely mad. "It's Ed, my husband. The divorce," she lied. Lately it was becoming her only answer.

"Oh," Edna Rothmann said, eager to transgress private boundaries, but appearing reluctant to do so. "I didn't mean to be pushy. But if there's anything you need. Anything I can do..."

"It's the divorce." Jenni insisted.

"You're valuable to us, Jenni," Rothmann said, leaving her chair and coming around her desk to stand beside her, looking down at her. "I think you've got a good future here. I don't want to see you hurt your chances. When you first came to us I thought I'd have to watch my ass. That you'd be after my job. It certainly doesn't seem that way now. Remember, I want to help, to work problems out. I'm always here for you."

Jenni didn't answer. She didn't know what to say that might make things better. Promises of more devotion to the job; they might sound, weak, ineffectual.

"Is it your love life?" Rothmann asked.

"Pardon?" Jenni said, hoping she didn't sound incredulous.

"Is it a man who's screwing you up?" Rothmann said bluntly.

Jenni couldn't believe the woman was so direct. "Don't you think my personal life shouldn't be brought up...?"

"If it interferes with your work, definitely it should. Don't let men get to you," the senior editor offered. "They're not worth it. They're all the same. They're only after one thing. Especially from an attractive woman like you. And once they get what they want they regard all women as shit. We become their victims."

Jenni hadn't heard such vitriol put quite so callously.

"Love," Rothmann continued, her tone icy. "Love and sex. How we all look for it. We need it. How important it is to us. Makes men seem indispensable to us, doesn't it?"

"I suppose so," Jenni said wearily, tiring of the direction the conversation was taking.

"Well, believe me, they are very dispensable. You'll find out someday that they are not that important in the scheme of things. It is very possible for a woman to live happily and sufficient without a man at all. I wouldn't give you the wealth of the sheiks for any man. I haven't met one who is worth the effort," Rothmann proclaimed vehemently. "They're nothing but trouble. Look at what the bastard is doing to you. You've lost weight. You're run down and you are worried to distraction. He is definitely affecting your life, maybe even ruining it."

Am I that obvious, Jenni thought? "If you say so," she said.

"Take my advice, Butler. Get rid of him. You'll be a lot happier person for it."

Jenni didn't respond. She realized that Rothmann's diatribe against men had not been spontaneously brought on by the situation at hand. Her words were barbed and laced with obvious invective. This woman despised all men.

"In the meantime, Butler," she continued, "I want you to shape up your work. Get some rest. Give it a fresh start. Remember what I told you. We are family here. We don't like to see one of our own in trouble."

This was the first subtle threat from Rothmann. The editor stood directly over her, intimidating.

"Do you live in the city?" Rothmann asked, her voice softening with a thickness that was heavy with implication.

"Yes."

"I assume you're living with this guy?"

Damn it! Jenni wanted to scream. But she refused to speak. Just because I work for you, she thought, doesn't give you the right to probe into my personal life.

Rothmann noticed the coolness that came into Jenni's attitude and did not push further. She stepped away from Jenni and sat down behind her desk.

"Butler," she said, "I want to help you. It does neither of us any good for you to be burdened with problems that affect both of us. They could be resolved perhaps by sharing them with others. I don't want you to think of me merely as your boss. Rather as a friend, a companion, if you will. Someone you can turn to in time of strife."

"I'll keep it in mind," Jenni said. She had expected worse. She thought about getting fired. "I won't let it get out of hand. I do like working here. It's just that I have to take care of a few things."

"I hope so," Rothmann said. "And I'm serious about coming to me any time for any reason."

Jenni couldn't be certain, but she felt the invitation transcended the practical advice between boss and employee. Jenni was now convinced that Rothmann was hitting on her. She cringed inwardly. She had heard that Rothmann was a lesbian and she certainly seemed to play the role as Jenni imagined it. Although, from what she had heard from other women in the office, the senior editor had never had an affair with anyone working here. Could she be the first? Was this considered sexual harassment? Jenni stood up, breaking the mood.

"Why don't we have lunch?" Rothmann said. "We can talk things out with more time."

"Today?" Jenni hoped not.

"No. Soon. You can see how it is," Rothmann said, gesturing to the stack of incoming projects on her desk.

## Mike Walsh

Jenni had lunch once before with Rothmann, she recalled. It had been shortly after she came to the magazine. Looking back now, she wondered if the luncheon then had been more than it had seemed. She tried to remember if Rothmann had gotten just a little too friendly then. If so, She had not picked up on it. Perhaps that was why almost eight months had gone by since then without another word from her boss.

"Maybe we can kill an entire afternoon," Rothmann said.

* * *

Jenni removed her black habit and hung it carefully in the bantam-sized closet. She then removed the head veil and placed it on the shelf. Her room was small, as were all the rooms in the convent, each planned to sufficiently accommodate one nun. They were more like cells, with barely enough space for a bed, bureau and the one chair allotted each occupant.

She stripped down to her panties and slipped into the bed, under the covers. It was only an hour until vespers and she needed to use the time for her personal gratification.

She would have to confess her sins once again. It seemed she was continually in the confessional. Yet, so were many of the other novices. It was their lot in life. The priest was sworn to a vow of secrecy and therefore she did not worry that he would tell the mother superior of her transgressions. He could not. But it worried her that he knew her secret thoughts.

It had been only last week that she had told him of her inability to contain her sexual desires. She had masturbated in the privacy of her little room. She knew it was wrong, a mortal sin. And yet, it did not seem so. The priest had dismissed her with platitudes, the expected penance, and she felt no remorse. Had she been sinning by admitting that she would not sin again, knowing she would?

She would have to hurry. Her hand slid down under the covers and found its way beneath the band of her panties. Her long, delicate fingers gently parted the already moist lips and probed deliciously into the forbidden depths. She sighed with sheer joy.

O God, she thought, how could this be a sin?

She closed her eyes and let her imagination soar as she slowly experienced the forbidden pleasure for which her body craved. In

34

*Dreams*

her passion the cover slipped slightly leaving her nakedness partially exposed.

"What are you doing?" cried out a harsh voice.

Jenni opened her eyes, startled at the intrusion, and sat up, clutching the sheet to her bare breasts.

"What do you think you are doing?" the mother superior said. She was standing in the open doorway, her face a mask of rage.

"Sin," the older nun cried. "Living with sin in this holy place. This cannot be allowed."

Jenni was horrified and ashamed. She didn't know what to do or say. Would the mother superior tell what she had been caught doing?

"The sins of the flesh will destroy you," the elder nun said.

Jenni woke up.

She had gone to bed early and had dreamed during the short time she was asleep. Her right hand was inside her panties and she had been massaging herself.

Damn it, she thought. I've been dreaming again. And I didn't even plan this one. Am I so sexually starved that I invented a dream of being a nun, deprived of the intimate pleasures of the flesh and yet satisfying myself?

As she sat up in bed and contemplated, she realized that the mother superior in the dream who had interrupted her was actually Edna Rothmann. Damn it! Was it possible that Rothmann could see through the thin barrier I present as a veil to shroud my inner sexual paucity? And why a nun?

35

# Chapter Seven

There were no windows in Johnnie Limbo's private room. It was an interior suite. He studied it as he had so often since his imprisonment.

If only there was a way to get out of here, he thought. And hide from them. It wouldn't be easy. The only exit from his apartment was a door that was always locked. And Limbo knew it could not be opened simply with a key. He might remove the hinges and slide the door off its moorings. But the hinges were outside, not inside as most doors have them. Nor was there was a handle on his side of the door.

As Limbo sat in his new quarters absorbed in a nineteen-sixties "spaghetti western" on TV, an astonishing event occurred. His life was about to change once again. A shadowy human image suddenly stepped into the room seemingly through the corridor wall.

Even though the only door in the apartment had not opened, a man was standing in front of him. Recognition came slowly as he stared at the intruder. Clad completely in black garb, Limbo's benefactor, Elymas, the demon, the man who had once freed him from prison, dramatically entered the room.

"Am I seeing things? Is that you?" Limbo asked, jumping to his feet, his face aglow with enthusiasm and hope. Elymas had come for him to get him out of here the same crazy way he had been freed from prison once before by this strange man. Elymas had entered Limbo's quarters now the same way he had entered that jail cell back then, through the bars. Limbo still couldn't relate to the explanation he had received, something to do with altering time. Crazy. But who the fuck cared how he did it? As long as he could pull it off. At last, he thought, he would be rid of this fucking place.

"Why yes, John," the man in black spoke softly, a grin on his astonishingly handsome face. "Don't act surprised. 'Tis I, for certain."

Limbo was elated. "I'll be damned," he said. "I haven't seen you in two years. I thought you were dead. Where the hell were you?"

"Busy, John, my boy. Busy," answered the demon. "But not in Hell."

"I just about gave up on you," said a beset Limbo to his mentor, referring to their previous collaboration involving kidnapping, murder and a face-off with the spirit of a medium. "When I came to on that boat back there in Maine, I didn't know what to do. You were gone and I was alone on the deck. That girl, Jenny, who we held prisoner on board, must have hit me with something damned hard. I was out cold for a while and when I came to she was gone."

"No matter about her. I am sorry, John," said the demon apologetically, "I, also, thought *you* were dead. I apologize that I did not go back for you. I couldn't wait around. How did you escape the police?"

"It wasn't easy. I took whatever money we had on the boat and made it to shore. I stole a car and drove away."

"Where is the boat now?" Elymas asked.

"I left it in the harbor in that town in Maine. I have no idea what happened to it."

"No matter," said Elymas. "As long as it can't be traced to me."

"How could it be? We stole it, didn't we?" Limbo said. But he did think that it could be traced to *him*. His fingerprints were all over the yacht. Perhaps by now the cops were on to him. Perhaps that was how these people had got to him and brought him here. But he never had a record other then that few hours in The New York City lockdown for a brawl in a bar. That was it. No charges. No record. No army file. No FBI file. And he never left a clue on any of his hits. Except that woman who saw him commit a double murder. Could she have fingered him?

"Stolen boat? Borrowed boat is a term more to my liking," said Elymas.

Limbo had enough of the small talk. "What are you doing here?" he asked. "You came to get me out of here, didn't you?"

"In due time. We have much to discuss."

"Discuss, hell. Just get me out of here."

"John, my boy, restrain your emotions. You will be staying here for a while. Under my supervision"

"What are you talking about? Why?"

"You are still with me. Still my protégé," said the demon. "You are here at my behest. This is my organization. I own it. One of my many toys. You are at home here. You are my guest."

"I don't get it. This place is yours and you got me locked up."

Elymas explained. "I lost track of you temporarily. Once I finally located you, I had you brought here. You are the quintessential archetype for the work we are planning here."

Limbo was confused. "Why?" he asked. "What is this place? I thought they were government. What do you have to do with this strange outfit?"

"Ah," said Elymas. "Not government. No. Only me, John. Completely me. I am the dream master, John. You must have faith in me. I have wealth beyond your wildest imagination. I have homes and castles along with business enterprises all over the world. I've had centuries to build wealth."

A statement like this puzzled Limbo. This enigma, this person, Elymas, claimed to have lived centuries. It didn't make sense in the real world. But then, he did things that were unreal.

"Just what is this place?" Limbo asked, thoroughly confused.

"Something that was in development stage years ago. It began as a profit maker. Dream psychotherapy; designed to help people find their way out of the torment of nightmares. It actually has developed a good reputation for just that, helping people who can't cope with nightmares. But, you know me. I had to find a way to use it against mankind instead of for mankind. I incorporated new technology into the program. A perfect way to disrupt convention on a broader level."

"Like what? And why me?"

"We kill people here, John. We make dreams of fear a reality. Here, we have a system that can create and alter dreams to our desires. Technology so perfect, that nightmares become real; no longer mere dreams to be forgotten and dismissed. We are able to create a dream that becomes deadly for the sleeper. We can kill people in their sleep because the dream is actual. Leaving no trace."

"I don't get it. What do you need me for?"

"Assassinations, John. We're talking about your business. You are an experienced assassin. You are my main ingredient in the mix. I guess you might call this place my version of a giant video game. Only we are stepping up in class from your level of killing."

"Class? My level? Don't insult me. I did well."

"Yes, John, you did me proud. You are as deadly as they come without prodding. But I intend to make a difference. Here we will concentrate on killings persons of international distinction. I plan to create wars."

"I don't believe this!" Limbo was still mystified. "I don't see you for years and I wind up your prisoner."

"No, John, you are not a prisoner. You are my guest," spoke Elymas. "All those others who toil here are my prisoners. They are pawns. Fools, to be used. Money can buy most anyone. But not you. You are different than those louts. You are the essence of my being. You are pure, uncorrupted evil. I searched for you and finally found you."

"I'm not sure I like being used this way. What am I getting involved in?"

"Hang in there, John. We are going to do great things. You'll be rich beyond your ability to measure. All you have to do is cooperate with my assistants. Do what they tell you and things will work. I plan new adventures on a grand scale. You will be the catalyst for my cause."

"How?"

"Every person has fears. They consciously fight those fears, manage to subdue them and live normal lives. But these terrors never really leave them. They are buried in the subconscious. That is where we attack them. By entering their nightmares we can increase their fears a thousand times. This power can be utilized in so many ways. One of them is on the astral plane."

"I know about that. I believe I've been there," said Limbo.

"Of course you have, John. You've already been tested here and have traveled on the astral plane."

"No," Limbo said. "Not that. I mean in my own dreams, before I came here."

Elymas's black eyes flashed red. "Why, John, my boy," he said enthusiastically, "please elucidate. Tell me what you know of the astral plane?"

"There is this woman..." Limbo began, and then paused, considering whether Elymas should be part of that innermost, secret place in his mind.

"And," prodded the demon.

"A while ago I hit a target on a New York street. I killed three people that night, the target and two witnesses. I thought it was a

39

clean hit. But another woman saw me. She was coming out of a building. Walked right into my action out of nowhere. I didn't plan on her. I had to cut and run. She got away from me. Later I tried to find her but there's no record on her. She was never named as a witness but I'm sure the police brought her in to ID me."

"Where is this going, John?" Elymas asked.

"I've had dreams about her since then, on and off. But I don't think they are my dreams entirely. I got this strange feeling that she is pulling me into *her* dreams. They seem real. Not like dreams that are so screwed up with symbols and stupid stuff. It's like I wasn't in a dream but I was actually living what was in my mind. And only last week, on one of the experiments here, I had her in my dream. I killed her in that one."

"She must be dead then," Elymas said.

"No. In the dream I dropped her out a window into a courtyard. But I watched her get up and walk away."

"Where is she?"

"I don't know. I came out of the dream. I woke up here. I never left the lab. It was when they were setting me up. You know, practice."

"John," Elymas said, "you never cease to amaze me."

"Is it possible that my subconscious traveled on that astral plane, you mentioned, to hers?" Limbo asked.

"Why not," Elymas offered. "Who knows what is or isn't possible? Far greater things exist in the universe than in our limited philosophy...to paraphrase."

# Chapter Eight

At two AM on a weekday morning, a private limousine deposited Senator Henry Montgomery in front of a massive elegant Victorian-era house that was DREAMS headquarters. The limo had driven north across the Henry Hudson Bridge into the Riverdale section of New York City located on the mainland side of The Harlem River. The residence was perched on the river's edge on four full acres of gated, fenced property on a long, sloping hill, eighty feet above the river. It was practically hidden from view by the trees that surrounded it. To the west was the much smaller Spytun-Dyvil Bridge, the last of the many bridges that connected Manhattan to outer boroughs. Beyond this low-level bridge, the narrow Harlem River joined the massive Hudson River. Below the building, at the base of the sloping acreage, the Metro North railroad ran along the coastline.

The structure seemed to passersby a well-kept edifice that was serene and posed no caveat to the community. Occupants and visitors who sometimes passed in and out of the elaborate, ornate double front oak doors maintained a low profile. Few neighbors gave any thought to the real purpose of their activities. There were vague notions that the dwelling harbored a group of medical people involved in some sort of research program; seemed logical. A harmless group, at best. If someone asked what the DREAMS foundation did, they might elicit a response like, "Damned if I know."

This was Senator Montgomery's first invitation to the research foundation. He had never been here before. For that matter he had never been to this part of New York. He was admitted through the main gate and he approached the double entrance doors. A bronze panel adorned the brick wall at the right door about shoulder high. In the center of the plaque was a silhouetted emblem that seemed to be made of transparent black marble, a sort of a black cameo. It appeared to be an eye with a teardrop shaped like a diamond.

It was a symbol Montgomery recognized but had no idea of its meaning. He thought it might simply be the logo symbol for DREAMS. Around his neck, tucked inside his shirt, he wore the medallion that had been secretly delivered to him at his home. It was a gold chain at the end of which hung a molded flat enamel duplicate of the symbol on the wall. Montgomery lifted the emblem in his right hand and placed it directly on the bronze wall-plaque as he had been informed to do. It fit exactly over the shape of the black cameo. An electronic code system recognized the symbol he placed there and unraveled an automatic lock that permitted entrance to the main floor. Montgomery knew he was on camera as he opened the door and entered the foyer. What he didn't know was that he was standing on an electrified system built in the floor that could have killed him in an instant if he was deemed an invader who had breached security.

Inside, he came to a second set of doors that were not as ornate as the outer two. They were unadorned and appeared to him to be made of stainless steel. He was informed of the procedure for entrance even though this was his first trip to the dream research center. The doors opened and two men, both dressed in similar dark suits waited inside. One of them extended his hand to him.

"Senator Montgomery," he said. "Glad to meet you. I'm Ken Raymond. This is Pete Foster."

Senator Montgomery pumped the offered hand and released it. He had to look up into the eyes of Raymond and Foster from his five-foot-nine-inch height. The two men were well over six feet tall, both younger than him by at least fifteen years and both slender and hard as compared to Montgomery's two hundred ten pound corpulent body.

"Welcome to DREAMS," Raymond said.

Senator Montgomery smiled. "Thanks," he replied. He thought about the acronym DREAMS. He had been told it stood for "Dream Research Employing Astral Manipulation Strategy." Appropriate. Montgomery was here by invitation from the director of the organization, Clayton Bancock. He glanced at his watch. Two AM. Hell of a time for a conference. But the subject matter seemed important in light of the condition of the present-day circumstances in the world. He had been informed he was to witness a unique exhibition. Because the latest enemy of the United States fought an unconventional war, news of any weapon that did not require an army became a hot item.

"Imagine," he had been told, "a weapon designed specifically to eliminate known enemy leaders for which they have no defense; a weapon that requires a very limited retinue of personnel."

Highly encouraged and highly classified.

DREAMS was alleged to have covertly developed a very secretive breakthrough in the use of paranormal technology. Senator Montgomery was here to witness a demonstration that claimed to command the human subconscious mind to act on a given order. The DREAMS organization was highly secretive in its experiments; so secretive that only a few select individuals had been made privy to the event about to transpire. Still, Montgomery entered the building with unsettled doubts.

"Follow us," Raymond said, leading the way through the modern, pristine halls of the institution that were in stark contrast to the exterior architecture.

They entered one of four elevators that were as gleaming white as the corridors they traversed. Senator Montgomery was taken to a large conference room on the top floor. Seated around a long, polished oak table were only two men he recognized instantly. Both were highly successful entrepreneurs involved in arms procurement. Apparently, he thought, he represented the military budget and these members of the private sector were specifically affected by defense spending.

Montgomery was grateful that he didn't have to choose a seat. He was placed opposite the two industrialists. The men greeted him as he sat down. He wondered if they, like him, put any credence in the development of a weapon that operated purely in the subconscious mind.

Two men entered the room from a door opposite the main entrance. One was tall, lean with close-cropped gray hair, while the other was shorter and portly, looking, Montgomery thought, much like himself. The tall man walked to the head of the table and dropped a file folder in front of him.

"Good morning, gentlemen," he said. "I'm Clayton Bancock. I'm glad you are here. I know it's a great sacrifice for you to show up at this early hour with your busy schedules, but I think what you will see today is worth the effort. I'll get right to the point. Then, we'll adjourn to the laboratory where our demonstration is ready to begin."

There was a murmur around the table as heads nodded in approval.

"What we are attempting to show you at this early hour is a major breakthrough," said Bancock. "In the past thirty or more years our enemies around the world have been trying to get an edge on our military in the development of psychic phenomenon as sophisticated weaponry. If successful, these techniques could be used to stalemate our defense systems. Think what it might mean if our adversaries were able to read the minds of our spies by telepathy or could enter the subconscious of an individual and rob secrets regarding our national defense. It's a new world we are entering, gentlemen. A world that opens avenues for exploration not yet thought of."

The men at the table stirred restlessly. They had heard this type of rhetoric before. Senator Montgomery wondered if this wasn't a waste of time.

Clayton Bancock continued. "We here at DREAMS are dedicated to the development of paranormal capability. Our primary motives are equivalent to the Department of Defense. We have developed dream technology as a formidable weapon. The possibilities are unlimited."

Senator Montgomery interrupted, his doubts prevailing. "Mr. Bancock," he said, "as you know, I am in favor of a strong defense posture. But I lean towards the more practical use of funds, for hardware, practical weapons systems. I favor 'dense pack,' 'drones' and 'bunker busters' I believe pursuing the development of esoteric weaponry of the type you are advocating is seeking reality where it does not exist. I have little faith in such an unproved science."

Bancock smiled and continued. "Today, perhaps your faith will be actualized," he said. "You are about to witness an amazing advance in controlling one of the psychic forces of the universe. A major step forward in new technology, so to speak. There is a thin barrier between the physical self and the spiritual self in all people. We enter that spiritual world every day. The ancients of China, Tibet, India all taught that the spirit wanders when we sleep, that it can reach the astral level through the subconscious mind. These scholars believed it travels on a higher plane than the conscious mind and can reveal many mysteries of the universe. And mystics of today believe that a soul can move forward or backward in time on this level. There are no boundaries."

Bancock paused, letting the thought settle in. "Let's assume the mystics are right," he continued. "Therefore, a spirit in journey may meet other traveling spirits or places and scenarios yet to exist in real terms. We have found that it is possible to target a specific time, area, or person and reach them on the astral level."

There were obvious frowns and sighs of skepticism from the three visitors.

Clayton Bancock smiled wryly and continued. "We have the ability to propel the subconscious mind to the astral level, invade the subconscious or dream of another person and place that person in a reality event of his worst nightmare. What he fears will kill him. We can make his nightmare a deadly reality."

There was an uneasy rustling among the men seated at the table. This revelation was remarkable, thought Senator Montgomery, a concept that the human subconscious could be used as an assassin during sleep. Astounding, if it were true.

"Can you prove that this research actually works?" one of the industrialists asked.

"This may sound unreasonable to you," Clayton Bancock answered, "but I assure you it is reality. This is not science fiction. We *can* do it. We have done it. Once we know where a target body is physically located, we can enter his subconscious while he sleeps. We can identify his greatest fear and kill him with his own concept of that fear. Through fear, the increased rate of adrenaline causes heart failure. Enemy leaders can be easily eliminated, with no evidence of foul play?"

The restlessness in the room grew.

"No enemy is immune from attack," Bancock continued. "No doubt about it. The target has no defense against absolute fear. He actually dies in his own mind. His heart bursts because he knows he cannot escape death. Assassination through dreams is the premier weapon of the future."

One of the men on the industrialist side of the table said, "I've a question for you."

"Yes?" Bancock said.

45

"Do you merely offer suggestions to the dreamer?"

"No, not at all. We will send the mind of an assassin into the target's subconscious. He will do the job."

"Is the assassin trained in any way?" came a second question.

"Not really," Bancock replied. "He merely responds to commands given him. He is induced by drugs and is ordered to respond to commands fed to him through a tiny device planted in his brain. The only training he needs has already been accumulated through his years of performing assassinations."

"What happens to the assassin after he has accomplished the killing?" the man asked. "I mean, are there any adverse effects?"

"There seems to be no physical change when this person comes out of the dream," Bancock said. "He is basically the same as he was before the experiment. Physically, he seems normal. But we cannot be certain of possible mental damage. There is no way of knowing how he has been affected without further experimentation."

"Does he remember what he has done?" came another question.

"At this stage we're not sure," Bancock replied. "We can't eliminate from his subconscious what we have programmed in."

"Wouldn't he present a danger to us, left alive with the information he accumulated?"

"Not at all," Bancock answered calmly. "The slightest indication that he has become a problem and we will eliminate him. No assassin is ever a danger to us."

"Isn't this akin to hypnosis?" another man asked. "And isn't it true that you cannot force someone through hypnosis to commit a murder unless he had a predilection to murder?"

"No. It's not hypnosis. But, as you suggest, we play it safe. We use only people who have a penchant for killing. Sociopaths, in their subconscious, will not rebel. Our killer is a sociopath, a man without a conscience, who murders with impunity," Bancock assured the questioner. "But not to worry. In our situation we can and will dispatch an assassin who balks. He is merely another tool for our use."

# Chapter Nine

At DREAMS headquarters the group assembled at the laboratory. The immaculate area was split into two large rooms divided by a thick one-way glass wall. On one side of the wall seats were arranged to accommodate an audience for viewing the activity on the other side. The inner room was composed of a myriad system of monitoring equipment. On a table in the center of the room a man lay unconscious, clad only in white pajamas bottoms. He was connected by a series of tubes and thin lines from his chest, arms and head to the compact, advanced equipment. Johnnie Limbo's blond hair bunched up behind his head and partially covered his ears. He was lean and tall and appeared to be in excellent physical condition. A scanning screen built into the wall above the glass divider in the theater faced the audience.

Bancock addressed the three men once again.

"The man on the table is a professional assassin. He has been a contract hit man for most of his adult life. He has agreed to conduct the experiment. He knows he must do it because his past life has left him vulnerable to intimidation. He is sleeping now, induced by drugs. He will be programmed to eliminate one of the suspected leaders of a terrorist cell ensconced in, would you believe, Cuba? We know exactly where he is located through tracking technology. It is so-called 'Data mining'; something you probably already are aware of. This process gathers and stores huge amounts of data and assembles it. We can pinpoint the whereabouts of practically anyone. We then translate the data into a viewable format."

Terrorists, Bancock thought. That's all you saw these days. It was all coming to a head, he mused, where nothing more than a worldwide cult of murderers had to be dealt with accordingly. Their vengeance aimed at the United States was, he was convinced, motivated primarily by unbridled jealousy. Their cultures were caught in the mire of religious fanaticism. As a result, they did not progress into the high-tech age shared by many leading countries of the world. They were, Bancock believed, neutered by the dictators who ruled them.

"Distance has no bearing on the experiment," he continued, "as

47

long as the target's position has been verified. We can hit a target in Iraq, Iran, anywhere we choose. It doesn't matter.

"Above you is a screening monitor which is linked to a device implanted in Limbo's skull. It reveals the subconscious thoughts that we program. The reason we asked you here this late hour of the night is that, obviously, our target must be sleeping in order to receive our input. We have to enter the target's dream while he is asleep. When Limbo enters the victim's subconscious, we will be able to visualize that dream on our monitor through Limbo's eyes. The chip in his brain will transmit those images to our monitor. You will witness a visual demonstration of what is actually happening on the astral level."

A murmur spread through the room.

"If there are no more questions," Bancock said, "we'll commence."

He waited a moment and then signaled to an assistant in the control room to begin the experiment. The lights in the viewing room went off and all eyes were focused on the man in the lab. It looked as if nothing was happening. Limbo lay perfectly still, breathing regularly. Just as it seemed the experiment was a failure, images appeared on the screen.

"The subject is hooked up to an EEG machine which measures his brain waves," Bancock said to his audience. "There are two levels of sleep, tetra and alpha. Limbo is now in the alpha stage, deep sleep. He had been there for some ninety minutes. He is receiving impulses to his brain that will dictate the pattern of his dreams. He will operate on this premise: he must kill the targeted victim. Limbo will be compelled to assassinate the man as if it were just another contract killing. As a professional hitman, he will obey. He need not have a motive for the killing. He merely responds to orders as he did in his conscious life. He won't refute or argue the commands he is given."

The images on the screen began to take form. Shapes appeared in shadowy outlines. A face slowly achieved definition of detail. All of the men in the room recognized the man who was to be killed.

"Limbo is now dreaming," Bancock continued. "His eyes are rolling around under his lids. He is in REM, rapid eye movement. This is where dreams occur. Although he is still asleep, his eyes see the images transmitted to his brain. Now, you see there. He has

48

entered the subconscious dream of the man we are targeting."

There was a collective gasp from the assemblage at the mention of Abdul Asim's name.

At first the images were vaporous, almost transparent, but quickly took form. The man who was to be eliminated was in the throes of a sexual fantasy. His head thrown back in ecstasy, he was dreaming a young girl was performing oral sex on him, In the vision of the dream, Limbo's own image appeared in a bedroom mirror.

"Remember," informed Bancock, "we are seeing this through Limbo's eyes. He is our camera."

Limbo drew closer to the couple on the bed. He reached down, grabbed the girl by the hair, and lifted her away from the target. The man's erotic thoughts were disturbed and the girl vanished. His eyes opened and stared at Limbo in disbelief. The hitman raised a pistol and leveled it at the man's head. The victim screamed but no sound was heard. The gun fired and his skull was blown apart. Still, he started to get up from the bed. He would not accept his death. Limbo put the muzzle of the pistol against the one remaining open eye of the victim and fired again.

The images on the screen blurred and faded.

"It's finished," Bancock announced. "The target is dead."

"Just like that," someone from the audience said. "But you say this is only subconscious thought. A dream. It's really difficult to believe that someone died because of a dream."

"You will have your proof in a day or two," Bancock said. "This is not just an experiment. What you saw here is actual documented proof. But it will be confirmed in the news. That man will have died of a heart attack."

As the men rose to leave the conference room Senator Montgomery noticed a man standing at the other exit door. Because the senator was focused on the action unfolding on the monitors, he hadn't noticed him when he entered the room during the demonstration. He was a strikingly handsome man, at least six feet tall, dressed entirely in black. Black hair combed straight back, black shirt, black tie. What struck Montgomery as strange about this man were his eyes. They were serpentine, also pure black, and he didn't blink. Montgomery swore the man was staring directly at him. He shivered, feeling a sense of trepidation as he left the room. Who the hell was he?

# Chapter Ten

Jenni was into the dream. She saw everything clearly. She was in a bedroom foreign to her. A man and a young woman lay naked on a bed. They didn't see her, apparently unaware of her presence. Jenni recognized him as a known terrorist leader who had lately made headlines. The girl was on top of him, her back to Jenni.

Jenni wanted to stop the dream, to get out of it. She didn't belong here. But she couldn't. She tried but her mind would not accept her commands. She could only watch in disgust.

Then she saw another man enter the dream through the bedroom doorway. Jenni gasped in horror but did not make a sound.

It was the blond man who haunted her dreams, the killer who had murdered two people in front of her on a city street. Once again, he was involved in a dream with her.

He appeared not to see her. It was as if she was only a spectator and did not belong here. Jenni realized she was in a dream not of her own making. Whose dream was she in?

The blond man had a gun in his right hand held by his side. His attention was directed to the man in bed. He walked into the room and calmly approached the couple. They did not see him.

When he reached the bed, he grabbed the girl by the hair from behind. He pulled at her and she simply vanished. The man on the bed recoiled in absolute terror as the gun was raised and pointed at him. The blond killer fired. The back of the victim's head exploded but he still tried to rise from the bed. The killer put the barrel of the gun against the man's eye and fired again.

Jenni stifled a scream and stepped back into the shadows. Her hand accidentally brushed against a small oil lamp on a table to her right. It toppled off the table, heading for the floor. She grabbed it in midair and held it before it landed. She clutched it tightly. Still, no one seemed to have noticed her.

Then, suddenly, the killer turned and looked directly at her. He had seen her. His eyes told her to fear him.

Was he going to kill me, she thought? But the blond man merely smiled and left the room. The dream ended.

# Dreams

Jenni awoke in her bedroom.

She was drenched in perspiration. She sat up in bed and turned on the light. Two-ten am. The blond man had entered her dreams again and brought death with him. The second time in less than a week. But this time he was not trying to kill her.

This was not her dream; she was sure of that. Somehow she had penetrated someone else's dream. Or had someone penetrated hers? What did this dream mean? Dreams could be interpreted; she knew that. Spendler had told her that dreams of death were usually associated with fear of failure, loss of ambition or change of lifestyle, an ending of the old life and beginning anew. That fit with the changes in her life in the past year. And death took the form of the man whom she felt was a threat to her.

But what significance could the latest nightmare have in her life? She wondered if Spendler could find a meaning to it.

Another trip to see Spendler? She wondered if he were tiring of her, if he doubted the credibility of her situation at all.

She got out of bed and walked to the bedroom window. Looking down at the garden below, the blond man once again entered her thoughts. A chill of apprehension stiffened her momentarily. Damn it, she thought. Had she created this dilemma herself? Had her planning and programming dreams so many times in her life led her to an astral level where she had somehow invaded a realm of other dreamers? What was going on?

In the bathroom she poured a glass of water and soaked her dry throat then glanced at herself in the medicine cabinet mirror. She did not like what she saw. Her eyes were strained and reddened, dark shadows under the lids. Did anyone at work notice what was happening to her?

On the way back to her bed Jenni saw light reflecting from an object on the floor near the edge of her bed. When she got closer she realized it was an object made of glass. She bent down and picked it up. She was holding the oil lamp that she had rescued from crashing to the floor in her dream.

She felt close to fainting.

* * *

The next day it was all over the news. At a newsstand, Jenni saw the startling headline on the front page of an evening "extra." She picked it up, not believing what she saw.

The headline read:

"TERRORIST DIES IN SLEEP!"

Beneath the banner headline was a photo of the man she had seen in her dream last night. She had tried to remember why his face was familiar. Now she knew.

She read the account inside the paper.

"The head of a known terrorist cell (name not given), was found dead this morning in Cuba. The terrorist, Asim, who had eluded authorities, was seeking refuge there. He died in his sleep early this morning of an apparent heart attack. Asim is believed to have been responsible for the ordering of many recent suicide bombings around the world. He had dropped out of sight as U.S. forces had closed in on him. He was believed to be hiding in Pakistan. It is now confirmed that he died in Cuba. His body was found in the bedroom of a small house located in the village of..."

There was no doubt. This was the man she had seen murdered in her dream; murdered by the blond man who had killed before. What had she witnessed? How could she have visualized Abdul Asim being murdered at the approximate time he actually died? And what did the blond man have to do with his death? Just who was the blond man in her dreams?

* * *

Once again, Carl Spendler listened attentively to Jenni Butler's latest disclosure. She seemed even more disturbed than she had the last time they met. He felt he was losing ground with her. Rather than relief from the burden of imagined persecution, she was having even greater visions of death and terror. Now it was a precognitive dream in which she saw a man shot to death, who, in reality, had died of a heart attack. His condescension was obvious.

"Dr. Spendler," Jenni said, agitation in her voice, "you really don't believe me, do you? You don't accept that this was more than just a dream. More so than the previous one."

"I believe you had a dream and you described what you remember to me. Yes, that I believe."

"But you put no significance in it. No truth. Just a coincidence that that terrorist died at the same time I dreamed of his death."

"Had you considered you have seen him in the news recently and put his face to the victim in your dream. Especially since you heard of his death afterward. Isn't it plausible that you believed he was the man you saw murdered after you saw the story of his death in the paper?"

"No," she avowed. "Not at all. The blond man killed the terrorist in my dream and then I learned of his death the next day. It definitely happened in that order. I saw the blond man do it."

It was difficult for Spendler to accept the preposterous claim that a human could affect the physical stability of another through dreams. He believed it was possible to connect to another's subconscious and relate on a metaphysical level. But to murder someone by a controlled dream, as Jenni Butler contended, seemed very unlikely.

"Let's be practical," Spendler said, his voice calm, soothing, professional. "We know that Asim died of natural causes. That is a reported fact."

"Couldn't that fact be false?" she interrupted. "Merely what his followers want us to believe?"

"It's possible, but doubtful," Spendler said. "If, in your dream, a killer shot him, wouldn't he have died of those wounds? Wouldn't there have been blood, traces of the assassination, if what you experienced was reality and not a dream?"

"Perhaps my dream was a vision of what really happened," she said. "Perhaps he *was* assassinated and somehow I was aware of it at the time it happened."

"Jenni, let's accept that he died of a heart attack. Remember, you have been pursued and attacked by the blond man in past dreams. It fits that you would see him in a dream again in the role of murderer. After all, the first time you saw him was in the commission of a real double murder."

"I wonder what are the odds of me picking that terrorist to be killed in a dream at exactly the time he died in reality?"

"I admit the coincidence is startling. But there are many possibilities. Perhaps you read about him the day before and buried his image in your subconscious. You say you were always able to tap your subconscious for your own dreams of fancy. Maybe you buried a latent desire to see Asim dead and brought the blond killer into a dream as his assassin. I can't explain, though, a connection of his death with your dream other than coincidence."

Jenni thought once again that she was being patronized. Did Spendler believe I made up this entire fantasy of realistic dreams?

"But I didn't choose this dream," Jenni said emphatically. "I know that. It was none of my choosing."

"Are you sure?"

"What do you mean? That I planned this dream and didn't remember doing it?"

"Not necessarily. But subconscious thoughts may have emerged, thoughts you might have planted there some time before. You admit having a vivid imagination in planning dreams as fantasies."

Jenni pondered his words for a moment. "Coincidence? No. I can't accept that. I know you are trying to help. And I am aware that I am obsessed with this killer. But it was too damn real."

After years of listening to patients relate their nightmares, they were all "too damn real," Spendler thought.

"Did the police ever identify this man when you reported him?" he asked.

"They showed me hundreds of mug shots. But he was not among them."

Spendler decided to try a different tack. If the patient wouldn't accept a reasonable explanation then coax her to tell you what she believed the symbols meant.

"What do you think happened, Jenni?" he asked. "Seriously. What do you think your dream means?"

Jenni pondered the questions for a moment. Then she answered, "I don't know. I wish I did know. If I did I wouldn't have to talk about it."

"You must have an opinion. You seem to be dodging an answer."

"All right, then. I think something did happen. A murder was committed and I saw it happen," Jenni said.

"Something happening? Like what?"

"I haven't got the right words for it. But I believe it was more than just a dream. I think I was contacted. I saw a vision that came to me without my input."

"The blond man played the role of death in the dream. But you weren't threatened in this dream. Do you realize that, Jenni?"

"But I was threatened."

"How?"

"The blond man saw me. He looked right at me. He recognized me. He knows I saw him kill those two people on a New York street a year ago. And now he knows I saw him kill the terrorist leader."

"One fact still exists, Jenni," Spendler said, his voice tractable. "Dreams are not and cannot be reality. They are dreams, nothing more. Chimera. Fantasies of the imagination."

"Something else you should know," Jenni added, her voice sharp and challenging. "I took a piece of your 'non-reality' with me out of that dream."

"What do you mean?"

"Something real," she affirmed. "Reality." She reached into the large handbag she had brought with her...and lifted the oil lamp out. She placed it on Spendler's desk.

"If you don't believe that dreams can be reality," she said, "then explain this. I took it from the dream."

\* \* \*

Carl Spendler laced up his favorite running sneakers and adjusted his shorts. He fidgeted with the sweatband around his forehead and stepped from his bedroom. The New York City Marathon, one more year, he thought, why do I do it? I have nothing to prove.

I'm forty-six years old, he told himself. What have I got to prove? Hell, just that I'm alive. In an instant he was out the front door.

Today was the big day of the year for runners, an adventure he could not pass up. He ran every year in the twenty-six mile trek, a feat he was able to accomplish once a year by running at least three to four miles every day that he could.

The trip by cab took him downtown to the Lincoln Tunnel, through it to New Jersey, south to the Goethals Bridge, across Staten Island to the base of the Verazzano-Narrows Bridge where the marathon commenced. Just before the bridge the cab stopped for a red light. People passed in front of the windshield. Suddenly, a man dressed entirely in black, stopped for an instant in front of the cab and stared into it, directly at Spendler. The ink-black serpentine eyes that caught Spendler's attention were absorbing and, they did not blink. His black hair was combed straight back from a sharp widow's peak on a high forehead. In that instant Spendler felt a chilling flash of peril.

The image seared Spendler's vision. He recognized the man at once. Mother of God, he thought. It was Elymas, the hellish demon with whom he had battled only a few years before and almost lost his own life in the encounter.

Spendler jumped out of the cab and looked to where he last saw the fiend. He was not in sight.

Spendler glanced around at the passing swarm. Black, he told himself. Look for black in a sea of bright colors. Elymas wore black. There. He spotted the demon in the throng, crossing to the opposite corner. He quickly paid the cabby, handing him money and not waiting for change. He rushed into the bevy. Don't lose him, he told himself. Mother of God, don't let him out of your sight. Evil incarnate exists again only to spread harm and terror. Catastrophe follows his appearance.

Spendler thought immediately of the people whom Elymas had murdered a few years ago, among them Spendler's friend and conspirator in studies of the occult, Father Gerald Stuart, a Catholic priest. His murder was a display of vengeance by the demon. At that time, he, Gerry Stuart and a woman, Laura Whitney, had conducted a séance temporarily stripping Elymas of his hold on them.

Now he was again relevant. The demon's reappearance was a portent of death and destruction.

Spendler was almost near the center of the bridge. He turned to look back. The crowd was massive, quickly filling in behind him. Many thousands of men and women would soon converge on the great bridge inexorably gathering at the center. Spendler had again lost sight of Elymas. By now it was impossible to find anyone in the grand surge of humanity. Perhaps, he thought, he hadn't seen him at all. Perhaps the fiend was still buried in his subconscious and had emerged now as a memory. That must be it, he told himself. No! He was real!

Spendler had arrived early. It was over an hour until the race began. He found a position with the sweeping confluence towards the foot of the bridge close to the Staten Island starting point.

Still, no sight of the demon, Elymas. People assembled quickly behind Spendler and it became so densely packed that it was impossible to see beyond the horde surrounding him. Every year he was astounded at the number of runners who converged for the run. By the time the race began, forty thousand human bodies were set into motion.

And now the demon, Elymas, might be among them. Why? What would a fiend from hell be doing at a marathon? It made no sense. Unless...chaos followed him...devastation! Death!

The race was in motion. Spendler was well up in the front of the moving horde and was across the bridge into the Brooklyn side when he heard the noise from above.

Dear God, no!

The sudden staccato buzz of an overhead engine came from the sky to the south. It was a large helicopter flying low, perhaps leaving from Newark Airport. No one bothered to look. A cruising helicopter is a commonplace sight over New York; news camera crews, police, passenger transport. But this one had no markings. A second chopper suddenly appeared to the north at about the same altitude. Both were heading toward each other from opposite directions.

The sea of heads spun in both directions when the choppers quickly changed altitude and dipped lower toward the crowd at the center of the bridge. Suddenly the air was ripped by automatic gunfire that burst from 50 caliber machine guns mounted on the open sides of each chopper. Panic instantly ravaged the runners as bloodied bodies fell. People broke. Trying to run, screaming hysterically in fear, urging the mass of humanity in a forward surge. They knew what was coming.

Spendler thought, Mother of God, not again!

He flowed with the now frantic masses. It was move or be crushed. People fell. Others charged over them. Both helicopters were descending at a rapid, unstopping dive aimed to hit at the center of the bridge. Spendler was now near the beginning of the bridge at the Brooklyn side. He was able to break away from the mass of bodies. He turned and looked back. In the sky, the choppers converged and dived into the bridge at the center where the runners had melded into a still, unmoving panicked crowd.

One chopper hit dead center. A colossal explosion fractured the air. The force of impact cut the bridge almost in two. Thousands died in an instant in the explosion and fiery holocaust.

A few seconds later the second chopper struck.

Flames spread over the runners at the fiery impact, killing even more. Under the devastating explosion, the bridge split and huge sections fell, snapping the suspension cables and plunging into the waters below, dragging with them thousands of flaming human bodies.

Spendler gasped in unbelieving horror. Each helicopter must have been loaded with a massive amount of high explosives to cause such devastation. This cannot be! This cannot be!

Spendler struggled out of the throng and stumbled onto a sidewalk near the bridge entrance. Others followed. There they stood watching the catastrophe unfold. Because of his proximity to the Brooklyn entrance he had not suffered from the explosions that were farther out on the bridge. The collapsing structure groaned as damaged sections continually separated and plunged into the waters of The Narrows. Hundreds upon hundreds of people clung to sections that were now ripping apart. Cables snapped, whipping across those who clung to the supported sections, killing hundreds more in an instant. The screams were agonizing, sounding like the fury of a merciless wind.

God in heaven! Spendler's mind screamed. This was so much worse than the Twin Towers disaster. Here, many more thousands died instantly. Where was Elymas? Was he involved? Why had he appeared at such an occasion?

Spendler drifted farther away from the bridge. Already the sirens of fire trucks were heard in the distance. Rescue units would soon be dispersed from all over the city and surrounding areas. But they would be too late for those on the bridge closest to the impacts. Bodies clinging to the structure lost purchase and one by one plunged into the fiery waters below.

And suddenly Spendler saw him. There was Elymas calmly standing by a lamppost smoking a thin cigar while raging, screaming people stormed all around him. Spendler charged across the turf to the concrete road where Elymas stood. The demon had not flinched nor moved. He grinned broadly as Spendler confronted him, his body a looming threat.

"So, we meet again, Spendler," Elymas said, grinning, a trail of smoke drifting from his mouth as he spoke. "Can you tell me if I am in a non-smoking area? I don't want to break the law. This damn city has so many restrictions. Don't you agree?"

"You did this, you murdering bastard, didn't you?" Spendler screamed at him. "You fucking madman. You killed all these people!"

"Now, now, Dr. Spendler, it's only for effect. You know! To get your attention."

"What are you babbling about, you sadistic monster?" Spendler cried out. "Look at the holocaust you created." He suddenly charged, reached out both hands and clutched the demon's throat. "I'll kill you, you miserable freak!" he cried.

As Spendler's grip tightened, his fingers melted into the dissolving form of his archenemy. In an instant Elymas vanished.

And Spendler woke from the dream.

He was on the floor of his bedroom, smashed against the wall by the window. He rolled over on his knees and got painfully to his feet. Looking down, he shockingly realized that he had on sneakers and a running outfit.

What the hell was going on?

He moved his sore body across the room to the mirror on his dresser. The image he saw there was unbelievable. His clothing had been shredded and scorched in spots. His forearms showed obvious layers of grime. What happened? Had he been present at the perimeter of a fire...or an explosion!

An explosion! The bridge!

But it was a dream! It must have been only that! When he went to bed last night it was still early July. The Marathon did not kick off until November. Yes, a terrible dream. Yet...he was dressed for running. Had he put on these clothes during the dream?

Elymas, the demon, was present in that dream and had spoken to him. Was it a revelation or did he imagine this horrific scenario because of the subconscious images of 9/11 buried in his mind?

It was early morning, hours before he normally awoke. He doubted he would be able to return to sleep. He went into the bathroom and splashed cold water on his face. As he raised his arms he gasped. In the mirror he saw streaks of blood on his left arm. With a wet washcloth he wiped away the still moist blood. The cleansed arm revealed several minor cuts. How the hell did they get there? What had he done during the night to cause these abrasions?

Had his vision been so real that he mutilated himself in the excitement of the dream? It couldn't be! But what of the scorched and tattered clothes?

He stumbled to the living room window, parted the vertical blinds and, in the dark room, looked out. His bedroom was on the third floor and he could not see much of the city from the window. Down the street, to the east, trees at the edge of Central Park by streetlights were still lit. Across the street the tops of brownstone houses and taller buildings behind them blocked the view to the north. Looking directly down at the street, there was little activity at five AM. An occasional car drifted by. A few people wandered home or left for early work. To the right he could make out the sparse flow of traffic on Central Park West. The city had not yet awoken.

Then, below on his street, something caught his eye. There, highlighted by a lamppost at curbside, stood a lone man looking up at him...clearly watching him, his eyes locked with Spendler's. Odd, thought Spendler, how unusual scenarios occur when you least expect them. The man was a distinct dark silhouette, entirely clothed in black, his eyes catching the glint of the lamplight, changing color and now revealing a flashing red glow.

Again, a chill invaded Spendler's body. It was Elymas. The demon *was* alive...and real.

# Chapter Eleven

Clayton Bancock sat at his desk, staring at the computer monitor. What to do about Limbo? Something was wrong and he couldn't put his finger on what it was. He had great hopes for this new technology. With it he could rise to heights of power and unimaginable wealth. But the bugs had to be eliminated before it progressed.

His thoughts shifted to his journey arriving here at DREAMS. The years he spent with the CIA in covert operations both as a field operative and later supervising and overseeing liaisons between hired contract hit men and military mercenaries proved to be a door opener. The assassination of adversaries was a sanctioned agenda that he considered job functions that "came with the territory." He still thought that way. There were no pangs of conscience.

And he received, out of nowhere, the best offer to advance his climb to power? The strange man in black, who brought him to DREAMS, was an enigma. Even with Bancock's extensive knowledge of veiled financiers and clandestine organizations, he could not find any background information on the man in black. How could this be, he wondered. How could this strange man, this Elymas, have no traceable background? DREAMS itself was an organization *with* a history. It had been a sleep research center for many years and had been linked to the study of the paranormal. The acronym "DREAMS" had not been applied until recently.

Was Elymas the catalyst to take the center to new levels of technology? It must be so, he thought. Somewhere there had to be a connection tying him to a source. Was he an enemy of the country? An ally? He seemed motiveless.

Enemy or not, how could Bancock resist the offer of five million dollars and a guarantee of more to come. It seemed no amount of money mattered to Elymas, the man from nowhere. The proof of his benefactor's sincerity came when the money was deposited in his personal Swiss account.

Right here, he believed, right now, this technology had opened a doorway to the future of a new military regime. Dream assassination through fear produced a new era of technology, invisible warriors, a mighty nation's fantasy. Where might it lead? The ability to take out key people without sacrificing manpower was mind-boggling. Its utilization was limitless. This experiment was the birth of power beyond his imagination. The fees for such a service worldwide could be incalculable. And *he* pulled the strings. He was at the rudder.

But what was the ship's destination? Right now it had to have an ultimate purpose. The mysterious leader, Elymas seemed intent open the dismantling of the existing military might of the nation. What had he in mind? Was he intent on establishing his own military structure? That seemed to make sense. It seemed too great a prospect to dismantle the existing military structure of the country. By establishing his own military might, once a weaker government existed, seemed logical to Bancock.

Here, today, he thought, by effectively dispatching one target, dream assassination was proven successful. That demonstration for the chosen committee had worked. And a terrorist was eliminated. Here was proof that the new contingent needed.

But there was the foul-up that must be addressed.

Bancock viewed the disk of Limbo's induced dream once again. It appeared to be textbook perfection. Limbo had been programmed to kill Asim and he had done exactly as ordered without qualms. But there was a problem. The system was not yet perfect.

Something that didn't belong had appeared in the dream. There, what was that? Movement slightly out of sync that bothered him. It was at the very end of the disk. He noticed it when the assassination was taking place. But it was so quick it had no significance until he replayed the disk a few times. Now, as the dream neared the end once again, he waited to assure himself that he was not imagining things.

Here it comes...there. He slowed the speed. Limbo kills the terrorist and turns away from the dead man. His attention focuses for an instant on a figure in the shadows at the other end of the room. A girl's face comes into view for an instant and the disk ends. She appears for only an instant; but Limbo sees her. Why didn't he kill her? She must have witnessed the murder. It seemed illogical that Limbo didn't take her out once he spotted her.

Who is she? And what was she doing in this programmed

dream? There was no input for her to appear. She had either been part of Asim's dream or she had been lodged in Limbo's subconscious and was dragged in by him. Could she be Limbo's sex partner? Could she be in tune with Limbo's subconscious and have somehow transferred his vision to her conscious mind? Bancock had to know the answers. He must find out who she is.

\* \* \*

When Clayton Bancock entered the apartment, Limbo was sitting in an armchair watching a video of a Dallas Cowboy football game. He snapped it off when Bancock entered the room. He got out of his chair and faced his warden. Limbo didn't like to admit it but he respected Bancock as well as feared him. The man represented power Limbo could not even dream of attaining. He did as he was told because he realized the vulnerability of his position for the time being anyhow. He knew Elymas was in his corner. There was a point of no return where he would be pushed to the limit and would use his mentor to rebel.

"I want to talk to you," Bancock said. He was carrying a cased disk in his right hand.

"Sure," Limbo said, sarcastically, "I got the time."

"I'm going to run a disk for you. Afterwards we'll talk about it," Bancock said. Limbo nodded and watched as Bancock loaded the disk. The images of the dream murder of Asim came on the TV screen.

Limbo watched in silence. Bancock sat in a high-backed chair beside him and observed Limbo's reaction. He was especially concerned about the hit man's response to the appearance of the girl in the disk. But Limbo did not visibly react when Jenni Butler came into view. Bancock turned off the machine.

As soon as Limbo saw the images on the disk he knew what Bancock wanted. He forced himself to remain placid and calm. He remembered the dream entirely, short as it was. He was an actor in a play, forced to perform without deviation from the script. But had he deviated? Had he brought the woman into the little drama purely of his own desire? At the time the dream occurred he thought that she existed only in his mind. But she had registered both in his subconscious and here on the disk. He wondered how they got the images on the disk. Did they bury a camera in his brain that registered what he saw in his dream state? Everything was seen from his point of view, as if the dream was seen through his eyes. As if he were the camera.

The dream involving that same girl with him in her apartment came to mind. But that dream had not been the result of DREAMS' technology. They had not planned to send him into *her* dream. He had not been set up with her as a target to kill. They knew nothing of her. He had thought about her in his conscious mind. She was the one he sought. And here she was again.

Perhaps, he thought, her appearance meant that she was nearby. He believed she lived in Manhattan. That was where he first saw her at night. Maybe he was reaching into her dreams just as she was getting to him through hers. Why? Why now? It happened only since he had come here to the experimental dream research unit. Could she have buried him in her subconscious as he had buried her in his? Could the experiment have caused the two minds to somehow be linked together?

"Who's the girl, Limbo?" Bancock asked.

"How would I know the target's whore?" Limbo replied.

"Don't get smart with me," Bancock snapped. He had no tolerance for flippancy. "I'm talking about the other girl. Who is she?"

"I have no idea," Limbo lied. He showed no emotion and registered no change of expression, except that his mind screamed silently, "Fuck you, you flea!"

"How do you suppose she got in the dream?" Bancock said.

"She's not one of your people?" Answer a question with a question.

"Don't be a smart ass, Limbo." Bancock was frustrated and there was edginess in his voice. "No. Of course she's not. And you know that, don't you?"

"Maybe she was part of his dream. The guy in bed, I mean. Like this whore who was his fantasy. Maybe this one was a voyeur. Or maybe it was supposed to be a ménage-a-trois."

"I doubt it. She didn't look the type Asim would know."

"If you say so," Limbo said. "Sorry I can't help you."

"Don't toy with me, Limbo. She has no place in this experiment. This is highly classified material and has no allowance for anyone but you and the target. If I see her again you die and she dies. Understand?"

Be careful, you arrogant bastard, Limbo thought, that it may be you who dies. "But I told you I don't know her," he said.

Bancock was not satisfied. "We will find out who she is and what she has to do with you. You know that, don't you?"

"Sure, I figure you would," Limbo answered quickly.

"And you won't like the outcome," Bancock added, his voice edged with rancor.

Fuck you, thought Limbo. Push me too far and you won't like my outcome.

# Chapter Twelve

Gordon Aldrich had developed dream research techniques while a staff member of a research clinic at the neuropsychiatry branch of a giant hospital in Boston. Within those years he had progressed so far as to have the facility bear his name. When he had begun his career twenty-odd years ago as a psychotherapist he could not have conceived that he would now be both developer and operations chief at the DREAMS research project. Yet here he was deeply involved in what had become his life's work at this renowned New York institution. When he reminisced, his early endeavors seemed unaffected and temperate. He had never truly struggled to arrive at his present position. It happened through a progression of events piled one upon the other in a stream of uninterrupted order.

Long aware of DREAMS, his association with the organization began during a class lecture on REM. As Aldrich spoke to students in attendance, he couldn't help noticing the distinct, unfamiliar figure, dressed entirely in black suit, shirt, tie; sitting in the back of the class at the highest row. At first Aldrich believed the person to be a guest of the faculty. Later he discovered the true reason for Elymas's appearance at his lecture. Aldrich could not break the constant stare of the enigmatic man and spoke to him rather than the class.

"Acquaintance with the REM phase of sleep in the early 1950s opened new doors to the exploration of the subconscious mind," he said, repeating by rote what he had elucidated so many times. "It established that a sleeping person comes out of deep sleep, or the Alpha stage, every ninety minutes and moves up to a lighter stage of sleep. This stage lasts about twenty minutes. During this period, or REM, which stands for 'rapid eye movement,' the mind sees images that the eyes follow under the closed lids. This is when dreams occur.

"Every sleeping person dreams during the REM phase of sleep as a relief of the pressures of life which the mind brings into sleep. It is a way to let out the frustrations and disappointments in life and actually go a little mad. Discoveries show that when drugs suppress dreams, the REM pressure is not expended in dreams and is carried forward into one's conscious life. This unrelieved pressure could be dangerous. When people do not dream they risk madness.

"The amazing thing is people who die in their sleep from cardiac infarctions always die during REM. One of the main causes of death during this phase is fear. Pressure can build to an extreme during the victim's REM cycle. An inescapable fear of death can cause the dreamer to die of heart failure while he sleeps." Gordon Aldrich finished the discussion by introducing the audience to lucid dreaming, a concept that was growing in research groups.

"If," he stated, "a person who practices lucid dreaming, that is, creating a dream and consciously entering it, may be able to travel on the astral plane. Once there, it is possible to become part of the dream of a second party. He or she might enter the dreams of others. It is here that damage could be done to the dreamer's psyche."

Aldrich entered the field of dream research with the belief that dreams could be altered. If drugs could suppress or change visions in REM then he felt it was possible to alter their content. Technology of this sort, he felt, might possibly reconstruct the demons buried in a tortured mind, and hope for the mentally impaired.

While working in the psychiatry arm of the Boston hospital he became involved in dream research through years of convincing those in charge that there was merit to his theories. Limited funds restricted his ability and a dozen years elapsed before he made his breakthrough. With the advent of a mind-altering drug, ingylorim, and advances in computer technology, Aldrich had found the right combination. It was akin to hypnotizing a subject, feeding him suggestions and forcing his subconscious to enact an idea in his dreams. On command, he was rendered unable to disobey.

The breakthrough that changed his life happened as a series of accidents. A drug-induced female patient was linked to a monitoring unit for a routine test. Aldrich realized that the patient had somehow ascended to the ultimate experience; she was dreaming on the astral level. She had traveled out of the dream that had been fed to her, out of the confines of her own body.

Aldrich's imagination soared. He realized that if he could control the ideas implanted into the subconscious mind of a patient who achieved the astral level then he might be able to penetrate the subconscious mind of others who dreamed at the same level and were somehow targeted. It took years but he finally had devised a tiny computer RFID chip, no larger than a grain of rice, which would trigger a response from a second party when inserted into the skull of the dreamer. He could now redefine the thoughts of man. His own mind was dazzled by the concept; program the subconscious mind with a mission to penetrate the mind of another. Subtle command suggestions could affect the targeted mind and change terror to tranquility, sadness to happiness and evil to good through the subconscious.

The offer to join DREAMS came unexpectedly. Elymas, the man in black, appeared in his life suddenly. After the lecture, Aldrich walked to his car in the parking lot of the institute when Elymas approached him.

"Dr. Aldrich?"

Aldrich turned to face the strange person who spoke to him.

"Yes," he said.

"I have an offer for you," said Elymas.

"What kind of offer?" queried Aldrich, unsure of what was about to happen. He recognized him as the mysterious man in the audience.

"I am aware of your efforts in dream manipulation. I am here to guarantee you the vehicle to pursue your research fully with the latest and most sophisticated technology at your disposal."

"Is this a joke? Are you serious?" Aldrich asked warily.

"I most certainly am. Serious, that is."

"Who are you?"

"I am your benefactor."

"Do you represent a research clinic, government, what?

"I wish to remain anonymous. I must do so. But the offer is genuine."

"What makes you think that I am looking to change my position? I am content with what I am doing," Aldrich said.

"I will give you riches that will provide for your family beyond your expectations. And you can build the facility to your needs. Unlimited funds will be available to you. Does that answer your question?"

"This sounds illogical. I will not work for anything illegitimate. No enemies of the country. Be assured of that," Aldrich affirmed.

*Dreams*

"Believe me, I do not represent an enemy."

"What would I have to do?"

"Simply join me in New York."

As he stood by his car Aldrich was spellbound by this man of mystery. It was the eyes that held him captive. The pupils were as black as midnight. They did not blink. They pierced his soul and left him in awe. They told him he dared not refuse.

"But what of my position here? What am I to do?" asked Aldrich, a tremor in his voice.

"Give this up," said Elymas. "My offer is genuine. It will take your lifetime, if ever, at this establishment to achieve what you can accomplish in no time at all with me. I offer you guaranteed success. With me you achieve immediately what you may never attain here."

He accepted the offer to work at the DREAMS headquarters in New York City. To Aldrich this was an opportunity he could not disregard. He had been sworn to secrecy and had virtually disappeared when he left the hospital. It was the culmination of the years of hoping for a position with an outfit that lead the way in dream research. It seemed his initial breakthrough was the reason for his recruitment.

\* \* \*

Gordon Aldrich moved his family from Boston to New York. His fifteen years of marriage had produced but one child, a daughter, Nancy, who was just turning ten years old. Aldrich realized that relocating to New York might be a problem but the opportunity to spend his days and nights in dream research at DREAMS overruled any contingencies.

His wife, Helen, had been slipping into a dependency on alcohol over the years. He knew her alcoholism was a result of the life he had chosen. Little of his waking hours were spent with his family. Nothing he tried seemed to end her dependency. And, once they settled in New York, it became obvious to him that the powers behind DREAMS were aware she had a problem. He had a sense about them, a feeling that they would take no risks. It seemed all relatives of project employees were continuously under surveillance. He had been warned that a careless family member would jeopardize the success of DREAMS. Aldrich felt that the

69

people who hired him would not shirk their goals for mere sentimentality.

What might they do, he wondered. Now that he had experienced their true purpose, the organizational name DREAMS held little inspiration for him. His "dream" bubble had burst. Within a few months he knew his family was definitely in jeopardy. It was a dilemma that limited his options. He could simply walk out; take his family and leave. But the dream project had grown too important for the controlling interests to allow one person to stall it. You couldn't hide from these people. Their alliance reached too far for a small fry like him to escape. He was convinced they would find him if he ran.

On the other hand, he mused, he could stick it out, try to salvage what was left of his marriage and wait for an opportunity to...to what? What could he do, one weak human without the ability, the training or resolve to combat the mega-force opposing him?

The idea of harm to his family lingered in his mind. His wife and child were virtual prisoners of the research project. And he was as much a prisoner as well. He dreaded to think what might happen to them if he objected to the deadly direction the dream project had taken.

After only one year he no longer felt secure with DREAMS. He had already seen his discovery evolve into a death machine for political gain. The benefit that he had envisioned early on was now a lost dream. His intention was to serve mankind with worthwhile causes. Now his work had been corrupted and turned into a weapon by the very caliber of people he wanted least to prosper. He felt betrayed. He felt personal guilt that overwhelmed him.

Before he came to DREAMS Gordon Aldrich had heard rumors that the government had allocated a substantial budget for developing sophisticated weaponry by studying the application of parapsychology. Many disregarded this blabber with no more validity than the discovery that man could become invisible, that he could breathe underwater without appropriate apparatus, or that he could travel forward and back in time. Aldrich remembered hearing at one time that the KGB was regarding the study of the paranormal as science. The United States was forced to keep up. Just in case.

In his research he knew that tests in parapsychology were not new. Both Russia and the United States had conducted experiments for years. But after some minor success and many mistrials, future studies had been abandoned. While he worked at his Boston lab, terrorist strikes on America's homeland changed the general attitude towards tested ideas that could work against such a threat.

At first Aldrich believed solely that the United States government, perhaps the Pentagon or the CIA, employed him. But he was not certain of the money source. The mysterious man who had come to him with the initial offer of wealth had certainly delivered on his offer. He now had an account of over a million dollars in the short period of time that he had been with DREAMS.

Aldrich had come to the DREAMS project as an idealist. When he realized the depth of involvement by private industry, he knew he would have little control over the project's ultimate use. When Clayton Bancock forced him to consort with a special medical/scientific team Aldrich knew his noble ideals had little place at DREAMS. Bancock revealed his true purpose once Aldrich had coordinated the project in working order. DREAMS itself was no more than a sophisticated terror organization. Not in the sense that it seemed anti-American, it was simply anti-human.

Clayton Bancock came to see him in his lab.

"I want you to explain something to me," Bancock said. "There was a woman in the terrorist dream who didn't belong. At the end. She was framed in a doorway."

"You mean the woman in the background who appears for an instant?" Aldrich offered, having seen Jenni Butler when he studied the disk.

"Exactly. What do you make of her?"

"I'm not sure. Something went wrong I suppose."

"You must have formed some opinion," Bancock said.

"She might be someone your assassin knows," Aldrich answered. "Or a friend of the victim. She could be someone buried in either subconscious. Maybe a lover."

"Maybe. I have a feeling it's more than that."

"I don't know what to tell you," Aldrich said. "I can't know what is in their minds."

"How could this happen?" Bancock demanded, obviously perplexed. "I thought you had this project under control. How do I know what else might go wrong? How can I depend on it to succeed?"

The icy tone in Bancock's voice sent a ripple of fear through Aldrich. Again, he thought of his wife and child.

"The project isn't perfect," Aldrich insisted. "We are still experimenting. We didn't know for certain that Asim's death would actually occur. I have never gone this far before. You've forced me to kill a man in his own dream. I'd say you got what you set out to accomplish."

Bancock stared at him. "We had no interference from outside sources in preliminary experiments. No foreign element, like this girl, showed up before in a programmed dream."

"We didn't use your guy, Johnnie Limbo, in those early experiments. We didn't assassinate anyone. This is a new world we're into. We're in the habitat of ghosts, Bancock. How the hell do I know what might happen? We're learning as we go along."

"All right," Bancock said, his tone mellowing. He was no fool. He knew Aldrich's value and he could go just so far with him. There was always the possibility of him lessening his efforts and Bancock could not allow that. "How do we find out what went wrong?"

"We work out the bugs," Aldrich replied. "Just like any experimental project. These are experiments. Nothing more."

"I want you to assure me that this won't happen again."

"How can I guarantee such a thing?"

"I have faith in you," Bancock said harshly. "Find out where she came from, and who she is."

# Chapter Thirteen

It was raining heavily. Jenni watched the evening summer shower from her apartment as it rattled on the courtyard below, quickly forming into puddles. The water brought to mind her sister, Lottie. Lottie feared water. She couldn't stand to be in deep water. It was something she learned about her sister early in their lives. Once, when they had been visiting an aunt, Lottie almost drowned in her backyard swimming pool. She was eight years old at the time and the event was so traumatic it affected her future attitude towards being in deep water. While other children frolicked in the water, Lottie sat on the sidelines.

"I still have nightmares about drowning," Lottie had once explained. "My one terrible fear."

Jenni could never truly comprehend Lottie's fear of water, but she respected her sister's decision to forever remain on terra firma. In Jenni's instance, swimming was learned early on and water became coupled with pleasure. Jenni had gone on to become a champion swimmer in high school and eventually a lifeguard during her college years.

Jenni never insisted on her sister joining group pool activities whenever Lottie and her new husband came to Connecticut to visit. Lottie usually sat in a lawn chair by the pool and would occasionally sit on the steps with only her feet in the water. She simply would not go near the deep end of the pool.

She and Lottie had been very close during their teens and had often spent hours discussing many subjects, religion, literature, morality, the ideal man with whom to spend their lives. The irony was that, back then, Lottie had considered a man like Jenni's Ed, a business executive, ambitious, who could easily provide her with a degree of luxury, as the archetype of her dreams. Jenni, on the other hand, had alluded to no such aspirations. She said she would settle simply for a man she loved. But, ironically, Lottie married a policeman, her childhood boyfriend, Bill Chambers. They lived in a modest home on a tree-lined street in Queens. Lottie married, not for the material advantages she sought early on, but rather because she was completely in love. Jenni, on the other hand, who never possessed the craving for luxuries, had inherited them as part of her bond with Ed, whose business acumen brought them to where they were.

Yet, in spite of unattained goals, Lottie seemed forever happy. She apparently did truly love her husband, now a detective, and found the happiness he gave her was a meaningful substitute for status. Jenni often wondered what Lottie's sex life was like. Was it so much better than hers? She assumed it was. Is that why Lottie always seemed so happy?

Right now she longed to telephone Lottie. She wanted to talk to her sister whom, she felt, understood her. But she looked at the illuminated hands of the clock on the end table. It was now almost midnight. She vowed to call Lottie in the morning. She hadn't seen Lottie in a while and she so desperately wanted to speak with her, to have one of those sessions they used to have, talking things out, spilling their secrets to one another, finding strength and consolation in their relationship.

It wasn't until ten AM the next morning before Jenni was able to call Lottie. Her workload kept her too busy. She dialed her sister at home. Four rings. Please be there. Lottie answered on the sixth ring just before the answering machine kicked in.

"Hello," the gentle voice seemed winded.

"Lottie. Hi, it's Jenni."

"Jenni," the voice was pleasantly excited. "How marvelous. I was thinking about you."

"I thought I might have missed you," Jenni said. "The phone kept ringing."

"I was out back. Would you believe working in our garden?"

"Sure, I'd believe that. Why not?" Jenni could imagine Lottie pruning flowers with the same care and attention she gave to everything in her life.

"How are you these days?" Lottie asked.

"Okay, I guess," Jenni said, then paused. "No. I'm not. Not really."

"What's the matter?" Lottie asked, the sound of genuine concern in her voice.

"Oh, nothing serious. I don't want to upset you. It's just things in general. Can you have lunch with me in town today?"

74

*Dreams*

There was a moment's hesitation on the other end of the wire. "Bill's home..." There was another pause. Then Lottie said, "What the hell am I saying? Of course I'll see you. Bill won't mind if I take a few hours off and go into the city."

"What about the kids?" Jenni asked.

"No problem. They're at his parents' house right now. Won't be back until tomorrow night."

Visions of Lottie and Bill spending an entire day alone in their house raced through Jenni's mind. She had ruined her sister's all-day sex romp. Jenni wondered now if Lottie had really been in the garden. She must have said something to Bill and he whispered for her to go ahead and have lunch. That was why she was so hesitant. Jenni wondered if they were lying naked in bed right now. Was Bill Chambers fondling her as she spoke to her? Was there an expression of complete satisfaction on Lottie's face?

"Listen, Lottie," she said. "I'm sorry. Forget it. I don't want to ruin the day for you and Bill. It's not that important. We'll do it another time."

"Hell, no," Lottie said. "It is important. We'll do it today. It's a beautiful day. I want to see you. It's all right, believe me."

"You're sure?"

"Yes, I'm sure. Now where shall we meet?"

* * *

Jenni met Lottie in Grand Central Station at eleven forty-five. She had made noon reservations for lunch in a small Italian restaurant on Lexington Avenue. Jenni saw Lottie coming towards her through the crowded station, her face beaming with a broad smile. Jenni thought how her sister suggested joy. She was one of those persons in life you meet who truly understood the essence of happiness.

Lottie threw her arms around Jenni in a sincere show of affection. "I'm so glad you called," she said. "I wanted to see you."

"Me too," Jenni said. "It's been a while since we got together."

"Over three months."

"It can't be that long," Jenni said. "How are you, Lottie? You look just great."

"I'm fine, Jenni. Is the divorce final yet?"

"Not yet. But it won't be long. I thought you knew. I should be ashamed of myself, not calling you sooner. How's Bill?"

"Bill's pretty much the same. Nothing fazes him. You know him."

"You love him a lot, don't you?" It was a statement rather than a question.

"Yes," Lottie smiled. "A lot. Hey, let's not get so serious. Where are we going for lunch?"

Jenni escorted Lottie to the chosen restaurant. It was already crowded even though it was just noontime. The girls sipped drinks and ran through small talk as the waiter took their orders. Jenni wasted no time in dropping the bomb on Lottie.

"Something odd has been happening to me lately, Lottie," she said flatly. "I can't explain what it is or why it's happening, but something frightening is crawling around in my mind."

Lottie was puzzled. "I don't follow you, Jenni. Does it have to do with the dreams again?"

"Yes and no. I don't know the exact terms," Jenni explained. "I've been seeing a psychotherapist because I've been having dreams of that man, the killer I saw. I've had dreams of him pursuing me during the year. Lately, though, I've been ravaged by nightmares that I can't explain."

Lottie relaxed. "Nightmares," she sighed. "Hell, it's probably because of the problems you had with Ed."

"I don't think so, Lottie."

"Then it must have been seeing that man kill those two people," Lottie added, her concern obvious. "You've had a rough year. Your emotions are probably being revealed in your dreams. Darn, just listen to me. I sound like I know what I'm talking about."

"No, Lottie, it's more than that. These are different than simple nightmares. They are real. Visions."

"Visions? Of what?"

"Did you see the papers about that terrorist who died?"

"Yes. But what...?"

"The other night I had a vision. I saw that man, the terrorist leader, being murdered. I woke up. When I looked at the clock it was two in the morning."

"But didn't the news media report that he died of a heart attack? Why would you imagine he was murdered?"

"But did he really die of a heart attack?" Jenni suggested. "That's what the papers say. But I saw him shot to death in my dream at the same time that he actually died."

"What are you saying, Jenni? Are you actually suggesting that man was murdered and did not die of a heart attack? That the heart attack story is some kind of cover-up?"

"Lottie, he was killed by the same murderer I saw when Bill drove me into the city that night."

"That same guy?"

"Yes! Exactly!"

Jenni realized that Lottie was staring at her, incredulity built into that stare.

"Lottie, when we were young, do you remember how I could daydream? Fantasize?"

"Yes. How could I not remember?"

Jenni knew Lottie did not put much credence in anyone's ability to manufacture dreams. Fantasy was not in her lexicon. She was the most practical person Jenni could imagine. She accepted life as the essence of practicality. Jenni had never proposed the seemingly impossible as reality to her sister. Now she felt she must unload her burden to the singular person in her life whose opinion she most respected.

"You know I was always able to control my dreams. I could customize them to about whatever I desired."

"Jenni, dear," Lottie interrupted, "you know I always found it difficult to understand what you claimed."

"But you saw me wake from dreaming. Many times I explained to you how I took myself into my own dream world."

"Yes. Of course."

"Well, I programmed them even then. I used them to take journeys inside my mind. Pure escapism. I could weave a dream any way I wanted. You see what I'm getting at?"

"I'm not sure I do, Jenni. Are you telling me you have been creating your own nightmares...on purpose?"

"No. Not that. I have created fantasies...sexual fantasies mostly, into which I escaped. Since I saw those murders on the street a year ago, I've had nightmares. What started as sweet, desirable dreams, the fantasies that I created evolved into nightmares. Lately I'm afraid to go into a planned dream, Lottie. I can't handle it any longer.

It's him. I believe he's taken over my dreams. He's becoming the one in control. Not me. Now I think he's bringing me into *his* dreams. I'm scared. I don't know what it all means."

"Jenni," Lottie said, "I'm no good at this. I haven't the slightest idea what these things mean. I wouldn't know how to advise you."

'Oh, dear, I'm not looking for answers from you, Lottie." Jenni realized suddenly that her initial reason for seeing Lottie now surpassed comfort. She *was* asking her sister for a solution. "I'm venting. I needed to speak to you in particular about it."

Jenni looked across the table into Lottie's eyes. They were noticeably somber. Jenni realized then that she was ruining their luncheon. She had intended to tell Lottie about the lamp she had taken with her from the dream to reality. But now...it seemed a moot point that would only worry her sister even more. And what did she expect from Lottie? Dr. Spendler had no answer for the appearance of the lamp except an indulgent remark. "Jenni, can you be sure that you did not possess the lamp before your dream? " was his answer. Even he had no solution.

The waiter arrived with the food at that instant, giving Jenni the perfect opportunity to get off the subject.

"I'm sorry, Lottie," she apologized. "I haven't been much fun to be with today. It's not fair to you."

"It's all right, Jenni," Lottie said. "Just being together is enough for me."

"You must think me terrible. I haven't asked anything about you or the kids. I've been so wrapped up in my own problems I just ignored you. Is everything all right in your life? "

"Everything is fine," Lottie said. She sipped her Margarita and stared solemnly at Jenni. She decided to be candid. "I'm worried about you, Jenni. Should I be worried?"

"Damn," Jenni swore. "I'm fouling this up. I should have realized it would have this effect on you. I've been dropping my problems on you, looking for sympathy. I didn't mean for this to happen. What was I thinking?"

"Jenni," Lottie said, reaching across the table and grasping her sister's hand, "why don't you take a few days off and come home with me? Get away from the job. We'll go shopping, talk. It'll be good for you."

"I would like to come, Lottie. Believe me I would. But my

swing moods can be overpowering. I'm sure you don't need that."

"You could never be a burden."

"Besides," Jenni continued, "I don't want to ruin Bill's time home with you. I'd only be in the way," Jenni said.

"Believe me, you wouldn't," Lottie quipped. "We don't spend all our free time screwing."

Jenni smiled. "I don't know. I know you're concerned. I didn't mean only to unload my troubles on you. I wanted to find a sense of normalcy in life. You give me that."

"Think about it," Lottie smiled. "And call me. Keep in touch."

"All right. That much I can promise."

After lunch Jenni was responding to Lottie's encouragement. She had come to her sister with an unmanageable weight on her shoulders and she left at least smiling.

# Chapter Fourteen

Ed Butler called Jenni at work early in the morning.

"How are you, Jenni?" he asked.

"I'm all right, Ed," she answered abruptly. "What do you want?"

"I've got a buyer for the house. I've got some papers for you to sign."

"Where? Not in Connecticut I hope. It would mean taking time off. That I can't do."

"No. At my office in Manhattan. You can meet me there at lunchtime. Our lawyer will be there. You can avoid the closing on the sale by signing over power of attorney to me if you think that would help."

Jenni smiled. How crafty, she thought. "I don't think that will happen, Ed. I'll meet at your office. What time?"

"Noon. Is that all right?"

"Yes."

"But you will still have to come to the closing at the bank when the final papers on the sale are ready."

"I'll deal with that problem when it comes," she said as she ended the conversation.

She was determined to end the marriage. Frustration and, finally, humiliation had settled in. Jenni had made contact with a lawyer of her own in Manhattan. There was no way she was going to sign a contract for the sale of the house without her lawyer reviewing it.

She showed up at Ed Butler's office precisely at noon. Miriam, seated behind her desk outside Ed's office, smiled insolently at her. "Hello, Mrs. Butler."

"Tell your lover that I'm here," Jenni said coldly.

When she entered his office, Ed came around his desk to greet her. It was the first time they had met since she walked out on him. So much had happened to her in that time it was hard to believe how quickly it had passed.

"Have a seat, Jenni," Ed said excitedly, seeming pleased to see her again. He gestured to one of the two leather chairs on either side of his remarkably uncluttered desk. "It's good you came. You know Hank Wright." He pointed to the man standing beside him. Henry Wright was their lawyer who also worked for Ed's employer. He had represented them on the purchase of their house. Without her own lawyer present she knew the deck might be stacked against her.

Jenni nodded and said, "I'd rather stand. Where are the papers?"

Henry Wright pulled some papers out of his briefcase and handed them to Jenni.

She glanced at them. "One million two hundred thousand for the house?" she said. "Not bad." She knew Ed carried a five hundred thousand mortgage on the property, so there would be about three hundred thousand coming to her when the sale was finalized.

She lifted the contract papers, folded them and said, "I'll want my lawyer to check these out before I sign."

"Of course," Ed said. "But don't delay. We've got to move on this."

"I'll get them back as quickly as I can," she said. "I'm just as eager as you are, Ed."

"Good," Ed said, forcing a smile.

"Is that it?" she asked.

"For now, yes," Wright said. "Until the closing date."

"How long will that be?"

"Probably a month or so."

She turned to leave. Ed followed her to the door. She stood in the open doorway and turned at his voice. "Jenni," he said, "I have so much to say to you. Can we meet for dinner and talk? Can't you give me that much?"

"What good would it do?"

"Maybe we can reach an understanding. I hate to see us end like this. Our marriage must have meant something to you. It did to me. I don't want to lose you."

Jenni restrained the need to explode. She did not want a loud confrontation to occur and was afraid it might. Surely Ed did not want to get into an ugly verbal battle over the shortcomings of their sexual life in his office with his lawyer present. Why did he insist on encouraging an outburst?

"Don't make me laugh, Ed," she quietly commented. "What could our marriage have meant to you? Why did you find it necessary to have a mistress when you had a wife at home begging for sex? It makes no sense."

"Jenni," he said, his voice faltering "I don't know how to explain what I did or how to make it up to you. It was a terrible mistake on my part. It just happened and got out of hand. I never thought it would go so far."

"How far is that, Ed?"

"I mean wrecking our marriage. I didn't mean for that to happen."

"Damn you!" she snapped. "You would have gone right on with your escapade if I hadn't caught on to you. Was it part of your image that you cherish so much? Did it make you appear more successful if you had a wife *and* a mistress? Big accomplishment. Brag to the guys?"

"No, Jenni, that's not true. It was a mistake. I don't want to lose you. I love you."

"It's too late, Ed. It's more than just Miriam. You know that. I've told you how I felt. I was just another one of your possessions. You weren't interested in my needs. You ignored me for too long. I should have left you sooner, but I kept expecting, or hoping for some indication that you really cared."

"But I do, Jenni. I do care."

"At this point, Ed, I don't."

She left abruptly, before he could say another word or try to stop her. She stormed through the open doorway. Heads turned as she exited through the large, open office exterior. Heads popped up out of cubicles and turned toward her. She felt suddenly conspicuous now that she *had* created a scene.

* * *

As he watched Jenni leave his office Ed Butler felt a wave of despondency overcome him. He ushered his lawyer out, shut the door behind him and settled into the reclining chair behind his desk. He tried to convince himself that he wouldn't let his mood overpower him, but he couldn't shake it.

He hadn't realized how much he loved Jenni until she was gone. He had tried, at first, after recovering from the initial shock of her final farewell, to fall back on his macho reserve and persuade himself that he would survive without her. Life would go on. At first, it was a stunning blow to his pride that Jenni walked out on him. He now blamed himself entirely for not listening to her complaints, but he couldn't believe that she meant what she had said. It didn't seem possible that she would actually leave. Didn't she have everything a woman could want?

When the damage to his pride wore off, the absence in his life became overwhelmingly evident. He had almost purposefully forced the woman he loved out of his life.

He felt alone, unable to face the future on his own. He was consumed by a sense of vulnerability that reminded him of the most frightening time of his life when he was alone and consumed by fear. It was during an incident in his senior year of college. Then, it was the force of nature that had rendered him as helpless as he felt now. He was attending college in Massachusetts and had accepted a ride home during the Christmas holidays in a small plane owned by his roommate's father who was a pilot. Because a storm was forecast to hit the east coast at about the same time they were due to take off, Ed had considered taking the train to New York. Ed's roommate and his father had insisted they would encounter no difficulties and reluctantly he gave in to their pressures.

Their plane crashed on a mountainside in Vermont. Ed's roommate was killed instantly and his father died a few days later in a hospital, never having regained consciousness. Ed was lucky. He had been sitting behind the two front seats and was spared. His left leg was broken and, for two days and two nights, as the plane hung precariously on a snow-covered cliff, he lay hopeless, waiting to die. Rescue choppers found him and saved his life.

The terrible memories of such a near-death experience haunted Ed Butler the days of his life. As a result, he hated anything to do with snow. He suffered through winters. In his mind there was always the horrible dread of how easily he could have died back then, hanging on the edge of that cliff, totally helpless. The way he now felt without Jenni in his life.

# Chapter Fifteen

Something was terribly wrong. Carl Spendler was certain. The appearance of Elymas in his dream and the reality of the horror that image invoked left him worried. He felt this archfiend was truly capable of mass murder. A few years ago he had experienced at first hand only a meager portion of the terror he believed Elymas might dispense. The murder of tens of thousands was not beyond belief.

If, indeed, Elymas still existed in reality—which Spendler believed him to be—then he was once again plotting some monstrous horror to unleash on humanity. In his encounters with Elymas, Spendler learned that the demon's raison d'être was to promote the augmentation of evil in mankind. Elymas' purpose was to see chaos reign on Earth.

How to stop him? Spendler had not forgotten his first attempt. He had teamed with Father Gerry Stuart, a friend, and Laura Whitney, an artist whose life had been endangered by Elymas. They formed a séance that summoned the spirit of a dead medium, Vera Lancaster. She had brought the demon into existence during an earlier séance that resulted in her death. Her spiritual force helped eliminate the physical body that Elymas possessed. But apparently the demon had not been completely destroyed. Now, Spendler felt once again that old fear resurging. He believed his enemy *had* reappeared in physical form. Who? Where? How could he locate him?

He recalled speaking to a New York City detective two years ago. At that time, Elymas had murdered a family in a house on the Upper East Side of Manhattan. Spendler shuffled through calling cards he kept in a desk drawer. He dialed the number of the precinct and asked for Detective Hodges.

"Hodges retired a few months ago," the officer on the phone told him. "Is it a personal call? Perhaps I can help you."

"Maybe you can," Spendler said. "I wanted to get some information about a case he worked on a few years ago."

"Why don't I have him call you?" the policeman offered.

That afternoon Spendler got a return call from Detective Hodges.

"How are you Mr. Spendler?" said the detective.

"Fine," Spendler replied. "Do you remember me? It's been a couple of years."

"How could I ever forget you and Father Stuart. You know, we never did find the perpetrator of his strange death," Hodges said.

"I'm sorry to hear that," Spendler said, knowing how difficult it would be for anyone who sought Elymas. He didn't expect that the police would ever discover who had killed Gerry Stuart. But he knew Elymas had murdered his friend. The murder still haunted him. Gerry had been crucified, nailed to a massive wooden cross that hung high from the ceiling above the altar in his parish church. No one but Elymas could have executed such a grotesque crime. It would have taken more than human ability to accomplish such a task. Spendler knew his testimony that a demon from Hell was the murderer would not bide well. He had seen or heard nothing of Elymas for the past few years and therefore assumed he had returned to whatever netherworld from which he had come.

"What can I do for you?" Hodges asked.

"There was an FBI man involved in a kidnapping case around the time of Gerry Stuart's murder. The victim's name was Jenny Douglas. She was a friend of Laura Whitney, the artist."

"Yeah, I sort of remember the case. The woman turned up a few months later. Seemed some weird guy who took her to Maine held her prisoner on a boat. Strange case. The FBI never found the guy who took her. Hold on a minute," Hodges said. "Let me go to my desk. I've got the FBI guy's name on my Rolex."

A minute later Hodges was back on the phone. "Here it is. His name is Walter Farrell. He's still in the New York Division in Manhattan." He gave Spendler the number. "Nice guy. Easy to work with."

"Thanks," Spendler said. "I'll get in touch with him."

"What's this all about, Mr. Spendler?" Hodges asked before Spendler could hang up. "Do you know something the police should know?"

For an instant Spendler almost opened up to Detective Hodges. Then he thought better of it. First, I talk to the FBI, then I'll get back to Hodges.

"Not really," he said. "There's something about the case that puzzled me. I wanted to ask him."

"Maybe I can help you," Hodges persisted. "I'm still interested in the murder of Father Stuart. There's no statute of limitations on murder, you know. These cases are related. I'm sure you know. Laura Whitney was tied to three cases at that time. Her friend's kidnapping, the murder of the priest and it seems this same perpetrator was involved in the slaying of a family in their own home in Manhattan."

"I don't know what I can tell you that you don't already know," answered Spendler.

"Why did you call me then? You could have called the FBI directly if you wanted Walt Farrell's name."

"True. But I didn't know his name. Now I do."

"All right, Mr. Spendler. But if there's something new about any of those murders please call me. Don't try and do anything by yourself. You're not qualified."

"Detective Hodges," Spendler asserted, "you will be the first to know anything I learn."

\* \* \*

Before Spendler contacted FBI agent Farrell he dialed Laura Whitney's number. He had two numbers for her. One was her apartment in the Murray Hill section of Manhattan. The other was her studio in the Flat Iron District farther downtown. Laura Whitney was a successful artist and it was midday; he expected she would be working. He was right. She answered on the second ring.

"Laura," he said, "Carl Spendler here."

"Carl," her voice was cheerful. "How are you?"

"Fine. And you?"

"I'm just great," she said.

"And Frank?"

Frank was Laura's husband. He and Laura had undergone a difficult period three years back when Elymas came into their lives. Frank had almost died at the whim of the demon. While hospitalized she and Spendler had participated in a séance that, at the time, apparently ended Elymas' hold on the Whitneys. Laura and he had become friends who kept in touch.

"Frank is great. He's completely his old self again. Knocking them dead at the ad agency. Like nothing had ever happened to him."

"Tell you why I called," Spendler said. "I had the strangest thing happen to me. It was a dream, a terrible one. It involved Elymas."

He swore he heard a slight intake of air on the other end of the line. "What...what about him?" Laura said, a tremor in her voice.

"There was something unnatural about it. Can I see you?"

"Certainly," said Laura. "When?"

"How about lunch. Today?"

"I'm at the studio. Can you meet me here at noon? I'm pressed for time. I have to be at the printer to check proofs of my book cover this afternoon at two. We can grab a bite nearby."

Later, near the Flat Iron Building, Spendler headed west on Twenty-Third Street. Laura Whitney shared a studio with a photographer in a loft building that was at least a hundred years old. The combined studio occupied the entire top floor and had marvelous light streaming in through broad skylights on either end of the roof. Laura Whitney greeted him as he got off the elevator.

"Carl," she took his hand in both of hers, obvious affection in the gesture. "It's been too long since I saw you last. How have you been?"

"I'm fine," he answered. "And you?"

"I'm doing well," Laura Whitney answered. "As is Frank."

"You certainly haven't changed," said Spendler. It had been a few years since their ordeal with Elymas, during which time Spendler had joined Laura and her husband, Frank, on a number of occasions for dinner. "It's been about eight months since we got together."

"Too long," she said. "Come in."

She escorted him into the expansive interior. They passed along a corridor that led first to the photo studio and ended at Laura's space. When they entered Laura's studio, Spendler caught his breath. Her paintings were everywhere; on the walls, stacked up in corners, framed, unframed. A work in progress was on an easel under the skylight. It was a large painting of the city at night, at least six feet wide. Sparkling building lights glistened from a spectacular but unfinished foreground and dwindling to a vanishing point at the top left. The contrast between light and dark was done in a variety of shimmering colors. Spendler was dumbfounded. The amazing thing about the painting was that there were no distinctive outlines of the buildings. Only the lights of other buildings created each

# Mike Walsh

definitive building's shape. These windows were done as squares and rectangles, ranging in size from small to tiny.

"Laura," Spendler gasped, stunned by the brilliance of her work, "this is magnificent. I always knew your work was good but this...this is genius."

"Thank you, Carl," she said. "I appreciate that since it comes from you."

"How do you do it?" he questioned.

"I don't know, Carl," she answered unabashedly. "I just work."

Spendler walked around the studio, seriously enjoying the power in Laura's work. He never seized to be amazed at her efforts. "You've certainly been busy," he said.

"The painting on the easel is to be a centerpiece for my new show. I'm struggling to finish it in time."

"Looks almost done to me," offered Spendler.

"Not quite," she smiled.

They left for lunch. In a local restaurant, they sat at a window table looking out on the street and sipped twin glasses of port as their sandwiches were being prepared.

"Now what's this about Elymas?" Laura said.

"Have you had any sight of Elymas lately," Spendler asked. "Dreams or otherwise?"

"No, thank God," Laura sighed. "I hoped I'd seen the last of him."

"I told you, of course, of my miraculous survival in Central Park when I fell in a soft spot he created in the tarmac."

"Yes."

"When I survived, crawling out of the hole he provided for me to almost drown in — I never mentioned this to you — but I was sure I saw him standing on the lawn under a tree."

"You think he might still be alive? Among us?"

"I'm not sure. I had a recent dream involving him," Spendler said.

"You mentioned a dream," Laura said. "Thank God it was only a dream and not a sighting."

"I'm not sure it was merely a dream. This dream was more frightening then the prospect of Elymas appearing in reality. It was much more than the murder of one man, him attempting to kill me. I think he might have been sending me a message. It was a classic

88

nightmare. In our experience, his terror had been limited to a few victims. Well, this dream transcended numbers."

"What do you mean?" Laura asked.

"I saw a vision of thousands killed at the New York Marathon."

"Mother of God!" Laura exclaimed, her eyes wide and filled with terror. "What a thought!"

"I can't tell you how the horror of such a catastrophe appeared. I saw everything so vividly."

"And...what did Elymas have to do with your dream?" Laura asked, a quiver in her voice. But she felt she knew what Spendler was about to tell her.

"That's the point. It had to be *his* dream. Not mine. Elymas was there in the dream. I was in a cab on the way to the race. I saw him pass in front of the windshield when we stopped at a light. I got out and ran after him. I lost him in the crowd. He led me to the thousands on the bridge and then...the bastard unveiled a disaster. Just like the Twin Towers, two huge helicopters, apparently loaded with explosives crashed into the bridge and blew up. Thousands were killed. I escaped. I had already crossed the bridge because I started early and was at the head of the runners. I believe Elymas created the vision I saw. I don't know how or why."

Laura shuddered. "I don't think I could face him again in my life," she stated.

Spendler continued, "The reason I believe he was involved in this vision is this, Laura. When I woke up I was still in my bedroom but I found evidence that transcended reality. I was smeared with blood and minor cuts and my pajamas were scorched by smoke."

"How could that be?" she said, puzzled.

"I don't know. I wouldn't even guess."

"This is frightening, Carl," Laura said. "Could you have hurt yourself falling out of bed? Sleepwalking."

"Perhaps. Or...Elymas created an illusion and inserted a little reality into the dream. But that wouldn't explain the scorched pajamas. I just can't figure it out. Is he able to enter dreams? Is he able to create a dream and make it reality? I dread the possibilities. He has some demonic power. You know that. And here's the irony of this dream; here I am a practitioner of dream therapy and I have no answers. I tell people how to cope with their own nightmares and I have no resolution for my own."

"I shudder to think we may have to face him again," Laura said. "Do you think he has returned?"

"I do," Spendler replied emphatically. "I went to the window after the nightmare and looked down at the street. Laura, he was standing under a lamplight looking up at me."

"Dear God!" she exclaimed, obviously perplexed. "If he is back in our lives, what can we do?"

"I don't know. But I wondered if...if it's possible to once again recall the spirit of the medium, Vera Lancaster...through a séance if need be. She demolished him last time."

"That's a strange request. I couldn't say, Carl. But I wouldn't care to go through that again. Vera Lancaster's spirit seemed to have vanished once she was through with him! And even if we could summon her spirit, what good would it do if he returns again?"

Suddenly Laura gasped, as her hand flashed to her mouth.

"Carl!" she exclaimed, suddenly alarmed as she pointed to the street. "Am I seeing things? Look, there, on the street!"

Spendler turned, his eyes following the direction she had indicated.

"What is it, Laura?" he asked. "What did you see?"

"I thought I saw..." She paused. "I thought I saw *him* for a moment, on the street looking at us."

"Whom did you see?"

"Elymas," she said, her voice agitated. "But that's insane. My imagination must be running wild."

Spendler turned again and strained to recognize the dreaded form in the passing throng. Nothing.

"Tell me, please," Laura Whitney said, "that it is my imagination."

"I truly hope so," Spendler said.

# Chapter Sixteen

Clayton Bancock was right about the DREAMS project's effectiveness. The terrorist's death was reported on TV news and in all the major newspapers shortly after he had witnessed the man's actual demise. The dream research project was a proven success. With this breakthrough he surely would be able to get the government involved. Bancock took his orders from Elymas, the enigmatic one whom he truly didn't understand. He could not grasp the overview of this mysterious person who always lurked in the background. The man had his own private suite on the top floor of the DREAMS mansion; so private that no one was permitted to enter. He seemed not to care when Bancock brought the contingent of business and government personnel to the meeting to witness the terrorist's death.

But now Elymas doubted Bancock's intentions. He appeared, as he always seemed to, suddenly and silently, as if he was nearby at all times.

"There *is* a political motivation in what you are doing here, isn't there?" Elymas questioned Bancock. "By bringing the government into our situation."

"No," Bancock answered. "I don't take sides. The money can come from either political party donor. But I believe the funds will come quicker from government than from private sources. Government is more motivated."

"You may be out of touch," Elymas said. "Don't overrate the government's interest. And don't underrate private investment. Especially foreign money. Funds are not a problem. Merely let me know where you think we can take these experiments. Just whom do you plan to assassinate?"

"I won't betray my country, if that's what you're suggesting," Bancock said. Not that he was patriotic. He believed the government was the proper place to secure such a weapon. Elymas, on the other hand, saw the enormity of the project as a grand extenuation of his function as an ambassador of evil—that placed DREAMS as one monster organization whose purpose was no more than that of a

91

hitman bringing evil to a new dimension.

Daringly, Bancock asked Elymas, "What is *your* motivation?"

"I betray no one," Elymas said. "Betrayal is not in my idiom. I have no allegiance to mankind. All humanity is a mere pawn. To be used in an immortal game. Does that answer your question?"

"And just who are you?" Bancock pushed it, speaking boldly.

"I am who is not. My world is not your world."

What the hell did that mean, wondered Bancock. What did Elymas truly expect DREAMS to be? How big could it become?

"I see DREAMS as a tremendous weapon," Bancock said. "Better in our hands than in the hands of terrorists."

"Fine," Elymas said. "We'll go that route for now. Use it as a weapon. But never betray my trust in you. I have not yet decided how to apply it to total chaos."

Total chaos? Bancock blanched at the words. Just who the hell was this lunatic? What power did he wield? And just how dangerous was he?

\* \* \*

Senator Montgomery arranged a meeting at a spot not yet decided for a private talk with Bancock who furtively agreed and was to be picked up at dusk by a black limousine at the entrance of DREAMS headquarters.

Bancock wondered what the senator had in mind. What did this man want? The meeting had to refer to the DREAMS project, of course. But to what end? Prior to Senator Montgomery's involvement, Bancock recalled he hadn't spoken to the senator more than half a dozen times. He had invited Montgomery into the project because of his commitment to one party government and his contacts in both government and private sectors. Perhaps, Bancock thought, Montgomery had raised the government funds to propel the project into its next phase. But that was no reason to be so secretive. The senator should come through normal channels, shouldn't he? It had to be something more. Something for his ears only.

He waited on the assigned corner. He didn't like this.

Where was DREAMS heading, Bancock wondered. What was its ultimate purpose? He knew Elymas was not anti-American. He proved that by encouraging the elimination of the terrorist. And didn't he allow politicians into the alliance? So far, though, he seemed not to be political. But political parties didn't matter to Bancock, whose only consideration was monetary. He did not trust Senator Montgomery. It didn't sit well with Bancock that he was asked to wait on a street corner to attend a secret meeting.

The car came quickly. Senator Montgomery sat in back and swung the door open for him.

"We're going to a place on the East River," Montgomery said. "Not too far."

"Really, Senator, I don't know if I can spare the time," Bancock said. "I've got a busy schedule. Can we make this quick?"

"I'm sure it will prove worth your while," Montgomery said.

"What the hell is this all about?" Bancock was brusque.

"It's about power," Montgomery said just as bluntly.

Bancock paused a moment, his hand on the open car door, then got in, curiosity ruling out caution. The senator didn't speak again until they came to a tall, prepossessing, prewar building on the edge of the East River in mid-town Manhattan. Montgomery had arranged a meeting in a private room in a penthouse restaurant thirty-five floors above Manhattan. It was dusk and the lights of the city and the Fifty-Ninth Street Bridge over the river presented an unrivaled dazzling view.

There were four men already seated when Montgomery and Bancock entered the private room. Montgomery introduced the new participants. Bancock recognized the men as prominent government officials. He knew some from his period with *The Company*. They, like him, were involved in the procurement of mercenaries as covert operatives.

Greetings were made and, when all were served drinks, Montgomery spoke again. "Gentlemen," he announced, "this may well be an historical meeting. Tonight, what is decided here may well change the direction of our nation for the better."

There was a general murmur of assent as Montgomery continued. "I know you all have been apprised of the situation confronting us and our plan to resolve that specific problem."

Bancock waited for an explanation.

"You are aware of the potential of our newly acquired...ah, weapon," Montgomery said.

Bancock winced at the possessive inference. Montgomery had

obviously already included himself a partner in DREAMS.

"Its uses are boundless," Montgomery went on. "It can bring unbelievable power to the people who control it."

Bancock was now perturbed. He was uncomfortable with the direction Montgomery seemed to be heading. The senator appeared to have taken the reins. He was taking over. Bancock said nothing, waiting for Montgomery's disclosure to continue.

"Our movement must benefit absolutely from this new technology," continued the senator. "And we can be rewarded in the process. I believe I can trust you all implicitly."

There was an all around nodding of heads.

"I am offering you the chance to seize this power and use it for our own singular purposes," continued Montgomery.

"What purposes?" Bancock interjected.

"Why, to save the country from this antiquated two-party system, of course," the senator responded quickly, an eyebrow rose at Bancock's insolence. "To put America back in its proper place in the world, of course, as the only true superpower. In light of the enemies we now face we need every new weapon available."

"That's what we're doing now," Bancock said, still puzzled.

"I want to use this tremendous force to make sure the country remains the most respected and feared nation in the world," Montgomery said. "I want to insure this purpose. We cannot allow the nation to be sidetracked by either the left or the right."

Bancock pondered. He touched his fingers to his chin pensively and said, "Sidetracked by what?"

The men at the table stirred restlessly at Bancock's comment.

Montgomery continued, calmly suppressing his annoyance with Bancock, "Weakness. There *are* people in this country whose ill-conceived motives can destroy the United States. They will weaken it from within and topple it from its once lofty position. By capitulation, they will make us vulnerable to even more terrorist attacks. They will prevent us from defending against our enemies. These people should not be allowed to continue in pursuit of their dangerous and devastating goals."

Bancock interrupted. "I take it everyone here has been secretly briefed on the technology we're talking about," he said.

The men nodded. "Generally," one said. "Not specifically."

"Very well," Montgomery jumped in. "The value of

assassination on the astral plane is undeniable. This formidable weapon is a proven groundbreaking forerunner of a new age of sophisticated technology. A target can be hit anywhere in the world and eliminated while that person sleeps. And the result is that he apparently expired from heart failure.

"That's why we're here," continued the senator, smiling broadly now. "Let me be specific. As you know, there is a large contingent that wants to control our country; a new wave of political treachery. They regard covert activities, specifically assassination, as anathema to their goals. These conciliators seek negotiation with our enemies rather than taking action against them. They will weaken America's efforts to remain the most powerful nation in the world. Teddy Roosevelt's comment, 'Walk softly but carry a big stick' I believe should be 'Carry a big stick and damn well use it'."

Bancock had suspected Montgomery had a more devious purpose than merely a strong defense; a secret that suited his political bent more than just a defense posture.

Montgomery confirmed this belief by continuing to speak. "Appeasement only increases animosities toward America," he said. "I am a staunch advocate of an unlimited defense budget. I say scrap the damn social programs that are choking us. Think of it, the trillions of dollars in the national debt is now equal to the amount spent on useless social programs over decades. If those wasted dollars were not spent so uselessly we would have no national debt. And what has all that waste accomplished? Only to weaken our power.

"A strong defense posture is the only true deterrent to attacks from our enemies. No other way. I say more money for missile programs, nuclear weapons, aircraft carriers, nuclear submarines, drones and, yes, sophisticated instruments of death. I firmly believe that no major enemy would risk attacking us if they perceived us as infinitely strong. The surest way to deter attack is to instill an overwhelming *fear* of retaliation in all enemies and to prove it. Carry an even bigger stick."

"Exactly right," said the man seated to Montgomery's right. "But a great defense requires a great budget. That budget must be approved."

"That's our job," Montgomery said. "You men. That's what we're here for; to make this weapon ours and no one else's. We can't allow these pacifists to crush this or any other weapon of the future. It would spell doom for America if they grabbed power.

"The anti-military movement gets its supporters from all economic levels," Montgomery continued. "We must combat that element. They believe we are guilty of antagonizing and arousing terrorists to action. They believe these enemies must be assuaged through negotiations and hand holding, not through military action. They band together to protest our defense spending. We are, in essence, at war with ourselves.

"And the news media gorge on the obvious rift in American politics and have branded militarists as dangerous hawks betrothed to war. The political right is not much different than the left. The 'Peace Now' movement has expanded rapidly and now constitutes almost one third of all voters.

"This movement can trace its origins to the Vietnam War," Montgomery continued. "The concept of dissension started in the universities by students seeking to avoid the draft. The masses learned to rant against military action. And protesters had the cooperation of the media to spread their diatribe."

Bancock had a suspicion of where Senator Montgomery was taking this and, as he continued, his suspicions were confirmed.

"It follows," continued Montgomery, "that, at this time of conflict, a leader would emerge among them; a harbinger of this *new* order. I'm sure you know of whom I am speaking. He has spearheaded the 'Peace Now' movement as the nation's misguided effort to rid the world of wars by eliminating the weapons that we need to set the world straight.

"He is a governor, no less. Who else but 'Peace Now' would propose such madness? Who else but pacifists would vote for Charlie Washburn? He now has aspirations to make a run for the presidency of the United States."

Montgomery was obviously distressed by this development. "A weakened defense position is the ultimate end to the United States," he continued. "Major powers are not the major problem. Third world nations who are developing nuclear weapons are the real threat. Imagine what might happen if these countries with the bomb, who hate us, banded together to attack us. And don't deceive yourself into believing this scenario could not occur. Terrorism has become the fashion of the times and there is no way to control

96

rampant strikes at the United States.

"If Charlie Washburn is elected to the presidency the end will come a lot sooner. Putting the situation in perspective, I feel, as do many others, that we *can* halt this tidal wave."

A silence of incertitude took over for a brief moment in the room. This then, thought Bancock, was Senator Montgomery's hidden agenda. He spoke up.

"What are you suggesting?" Bancock asked, already sure of the answer.

"Let us not mince words," Montgomery said. "I propose that we eliminate Charlie Washburn in our next DREAMS assassination."

"Now just a minute, senator," Bancock responded emphatically. "I'm in agreement with you that the 'Peace Now' movement must be stopped. But I can't give you an answer right here and now. Do you realize the severity of such a proposition?"

"Don't waste our time, Clayton," Montgomery urged. "We are approaching crunch time."

The meeting ended and Montgomery's associates rose to leave the table. The men departed and Senator Montgomery let them enter the elevator without him. He took Bancock's arm and held him back.

"Sit down," the senator said to Bancock. "Stay with me. I want to talk to you privately."

"What about?" Bancock said. "I've got a busy day."

"It will only take a few minutes."

Settled in their seats, Bancock said, "Why should I get involved in such a drastic event? You propose killing a presidential candidate. They'll hunt us like dogs."

"No. Actually, that dog won't hunt. Washburn will die naturally of a heart attack."

"Why should I do such a thing?"

"We work well together. I believe you feel as I do."

"And just how is that?"

"Power, Mr. Bancock. Just like me. You seek power."

"Did your homework, did you?" Bancock said. "What do I personally get out of this venture?"

"You'll be my partner. We'll share the rewards."

"Just how safe are we?" Bancock asked. "Can you trust your cohorts?"

"With my life. We're perfectly safe."

"How the hell do I know I can trust *you*? This situation smacks of a setup."

"How can I convince you?" Montgomery asked.

"Before we talk," Bancock said, reaching out with both hands and searching Montgomery for recording devices. "Do you mind?"

Montgomery smiled. "Not at all," he said. "I don't think it's necessary. You have my word."

"At least now I feel we can talk," Bancock said, relieved that Montgomery was not wired.

They resumed their conversation.

"Be more specific," Bancock said. "You suggest power; the achievement of power. What do you have in mind?"

"First we take out Washburn. Then we slowly take out every leading figure in the 'Peace Now' movement."

"Are you serious? That movement is too damn big. It's probably impossible to stop."

"Nothing is too big. There will be an epidemic of heart attacks. They can't prove a thing. What I'm after is something traumatic to stall that movement's growth in this country. Take away its momentum. Then it will fall apart on its own."

"What do you propose, starting another civil war?"

"Nothing so dramatic. We can do this. We start with Charlie Washburn. Then we attack the opposite party. At a certain point the public will clamor for our protection."

Bancock pondered the concept for a moment. Then he smiled wryly. "Pretty ambitious, I'd say," he said. He was not yet amiss to the possibility of what may come.

"It can be done. We can do it," Montgomery insisted. "You know it. It would take the starch out of their sails. They wouldn't recover in time for the election. With the movement stifled the president probably would be reelected and defense spending would not be cut. In fact, it would surely be increased. The disarmament movement would take a back seat and maybe even fizzle out. Then we could work on the other party. Wipe out both of them. "

"How do we personally benefit?"

"The military will be on our side. There are already factions in the country who would back our action with all the money we needed."

"There are laws against what you're suggesting."

"We can work around them. It would be damned difficult to prove that we eliminated people when they die of heart attacks. Besides, this would be kept top secret. Only the right people would know. Strictly recruited personnel. We'd have to replace many of the personnel we now employ."

"Still sounds very risky."

"Wasn't the Kennedy assassination risky? And who knows to this day what really happened. We will set up red herrings. And we can deal with anyone who might be a risk."

"Can you guarantee that this will be our baby?"

"You and me. Absolutely," Montgomery said.

"I'll have to seriously consider what you've proposed. I've got my benefactor, Elymas, to deal with."

"Fuck him!" swore Montgomery. "Who the hell is he? Merely some rich guy I never heard of. He can be taken care of."

"I'm afraid he might not agree. He has to be informed. He could close us down. He is the money man." Bancock sighed. "Goddamn! You're asking an awful lot of me."

"Don't ponder it. Just give me an answer. This can't wait. It can't just hang out there. You know that. It has to be now."

"And if my answer is no?" Bancock said.

Montgomery did not pause to consider his response. "Then you would never know what you lost."

Bancock felt he was being threatened. "All right," he said. "I'm with you. But this is not going to be easy. We have people working for us who won't take kindly to this. Killing a foreign enemy, a threat, is one thing. Killing our own is another. I don't think it will wash."

"I don't consider Charlie Washburn one of our own. He's a threat to the country. Imagine what would happen to America if he became president. Good God! The prospect scares the hell out of me."

"Still," Bancock said, "people on the staff are not going to go along with it. Especially Elymas."

"We take him out too," Montgomery said. "We can start by trimming the staff to only those who must be involved. You've got the technology. Elymas provides funds. Taking him out merely means the funds have to be replaced. I can get you all the money you need. There are factions waiting to finance us. Get the project down to only the necessary people to run it. There are ways of handling them. Who do we need?"

"A few technicians. That can be arranged. We'll need Gordon Aldrich, the originator. For the time being, that is. Until we are really up and running. Apparently he has misgivings about our use of the technology. And, of course, there's Johnnie Limbo."

"Who is he?"

"The contract killer. The assassin. The guy who killed that known terrorist."

For a moment both men were silent. Then Bancock said, "Just remember what I told you. I don't think Elymas will be easy to kill."

"Don't deceive yourself," Montgomery said. "You apparently don't know who you're dealing with here. I've got the backing we need. No man is invulnerable, especially this Elymas character. Believe me, he can be eliminated."

When the two men finally departed, the restaurant help came to clear the table. In the midst of activity, the setting was suddenly disrupted by a piercing loud clatter. A busboy, startled when he saw movement in a shadowy corner of the room by the abandoned table, dropped the plates he was holding, sending them crashing to the tiled floor. A human shape had suddenly appeared from nowhere. A man, dressed entirely in black, suit, shirt, tie—even his hair and eyes were the color of tar—emerged from the solid wall.

Elymas had been part of the wall. All through the discussion, he was invisibly assimilated into the molecular structure of the wall and listened to every word. He stepped out of the wall and calmly left the room.

The busboy watched the strange creature in awe and quickly blessed himself with the sign of the cross. "Madre di Dei," he said. "It is the devil."

* * *

Elymas waited for Bancock to come to him at his private apartment on the top floor of DREAMS headquarters. Elymas had demanded of anyone in the building to make arrangements for an appointment to see him.

"What is it?" he asked as Bancock entered.

100

*Dreams*

"I want you to know about an extremely important dream contact I would like to try. I need your input."

"My permission, you mean," Elymas said derisively.

"Well," Bancock sighed, "yes."

"You want to assassinate Charlie Washburn."

Bancock tried not to show amazement in his expression but he failed.

"You already know?" he managed.

"Don't ever try to deceive me, Clayton," Elymas said, preferring to use first names when he spoke to underlings. "You can't outwit genius."

The arrogant bastard, thought Bancock. He must have spies everywhere. Who, in the restaurant might have betrayed him, he wondered. Not Montgomery. It had to be one of the others. How much did he know?

"All right, then," he said. "You are aware of what I'm proposing. Do you agree?"

"Sure," Elymas said flippantly. "I'm all for chaos. The more the better. This would make a great gimmick to set off massive strife. Go to it."

Bancock left Elymas with a feeling of accomplishment, thinking how easy that was, but harboring a sense that it might have been too easy.

# Chapter Seventeen

Charles Washburn backed into politics. He started as a lawyer defending people who could hardly afford to pay for his services. He embraced their hopeless cases and won so many he became known as a champion of lost causes. He took his penchant for the defense of the underprivileged into public office as the result of his popularity and because of the demands of his followers.

He was *the* definitive candidate for the new movement, the perfect person to carry the banner, the movement that was becoming the most popular in the nation, eclipsing all others. Its banner "PEACE DEFEATS MIGHT!" was prevalent everywhere.

Charles Washburn started his political career in the most unlikely role as mayor of a small city in Minnesota. From this office he made the jump to governor of the state. Both positions were entered into reluctantly, riding on the demands of his constituents. He had never considered becoming a leader, but he espoused the political philosophies people wanted to hear. He believed in what he said. He did not operate on polls, although he was constantly advised to pay attention to them. Timing, the news media called it. They applauded him as being in tune with the pulse of the people and always in the forefront of popular causes.

He caught the public's fancy. The press immediately picked up on his campaign for the presidency and he forged ahead of other candidates. He easily triumphed in the primaries and, according to polls, was currently running head-to-head with his incumbent opponent. It was expected that, as his campaign gained momentum, he would pull well out in front.

And the timely topic that would carry him to the presidency was the "Peace Now" movement, the concept of compromise. Its legions of supporters across the nation were gathering every day, recruiting new members as exposure to the public made their cause credible.

"Washburn is a person to be reckoned with!" the news media proclaimed. The women's vote was his to claim almost exclusively.

He was a tall, trim, attractive man in him late-forties. He possessed a seemingly honest nature and welcoming charisma.

People trusted him both by his appearance and his words. He was no common, run-of-the-mill politician. Charles Washburn did not say what was expected of a candidate. He did not make hollow campaign promises simply to get elected. He thought his presence in the White House could change the course of the cataclysm that he felt was to come if the nation continued on its present warlike course.

He stepped from the shower, dressed quickly in the bedroom of the hotel suite that his staff had booked for him in Chicago. Tonight's speech would be an easy one to deliver. He expected to be supported by an audience that consisted of many leaders from a variety of groups throughout the country. These people believed as he did that a continual arms buildup and aggressive foreign policy of the present administration was a sure path to national decline. But it was not just this captive audience he intended to attract. He wanted to gather into his tent women of the country who were yet undecided and the male population who agreed with him but did not believe he could win the election. But hell, didn't he carry the electorate and win the primary?

There were six people waiting in the living room and many more downstairs, all members of his entourage, setting up the grand ballroom for his speech on national TV. An end to his privacy, he thought. His life would never be the same again now that he had committed to run for the ultimate public office; the most powerful position in the world. He was catapulted into a completely strange and terrifying arena. A quiet man, basically, he was caught up in a wave of activity that carried him along in its wake. He did not make the rules, or the strategies. He was the fountainhead who espoused the rhetoric of a force that, by now, was self-propelled. And everyone listened, even his opponents paid attention.

Charles Washburn's wife—he had married his law partner— had gone all out for him when he announced his plans to run. There was no reason, he stated, why he couldn't be President of the United States. He believed he could make it all the way to the top. He smiled as he thought of her back in Minneapolis. He wouldn't be joining her for two more weeks; another of the disadvantages of campaigning.

He dressed swiftly. When he was ready he entered the living room where close members of his staff waited.

"It's sure looking good, Charlie," Bill Manning, his campaign manager said. "Better all the time. We've climbed two more percentage points on the polls. We're starting to pull away."

"I guess we have the momentum now," Washburn said. "I wasn't sure we would in the beginning."

"I was always sure," Manning said. "The movement has the votes. All it needed was the right person to spearhead it. You. You're the only one who could take it all the way."

"I'm glad you're so sure, Bill," he responded. "I think it's a case of merely being in the right place at the right time."

"Timing is the essence of any campaign," said Manning. "And we've certainly got that. We're on a roll. And they can't stop us. There's nothing in our way."

"Only the debates," Charles said. "I was never really much good at debating. It isn't my forte."

"I wouldn't worry about it," another of his staff, a woman, joined in. "The press will carry it in your favor. They're all for you. The format is rigid. You just have to stick to our program."

"Right. Peace in the world through mutual disarmament. People believe in you and the movement," Bill Manning said with authority.

"I know all that, Bill," he said. "But the debates are for all the marbles. It's gotten so that a candidate lives or dies by his or his exposure on national TV. If I don't do well there I might not win. All our work would be in vain."

"It won't happen, Charlie," Manning said. "You don't have to win the debates. Just make a credible showing. Hold your own. We've got so much going for us. It's the pulse of the nation right now. People believe in us."

"That's one of the things worrying me," he said. "It's not me the people are voting for. Any candidate would make it on this ticket. I wouldn't guess what my chances might be without the movement behind me."

"That doesn't matter now. We are on the verge," Manning stated. "You took a burgeoning movement and made it into a viable cause. You *are* the movement. Don't let it get to you. Don't give in."

"I didn't come this far to give in," Charles said in earnest.

Manning smiled. "That's the spirit."

104

His security men joined them and the group moved downstairs to the main ballroom. Every seat was taken and many people were standing in the aisles and in back. The crowd rose and unanimously applauded as he ascended the stage.

Preliminary statements were made and he was introduced to another thunderous outbreak of applause. When the clapping stopped he spoke in a quiet steady authoritative voice.

"Ladies...and gentlemen," he began, "Let me start with this concept...our children and our children's children must not be forced to live in the shadow of impending doom brought on by our own misguided leaders."

The opening line resulted in more applause. Bill Manning was right, Washburn thought. I am the fountainhead of a movement that has its own energy.

"I appeal primarily to the parents of the nation...of the world, for that matter," he continued. "We instinctively react to protect our children to the exclusion of all else. Why then, will we complacently stand by when their lives are in jeopardy by policies that must never come to pass?"

More applause. He waited until it subsided before continuing.

"Voters of America can lead the world now, once and for all, by fighting to end the continuing cycle of war between nations. We can do no good by canceling out each other's votes. United, with one purpose, we can change the course of inevitable disaster. We are a force to be reckoned with. United, we can lead the nation away from the inevitable road to war.

"This great nation now stands once again at a crossroads and a monumental choice must be made. We can choose one of the two paths before us; we can continue to manufacture weapons of destruction that will inevitably lead us to become the perpetrators of worldwide holocaust or we can take the true road to peace by carving a path to global disarmament. I believe this is the only way to let nations of the world know that we are at heart a peace-loving country and not the warmongers they believe us to be. The example we set can change the world for the better. We must take the lead and begin a program of disarmament that other countries will follow. This is the road we must travel; for us to lead the way."

A ring of applause exploded at his words almost before he finished speaking.

"Our founders wisely devised a future for all generations based on freedom, prosperity and happiness. But there is no freedom for future generations while we are held in bondage by a policy promoting the endless proliferation of weaponry. It is servitude of the spirit to a false concept; that might is right.

"There is no prosperity in the unending arms race. Some maintain that spending more billions upon billions every year on an endless accumulation of newer and more sophisticated weapons is good for the economy. Is it really? This money comes from our taxes. We pay for the arms build-up. The manufacture of weaponry is not the essence of a consuming economy. Military might is not consumer oriented. It is the product of special interests, schemers who get rich by lobbying and wielding power. The production of arms only produces riches for the few arms-makers.

"Think of the billions of dollars that would be saved by adopting no less than an arms freeze," he continued. "These many, and I emphasize the word many, billions would be put to use as subsidies for education and social programs which sorely need funds every year. An educated populace is the hallmark of a true economy.

"Where is peace and happiness when the threat of war is our only future? The arms buildup brings only disaster. We live in the shadow of doom as long as we follow this devastating path. Peace will come only when we cast off this unbearable yoke which drags us down. Let us lead the way for all nations."

He paused and sipped a glass of water at the podium while the applause rang in his ears. Charles felt good about his speech so far. He was really into it and he believed what he said. He didn't need the notes laid out on the podium; the words filled his mind and came to him easily.

He resumed his speech and spoke of the misguided belief that an unlimited defense budget and a superior military posture served as a deterrent to war. He saw the arms buildup rather as a provocation to the enemies of the United States. He even went so far as to say that like all wars of the past, paths of blind self-righteousness led to conflict.

He continued. "There are those who will tell you that the United States can win a war on two or more fronts as we did in World War Two. But our current flawed foreign policies prove that we will attract few allies as in previous wars. We will have to stand alone in situations perpetrated by us alone. The mindset of those weaned on victory through destruction is to create conflict during their time in charge to prove their worth. We all know there can be no victor after a nuclear war. The entire globe is the victim; all the children of the world will be affected.

"And, please tell me, what is wrong with the concept of peace through reconciliation...?" At this point he was interrupted by a spontaneous crash of applause. He smiled, took more water and waited for the roar to die down.

He resumed speaking.

"Peace through disarmament is the proper path for us to pursue. We have sold the world the idea that our nation is the greatest vestige of freedom and peace and yet we threaten those who disagree with us with the prospect of war. If we profess to be the peacekeeper of the world then let us practice what we preach. Let us advance world peace, not world war.

"The madness of war must stop. We can begin by effective conferences with all nations. We must convince them that the way to world peace is to set an example. Once our message is received —that we are serious—these nations will join us. It is in their best interest as it is ours. This is the new beginning we seek. From there we can expand until there is a true ban on all nuclear weapons worldwide. For I truly believe that deep down inside all people is goodness waiting to spring free.

"You hold the destiny of our nation in your hands. You have the voting edge that counts. Use that power. Use it as a beacon to light the true road for generations of warmongers. Show them the path of righteousness. Let them know we are coming. Vote to end all war. Once and for always ... PEACE OVER WAR!"

Again, thunderous applause filled the grand ballroom. The crowd was on its feet and was not only applauding, but also cheering. A feeling of overwhelming euphoria grasped Charles Washburn. He felt elevated to a state of accomplishment he had never before experienced.

Dear God, he thought, I'm going to win. Is it truly possible? President of the United States.

# Chapter Eighteen

"How long is this going to take?" Limbo asked Clayton Bancock when he came to see him in his room. "I'm going out of my fucking mind. What do you call it? Cabin fever?"

"It's going to last as long as it takes," Bancock answered. "The experiments are far from over. We've still got to get the bugs out."

Limbo wouldn't ask Bancock about the ultimate goal of the dream experiments. He knew better. Were they after bigger game than the singular assassination of a minor terrorist leader? These fuckers were CIA or some such thing and he was convinced they would kill him if he asked too many questions. But he had Elymas as his protector, didn't he? What was Elymas's goal? Was he, like them, after bigger things? Sure, he must be. Didn't he claim to have planned this experiment? Didn't he claim to have been searching for me?

The mock killing of the terrorist came easily. He believed that he was issued commands and, through his eyes, he saw the target's dream in visual reality. It had to be through the little device that that was implanted in his skull. There must be a mechanism of some kind set up in the building to receive and show those images.

At first Limbo wondered why they had specifically chosen him for the experiment. Limbo thought he had the answer when Bancock, seeking the girl's identity, showed him the disk. They believed him to have no conscience, a sociopath. There were many other contract killers who could have served as well. Or could they? The experiment was an assassination scheme utilizing the subconscious mind. Perhaps, in the subconscious state, he thought, the DREAMS crew needed a subject who was devoid of conscience.

"How are you feeling?" Bancock asked him. "Any after-effects?"

"Nothing I noticed," Limbo answered. He didn't want Bancock to know that he felt a tremendous change in perception right after the first sessions in the sleep lab. He wasn't sure exactly what it was he did feel; it would be difficult to put into words. It was purely psychological. He had a vivid sensation of power. He thought he could make Bancock's heart burst right now if he chose, without the DREAMS technology.

Bancock brought a doctor with him. The man wrapped Limbo's arm and was checking his blood pressure. He made marks on a clipboard and ran his stethoscope over Limbo's chest and back. The man performed a series of simple tests while Bancock sat patiently in a high-backed chair. When the doctor finished he spoke to Bancock as if Limbo wasn't there.

"He'll have to come downstairs for x-rays and blood tests," he said.

"All right," Bancock said, dismissing the man and closing the door behind him.

I could take his fucking head off right now, Limbo thought.

Bancock said to him "Have you thought anymore about the woman in the dream who appeared on the disk?"

"No," Limbo lied. "But I told you I don't know who she is."

"Don't shit me, hit man. I know she came from you."

"I don't know her!" Limbo shot back. "You either believe me or you don't."

"I want her name."

"I don't know her name." He wasn't lying now.

"Why are you protecting her? What's one girl, more or less?"

"Not much," Limbo said. "More or less."

\* \* \*

Gordon Aldrich realized just how trapped he was. Bancock came to him and took him to an apartment in a lower floor at DREAMS headquarters. Once inside, he gestured for Aldrich to be seated.

"This will be your home for a while," the ex-CIA officer said calmly.

Aldrich remained standing. "What do you mean, my home?" His eyes were wide. He was obviously agitated.

"You'll be staying here for a period of time."

"I don't understand. What's wrong? What's happening?"

"There is nothing wrong. Just consider this a security precaution. The secrecy of the DREAMS project cannot be compromised, no matter whom it concerns."

Mike Walsh

Aldrich looked around the room for a telephone. There was one on a small table near a sofa. At least, he thought, he could get an outside line to his family.

Bancock saw him glance at the phone. "That telephone will only connect you to inside lines. You cannot get an outside line without permission."

"What the hell is this?" Aldrich said. "What about my family?"

"They will be taken care of. Don't worry."

"What do you mean don't worry? And just how are they being taken care of?"

"Professor Aldrich, believe me, this has to be done," Bancock said. "You must have known that sooner or later we would have to lock down the project. We can't have our people going home every night. This has become a top priority. We are all volunteers here. All of us are subject to the same rules. Myself included. I won't be leaving either. I am under the same confinement as you."

"How long is this going to last?"

"We don't know yet. It won't be long."

Aldrich was becoming more nervous as he talked. His right eye twitched and he began to pace the room. "You've no right to do this," he snapped. "This isn't some communist country, damn it! I am an American citizen. I have rights. You can't keep me prisoner!"

"Calm down. You're getting overly excited for no reason. You're not a prisoner." Bancock was good at lying. He had spent a lifetime at it.

"I want to know the real reason I'm being locked up," Aldrich ranted. "You're deceiving me. Why can't I leave here? Not allowed to speak to my family? What the hell is going on?"

Bancock waited for Aldrich to calm down.

"This is a prison cell," Aldrich continued, his voice on the edge of panic. "Suddenly I'm treated the same as Limbo, a murderer, a known criminal. You're holding me here by force. I want to know what's happened to my family."

"Your wife and daughter are being looked after. We will provide a tutor for your daughter's schooling. They are protected until our mission here is finished."

"And just what is that mission?"

"You'll know soon enough," Bancock said. He turned abruptly and left the room. Aldrich flung himself against the door and tore at

110

the knob. Locked. He *was* a prisoner.

What had he gotten himself into, he thought. His decision to join the DREAMS research group now appeared to have been the worst decision in his life. He had been led to believe that his project would be developed and utilized for the security of the country. He sincerely believed the project was a legitimate covert arm of the government. It was, wasn't it?

But its purpose had been altered. By whom? Who issued the assassination order? How far to the top did it go? Was Bancock in charge? Did he make the decisions as to who would die? Aldrich couldn't believe that Bancock had that kind of power. He believed the former CIA officer was only a link in a long chain. He merely did as he was told.

Aldrich knew he could do nothing but wait. He prayed that no harm had come to his wife and daughter. He didn't want to believe that the members of DREAMS would harm them. But then, he had already seen what they would do to satisfy their aims. What did he or his family mean to them? They were merely three insignificant people who didn't matter; people who could be eliminated and never missed; who dared not interfere with the suposedly greater purpose of this secretive organization.

And yet, he considered "it" his program. It was he who had made the significant discoveries that made it possible. He felt he had hardly tapped the power he had unleashed. So far, Limbo had been able to actually enter the mind of a victim in REM sleep and burst his heart through fear. But where else could Bancock take his experiment? If this was the beginning, what was the next step; new horizons for a killing mechanism?

\* \* \*

They came for Gordon Aldrich the next day. He had spent a restless night. His eyes kept opening; he never got past REM sleep. He pictured his wife and daughter somewhere in a room, like him, prisoners, guarded, worried and fearful. And he could do nothing about it. He knew he would never have the opportunity to get to an outside phone line. They had taken his cell phone. He should have realized something like this was bound to happen. Someone would be with him all the time. Even if he could call out, whom would he call? The police? What would he say? That he was an employee on a research project and he was kept prisoner.

The two men who escorted him to Bancock's office were always visible in the building. He had met them when he first joined the organization and thought of them as Bancock's bodyguards. They left Aldrich in front of their boss, who was seated behind his desk. Bancock waited until the men left before he spoke.

"We are going to make another target hit," he stated. "You will prepare it."

"Who is it this time?" Aldrich asked dismally.

"Charles Washburn," Bancock replied coolly.

"Charlie Washburn!" Aldrich was incredulous. "The presidential candidate?"

"Yes. Exactly."

"You're crazy. This is sheer madness. Why?"

"We have good reasons. Let's just say it's for the security of the nation."

"I won't do it. He is no threat to the country; not like we eliminated a real threat, a known terrorist."

"Ah, but he *is* a threat, probably more dangerous than any terrorist. He will ultimately destroy this country. He must die. And, yes, I believe you will do it."

"You go too far, Bancock!" Aldrich cried. "There is a limit to all this. You've taken my discovery and made it into your own personal murder weapon. You can't get away with murdering innocent citizens at will."

"But we can. Charlie Washburn is not an innocent citizen. Anyone who is treasonous must be eliminated. I should be considered a great patriot for ridding the country of him."

Aldrich now saw Bancock as a power-hungry madman. "What gives you the right to determine such a thing?" he said. "Your views are not what this country stands for. You are nothing more than a murdering psychopath. I'm telling you right now, I won't do it! You can't force me!"

Bancock turned away. He punched a few numbers in a cell phone. "Put the woman on," he said and handed the phone to Aldrich.

"Gordon," his wife said. "Gordon, is it you?" She sounded perplexed, but sober.

"Helen, yes. It's me. Are you all right? How is Nancy? Have they hurt you?"

"No. We're all right. Nancy is fine. It's just that...they have us confined in a house somewhere. Out of the city..."

The phone went dead. Bancock took it from Aldrich.

"Did you get the message?" Bancock said.

"You bastard," Aldrich cried. "You'll pay for this."

"Just do the job you're being paid to do," Bancock said.

\* \* \*

Limbo was placed in the dream experimental room and the implant in his skull was once again linked to the system that would command him to attack a target. Clayton Bancock, Senator Montgomery and his retinue stood behind the glass window and watched as Gordon Aldrich and two assistants prepared Limbo for the endeavor. Both worked by Aldrich on either side.

Once sleep was drug-induced, Aldrich entered the code into a computer and set Limbo into action. The chip in his brain was activated and the coordinates incorporated into the system quickly pinpointed the destination he was to travel on the astral level. Within minutes images appeared on the screen. It was two-thirty in the morning and Charlie Washburn was asleep. That fact, along with his present location, had been confirmed.

The picture cleared, revealing that he was indeed dreaming. In his dream, seated behind his desk in the Oval Office, surrounded by close aides, he discussed matters of state with them. Such a dream at this particular time would logically be buried in the subconscious mind of the presidential candidate.

Limbo entered the dream just as the system ordered him. He walked slowly into the famous office and moved directly to Charlie Washburn. No one was going to stop him. The other figures in the dream had no control over him or the dream in which they were participants. They were present only in the candidate's imagination and would vanish as soon as he was threatened. Limbo invaded the dream entirely by systematic input.

Senator Montgomery held his breath as he watched the dream unfold. This was too good to be true, he thought. Within seconds Charlie Washburn would be dead. The "Peace Now" appeasement

Mike Walsh

movement would be dealt a tremendous setback to its astounding growth. Montgomery saw Limbo raise the pistol to a level position as the hit man drew closer to his victim. It's going to happen, the senator thought. Nothing can stop it now. He felt exhilarated by the power he controlled and was overwhelmed with the realization that he was on the way to greatness. With this technology he could eliminate any enemy.

He turned to Bancock. "This had better work," the senator said resolutely.

"Don't fret it," Bancock answered. "It can't fail. There's no way to stop us."

Charlie Washburn was having a pleasant dream, seeing and feeling the sensation of being ensconced in the Oval Office, in power, while solving a policy problem with his staff. It was going well and the dream contained an overall sense of accomplishment.

And suddenly, Washburn saw Limbo coming toward him. The candidate's eyes registered fear and, spontaneously, the dream was disrupted. Marginal people vanished as his attention focused on the intruder. He saw the gun in the intruder's hand and instantly recognized the situation. His worst subconscious nightmare was manifesting in what he perceived as reality. Close up. He had harbored the fear of assassination while in office because of his controversial stand on disarmament. And here it was, seemingly come true. His heart rate jumped to a bursting point and was about to slam a severe body blow inside his chest. He was going to die and he knew it.

The gun was raised and aimed at him and the steely determination in the eyes of the killer who approached sealed his doom. There was no escape.

And, as suddenly as the gunman appeared, another body interrupted the dream. A woman stepped out of the background and screamed a silent scream. Limbo was distracted. He turned to the intrusion and smiled at Jenni Butler. He knew her by sight. Here she was, once more in his dreams. Had he purposely reached her again while dreaming? It seemed she was an integral part of his subconscious; that when he dreamed she appeared. Had he no control over her materializing? But this time something appeared to be going wrong. Limbo was not controlling the actions of this dream. He turned away from Jenni and pointed the pistol at Charlie

114

Washburn. He pulled the trigger. Nothing. It didn't fire. He turned back to Jenni, puzzled.

She stood in the background, silently watching the action unfold. Only this time she was not passive. She had screamed. Although there was no sound, Charlie Washburn heard it and was instantly aware of Jenni's presence.

Jenni was winning. She had blocked the planned assassination.

Jenni approached Charlie Washburn, bent over the desk and said softly, "Don't worry. He won't murder you if I can help it."

At the laboratory Senator Montgomery cried out, "What the hell is going on? Who is that woman?"

"Damn it!" Bancock shouted. "Abort! Stop it!"

"What's going on?" Aldrich said.

"Look!" Bancock indicated the images on the monitor. "There. It's that same woman. The one who appeared in the terrorist's nightmare. Now she's here in this attempt."

Aldrich saw her now.

The appearance of Jenni Butler amidst the images on the screen startled both Clayton Bancock and Senator Montgomery as they watched. The dream had not gone as it should have. That woman. Again! Who was this person?

"She knows!" Bancock cried out. "Look at her face. She sees what is happening! How did she appear? Where did she come from?" He moved quickly to Aldrich.

"Stop the operation! Immediately!" he shouted.

Gordon Aldrich complied and ordered the system shut down. In the experimental room Johnnie Limbo's body convulsed on the table. In the dream he felt himself losing power. He faded from view in the dream like a burned-out circuit. He awoke, sat up. Clawed at the connections on his body. In that instant the dream was gone; its images faded and vanished from the monitor. The assistants inside the test room disconnected Limbo.

The dream was incomplete. Charles Washburn would be spared for the moment. Aldrich breathed a silent sigh of relief. He had gotten a reprieve. Perhaps he could figure a way out of his dilemma while Bancock and his team regrouped.

Bancock gave orders for Limbo to be brought to him. Senator Montgomery, who was now raging, caught him by the shoulder and spun him around as he marched out of the experimental room.

Mike Walsh

"Do something about this, Bancock!" he wailed. "Whatever is happening here has to be corrected immediately."

"I'll take care of it," Bancock assured him. "It won't happen again."

"It can't happen again," Montgomery said. "If Washburn realizes what happened here he'll go into hiding. We won't know when he's sleeping and where."

"It won't get to that," Bancock said. "No one could possibly realize what's going on."

"What about your guy on the table in there?" Montgomery pointed to Limbo. "Is he the cause of what happened?"

"We'll find out and correct it. I promise you that."

"You had better," Montgomery said sharply. Bancock knew he had just been threatened.

His strong-arm men hustled Limbo to Bancock's private office. Limbo did not like to be manhandled and he thought he could take out the two henchmen in an instant. As professional as they thought they were he knew better. Apparently things were not going exactly right with Bancock's experiment. His head ached more severely from this dream than the first assassination attempt. He stood before Bancock's desk and knew immediately by the strained look on his face that the dream had definitely failed. Bancock was infuriated.

Fuck him, Limbo thought. Let it come to a head right now.

"All right, hit-man," Bancock said, his voice ringing with acrimony. "I'm asking you one last time. Who's the girl?"

"How the hell do I know?" Limbo snapped back. "Are you still on that bullshit? I told you I don't know. What the hell do you want from me?"

"She showed up on the screen during the Washburn hit."

"So what!" Limbo snapped.

"The operation was canceled," Bancock said.

"Charlie Washburn is still alive?" Limbo actually sounded surprised.

"That's right. And only because of you and this girl who follows you into our dreams. She interrupted this dream because she made her presence known. She actually changed the outcome by her interference. You brought her into this dream, Limbo. I'm sure she knows what was going on. You fucked up this assignment, hitman. This was a major screw-up. There will be huge repercussions."

"How can you be sure this girl knows what's going on?" Limbo asked.

"We don't know. But we can't take the chance. She certainly must be suspicious. In this dream she went directly to Washburn and said something to him. If she remembers anything, our attempts will be in vain. Now, do I get her name or not?"

"You don't take no for an answer, do you, pal?" Limbo responded belligerently, a note of challenge in his voice, thinking of Elymas as his strength. "I don't know her fucking name."

"All right," Bancock motioned to the two men who remained. "Get him out of here. Lock him up." To Limbo he said. "We'll find her. You've had your chance. Once we find her your girlfriend is as good as dead."

# Chapter Nineteen

Charles Washburn awoke from the nightmare in a fit of horror and disbelief. The most feared occurrence in his life, since his campaign activities began, was that of his death by assassination.

And now he had envisioned a nightmare that was a heart-stopper. His pulse was pounding.

His eyes open, he could not believe what he saw.

Dressed in pajamas, he was seated in a leather chair behind a massive mahogany desk. On the floor was embedded the presidential seal. He looked around. He was alone. But this could not be, he determined. He must still be dreaming. How could he be in the Oval Office? This is impossible! Where is the assassin? Is he still here in the room?

He got to his feet and slid around the desk. All his senses were animated. Whatever he touched had solid substance; the desk, the chair, the floor under his feet, all felt solid. Madness! His mind could not accept what was seemingly unfathomable. But yet...it was true. This was not a dream! This was reality! How, in the name of God, he thought, had I gotten here? Was I drugged and brought here? No. White House security would have prevented such a happening.

Must get out of here. Quietly. Without anyone noticing me.

But how? Oh God! This cannot be!

In dreams everything moves quickly. Results take seconds to occur. And now, here in reality, the same was happening.

The doors of the Oval Office burst open and Secret Service men crashed into the room, their arms outstretched, pistols aimed at him, poised to fire.

"Freeze!" one man commanded.

Washburn froze.

"Hands behind your head! Down on the floor"

He obeyed the commands.

"Please," Charlie begged as he knelt. "I don't know how I got here. I don't know what happened."

"Hey, Pete," another Secret Serviceman said. "Look at this.

Don't you recognize him? It's that Washburn guy. The one who wants to be president."

Pete looked closely at the man kneeling before him. He laughed. "By God, you're right. This is one for the books. What the hell is going on?"

He was taken from The Oval Office and escorted to a private basement room somewhere in the bowels of the Washington complex. Because of his status he was treated with care and respect. He was given a robe and coffee was left alone in the room before representatives of the FBI and Secret Service arrived.

"Is there any explanation for what has happened?" he was asked.

"None," Charlie Washburn replied. "I'm as puzzled as any of you are."

"You are saying that you don't know how you got here?"

"Exactly."

"No one could have smuggled you in. Not one security position has been breached. No security personnel witnessed you or anyone else entering. Can you explain how that can be possible?"

"No. I can't."

"Mr. Washburn, this is getting us nowhere. We must know how you entered the Oval Office during the night."

"I'm telling you I don't know," he insisted. "I went to sleep in my own house and when I woke up I was in The Oval Office. You explain that to me," he challenged. "Look! For God's sake, I'm still in my pajamas. Explain that!"

The interrogator turned to one of his men and shrugged his shoulders.

"Can I call my wife?" Washburn asked. "She'll be worried."

"In a moment," said the interrogator.

Washburn decided in an instant that he must take charge of the situation. He was being treated like a common criminal, perhaps even a suspected terrorist.

"Now listen!" he insisted. "I don't know what the hell is going on here. This is some kind of trick. I'll deal with you after I talk to my wife."

The interrogator left the room. Washburn sat with the two remaining men and his thoughts.

Of course he could not tell them of the dream. They would not understand what he felt; how real and frightening it had been. Assassination; Charles Washburn's worst nightmare ever. He had entered a dream in which he was the President of the United States sitting at his desk in the oval office...and then, this.

Assassination. He shuddered with fear at the thought of dying this young. He remembered the steely, determined look of the assassin as he leveled the pistol directly at him, ready to kill. He wondered if the presidency, as the leader of the most powerful nation in the world, was worth it.

He was well aware that the political philosophy he had adopted, now favored by a majority, angered many to the point of permanently eliminating him. Even now, there were factions who wanted him dead.

And now he faced an even worse nightmare. Could it happen like this, a dream come true?

No! Charlie Washburn silently cried out, holding up both hands in front of him as if the gesture might hold off his adversaries. This isn't happening! Impossible! This cannot be.

The Oval Office and the men surrounding him suddenly dimmed. Then the vision faded. In an instant it was gone.

Charlie sighed in relief as he knelt on the floor of his own bedroom. His eyes adjusted to the darkness and he recognized the safe, familiar surroundings.

Thank God, he gasped. As he got to his feet he realized he was holding something in his hands. He went to the end table by the bed, snapped on the lamp. He looked at what he held. It was the personal penholder, with two pens in their respective receptacles, belonging to the president of The United States. The inscription on a plaque said, "To my loving husband, President of the United States, Kenneth Newland."

Dear God! Washburn thought, was I really there?

He labeled it a somnambulistic mishap; a sleepwalker somehow slipped through a crack in the network.

\* \* \*

Jenni Butler awoke in terror. In this dream she saw the blond assassin preparing to kill Charlie Washburn in the Oval Office. She watched the killer raise a gun and aim it directly at the presidential candidate. It was a repeat of the vision she had when the terrorist, Asim, had been killed in a similar vision.

Had she seen a prophetic vision of a future event?

Precognition? Or was it the same dream she had seen before, repeating itself with the characters and setting changing? Or was it a revelation of an event that had already happened? Good lord, was Charlie Washburn dead? Would she read a headline tomorrow that the candidate had died during the night? No, that couldn't be! This event had taken place in the Oval Office. And hadn't she intervened and prevented the murder?

She was sure she had been dragged into the dream of the murdered terrorist. She now thought this was true of Charlie Washburn's dream as well. How had she been able to invade this nightmare without willing it?

The blond man was obviously an assassin. She saw him kill two people on the street. No dream there. And now two more attempts to end human lives.

If she had actually witnessed a murder in her dream, who would believe her? Who could she tell? The police? The FBI? Hardly. She thought immediately of Dr. Carl Spendler. He had told her that she brought the killer into her own dreams because of her fear of him. Had she also manufactured dreams about that person murdering other people? Might the blond man be in tune with her subconscious and bent on luring her into his subconscious thoughts?

But she was afraid Spendler would not believe anything she told him. She noted a tone of skepticism at their last session. Was he patronizing her? She could almost imagine what Spendler might think..." Now she is seeing her dream killer murdering people other than herself in her dreams. First a terrorist and now a presidential candidate."

Dr. Spendler must believe her, she thought. He was her helmsman through this storm. She relied on him. He would have to listen.

The next day there was no news of Charles Washburn's death. Apparently she had not died as had that terrorist leader. Jenni went through all the papers looking for any news that harm had come to her. There was nothing.

Still...there was doubt. Finally, she called Carl Spendler.

"I must see you," she wailed into the phone. "I'm in a bad way.

I'm afraid. I've got to talk."

"Calm down, Jenni, please," Spendler said. "What is the trouble?"

"Something new has happened. It's the blond man again." Jenni's voice was cracking, on the edge of desperation.

"I'll see you, of course," the psychotherapist said. "But you're scheduled to come in at the end of the week. Can't it wait till then?"

"No. Please."

"All right, Jenni," Spendler said. "But the best I can do is tomorrow night. We'll resolve this thing. I can't give you any time during the day. But I'll wait at the office for you. About seven o'clock."

"I'll be there," Jenni affirmed.

\* \* \*

Charles Washburn's wife prepared breakfast while he sat at the kitchen counter sipping coffee. He had a brief two-day respite before resuming the rigors of the campaign trail in the northeast.

"Helen," he said, clearly concerned, "I had this terrible dream last night. Maybe you can put more meaning to it than I have."

"Tell me," his wife said, her voice tinged with sympathy.

"I dreamt I was in the Oval Office..." he said, "talking to members of my cabinet..."

"You were the President, of course," she said, smiling.

He reluctantly grinned. "Naturally. Anyhow, the session was interrupted by the appearance of a man with a gun..."

"What...!" his wife said.

"The assassin was someone I'd never seen before," he continued, "but was so distinctive and terrifying I can't get his image out of my mind. Damn, Helen, he was going to kill me. Pointed a gun right at me. Scared the hell out of me."

"I can believe it," Helen Washburn said. She was never completely convinced that her husband should pursue the path to the presidency. Now she felt that concern accelerate. Since he began his political climb their lives had been torn apart. Their lives were active and content until the transition to the political scene began.

"It seems to me that was bound to happen, honey," she said. "We've spoken about such a threat. There are madmen out there who don't like what you stand for. After what you've been through on the campaign, you were bound to have that type of nightmare."

"There's more," Charles said, a puzzled look on his face. "It wasn't just an assassination attempt with a gun. There was something that puzzled me. As soon as I felt threatened in the dream all of my staff vanished. You know how things like that happen in dreams. People pop in and out without control. Well, the oddity of it was that not everyone disappeared. The man with the gun raised it and pointed it at me. God, it was awful. I felt so near death. The fear was so strong it choked me. But then a young woman screamed. I turned. She was beside me. The gunman didn't fire. Whatever influence on him or ability she had, stopped him from pulling the trigger. I stood there frozen with fear, looking at that puzzled and frightened woman. She came very close to me and spoke. 'Don't worry,' she said, 'they won't murder you if I can help it.' Then the gunman vanished and the dream ended. It was chilling. I can still see that girl's face, screaming and yet talking to me."

"God, honey, it was just a nightmare," Helen Washburn said, soothingly. "We all have them. Results of buried subconscious thoughts. And you're stressed out."

"Probably, you're right. But this was more than just that. This person, whoever she was, was trying to...I don't know...warn me, I think. It was as if she knew the killer was coming for me and she was there to stop him."

"Dreams seem that way at times."

"What way?"

"You know, as if they had a secret meaning. Some kind of message."

"Perhaps," he said, pondering for a moment. Then he stated, "But the puzzle, worst of all, is not so much the meaning of the dream, but how did I get into the Oval Office without any knowledge of the journey there?"

"What do you mean, how did you get there? You were there only in a dream."

He lifted the presidential penholder from his lap and set it on the kitchen table. "Take a look at this," he said.

Helen Washburn picked up the holder and perused it. Alarm registered on her face. As she spoke her mouth was grim and unsmiling. "Where the hell did you get this?"

"You're asking me," said Charlie. "That is a true puzzle. Is it possible that I could have been sleepwalking and really was in the Oval Office?"

"That is impossible," Helen Washburn said.

"Yet here it is? Someone would surely have seen me and stopped me...even if I had been sleepwalking or hypnotized."

"Don't you remember anything else about than the dream?" Helen pursued the point.

"The dream was so vivid I remember every detail. But I have no knowledge of getting to where the dream took place. Could I have been drugged and taken there and brought back here?"

"Impossible. I never heard a sound in bed last night," Helen offered. "We fell asleep about the same time and I never heard you move. If you had gotten up to walk or someone broke into the house I surely would have heard some noise."

"I wonder," Charlie said. "Was this really only a dream? Or a premonition; a view of something in my future? Somehow sent as a warning by a psychic...perhaps? Maybe the woman I saw was a medium. Something of that nature."

"Do you know the woman you saw?"

"No. And that's strange too. Helen, I could see her so clearly. Just who is she? And her distinct words to me. Why would a total stranger appear in my dream involving a death threat?"

"Maybe you met her somewhere and her face was buried in your subconscious."

"No. I'm certain I never met her before. But I don't think I'm going to forget her face so easily. I have never before felt such downright terror in my life. There was no way to stop that gunman. I swear I felt close to death. Like I was going to have a heart attack, the fear was so great. If that girl hadn't been there and screamed, I thought I might have died on the spot. Helen, can people die of fright in their sleep?"

"I don't know that much about dreams. But I doubt it."

"Here's the thing that bothers me so much," Charlie said. "Assassination is the only fear I've had since I started this run for the presidency. I've got so many radical enemies out there. It is my one dread. Why was this dream the subject of my greatest fear? Last night was the closest I've been to the edge."

"What edge do you mean, Charles?"

"Death."

Helen sat silent and studied the pen set.

\* \* \*

Jenni got to Spendler's office at 6:45 PM. The building was closed and she had to wait for him to show up. She stood outside the office building. Earlier rain had stopped but the gray blanket of clouds over the city lingered. The building was located in mid-Manhattan and there were still many people on the streets. She watched for Spendler. The minutes passed slowly. A feeling of apprehension overcame her. She felt suddenly very vulnerable, aware of just how insignificant and helpless she was against the blond man. If he could kill people on the streets of the city and elude capture, kill victims in a dream and lord knows how many more, then what chance did she have, an individual with no support?

A hand touched her on the shoulder from behind. She jumped and gasped involuntarily.

"Jenni," Carl Spendler said softly, "I'm sorry I startled you."

"Mr. Spendler," she sighed, relieved. "It's you."

"Sorry I'm late," he said. "Some personal business to take care of. Let's go upstairs."

He unlocked the door and let Jenni into his office. She sat down in a familiar chair.

"What am I going to do?" she immediately asked, excitedly. "Something terrible is happening to me."

"Tell me," Spendler said.

"I've had another dream like the last one. The blond man was going to kill someone again."

"Is it someone in your life?"

"Well, no. It was Charles Washburn."

Startled by her answer, Spendler responded, "The guy running for president?"

"Yes. It was like the last one. Real. This dream was an attempt to murder him."

Spendler pondered for a moment, thinking of his own recent bout with a nightmare in which the demon, Elymas, had appeared. "You believe this dream to be reality, Jenni? How could that be if it was merely a dream? It was a dream, was it not?"

"I don't know. But I'm sure I was witnessing another murder attempt."

"When was this? Last night?"

"No, the night before last."

"But Charlie Washburn has not been murdered. Surely you know that. And there has been no news of even an attempt to kill him."

"I'm aware of that. But don't you see? It was the same as the death of the terrorist. An assassination. The same killer, that blond murderer. I was also in this dream. Washburn was going to be killed. The blond man pointed a gun at him and was ready to shoot hlm. If I hadn't been there...in his dream...I screamed and interrupted his attempt."

"He saw you and stopped?"

"Yes."

"You believe it was his dream and not your own?"

"It must have been his. Why would I concoct a dream in which he would be there and try to kill Mr. Washburn?"

"Perhaps you've taken him to a higher level of murder. Remember, he is a symbol of death to you."

"No. I'm certain this was not my dream." Jenni was adamant. "I was in *his* dream. He must have somehow dragged me into his subconscious."

"So you believe he was aware of you being in his dream?"

"Yes. Absolutely," she said. "I interacted with the content of his dream. I stopped him by crying out. I upset the routine. And he knows I witnessed this attempt on Washburn's life?"

"Jenni, were you aware all the time that this was a dream you were into?"

"Yes."

"Do you believe you actually *do* control or plan the action in your dreams?"

"Yes, I always could. I planned my own dreams for years. You know that. We've discussed that."

"Lucid dreams are rare and the ability to control them even more so. If, indeed, you are capable of consciously manipulating a dream in your subconscious, it is entirely possible that it was you who created these threatening dreams."

"But I'm telling you I did not create them. Not the last few.

Before that, yes. But they were dreams of mainly..." She paused, reluctant to say what was true. "They were sexual dreams. I created them to fulfill a need."

"Jenni," Spendler said softly, "these recent nightmares might simply be a matter of association on your part. Charles Washburn is a prominent figure. He has been getting a lot of attention in the media. You have had ongoing psychological problems with the blond killer buried in your psyche. In your subconscious you brought the two together."

"I don't believe that..." Jenni stammered. She began to vigorously clench and unclench her hands. Why would Spendler not accept what she told as fact? Why must she be questioned so? She saw the cloud of doubt in his eyes.

"Damn it!" she cried, provoked to respond angrily. "This is all wrong. You don't believe me at all. You never believed me. I can see it in your eyes. I can hear it in the tone of your voice. Have I been wasting my time by coming here, Dr. Spendler? All you're doing is patronizing me. If you don't help me, who will? Do you think I'm delirious, raving? A lunatic? Have me locked up? Is that what you're thinking?"

"Nothing of the sort, Jenni," Spendler replied.

"Then help me, dammit! Tell me what I should do!" she cried, jumping to her feet.

Spendler recognized the anxiety of his patient. She seemed to have dealt with an occurrence similar in his own recent personal experience that he could not explain. Spendler thought of his nightmare then, the unexplainable fact that he had retained visible indications of his ordeal when he awoke from the nightmare of the Verrazano Bridge disaster. To him, at the time, it seemed reality was somehow part of that dream. How could he censure Jenni Butler for her beliefs when he questioned his own sense of reality?

"First of all, you'll have to get control of yourself. This is imperative." He looked deeply into her eyes. "I don't want you to become overly excited. That won't solve anything."

"Is that all you can say? I didn't need a psychotherapist to tell me to get control. I know I have to get control. It's how to do it that's the problem. Can't you see what's happening? I'm seeing this madman commit murders and I have to somehow stop him."

Spendler frowned. He had lied to Jenni. He did consider

# Mike Walsh

recommending observation in a dream research institution for a short period. She was in a terrible state of depression brought on by her paranoid obsession with the blond man. Granted, she had reason to have such fears but now Spendler believed she might be dangerous to herself. He was certain her delusions would become progressively worse.

He couldn't let this continue. Lately, each time she came to see him, she presented him with a new twist to her dilemma. He couldn't attack that specific problem when she kept compounding it.

"Do you want to go to the police?" Spendler asked. "Tell them what you've told me?"

"I don't know," she answered. "Maybe the FBI."

Spendler thought of FBI agent Chambers, with whom he had dealings in the past. He could tell Chambers about Jenni Butler's unusual dream. But what could he tell the FBI agent? After all, she had only had a couple of dreams regarding assassination.

"It might be awkward to ask either the police or the FBI to investigate the truth or significance of nightmares. I don't think there is any precedent set."

"But these are not merely nightmares. These dreams are reality. They are visions of events that actually happen."

"Jenni," Spendler said, rising from his chair and sitting on the edge of his desk, "I would like you to visit a dream research center for additional therapy."

"I thought I was already into therapy by coming here to see you," Jenni responded. "What are we talking about?"

"I'm advocating specific therapy that may help you understand the cause of your dreams," he stated, thinking perhaps he also needed therapy.

"So you do want to have me committed," she responded.

"Not at all. I merely want you to undergo some research. There are many phases of dream studies; group sessions, individual head-to-head techniques which can resolve many problems. Today there are even drugs that might help."

"But I don't want to share my dreams with anyone else," she said. "How much time are you talking about?"

"I should say no more than a few days. There are many institutions around the country practicing dream research. But I

128

would insist that you stay close to home. Right here in Manhattan. The center I have in mind has achieved some rapid success. And I will come and spend some time with you during your stay. Would you agree to that?"

"What is the name?" Jenni asked.

Spendler handed her a card he lifted from his desk drawer.

Jenni glanced at it. "DREAMS," she read. *"Dream Research Employing Alternative Memory Surveillance.* Sounds appropriate."

"I'll arrange a stay for you," Spendler said. "Can you spare the time in the near future?"

"I'll have to," Jenni said, not at all enthusiastically.

# Chapter Twenty

Edna Rothmann smiled as Jenni entered her office.

"Sit down, Jenni," the senior editor said. She had a file folder on her desk and opened it upon Jenni's entrance. She slipped out the paper on top.

"You're sure about this?" she said.

"Yes," Jenni answered.

"Do you understand what it says?"

"Certainly. I am requesting a leave of absence for one week to attend to personal affairs."

"Unidentified personal affairs," Rothmann added.

"Yes. Personal. Unidentified."

"Well, you can guess that I'm not in favor of losing you for even a few days," Rothmann said, rising from her chair. She came around the desk and stood before Jenni, then leaned back and sat on the edge of her desk. "This is an unusual request, especially for someone who's just breaking back into the job market."

Jenni didn't reply. Rothmann towered over her. "Well, I approved it," Rothmann added.

"Thank you," was all that Jenni could think of to say.

"Now let me get personal, Jenni," the editor said, in a soft yet stern voice. "Is there anything I can help you with? As I've said before, I consider my staff as family. If there is any way I may be of assistance in whatever problems you are facing, I am here for you."

"Thank you very much for the offer, Ms. Rothmann..."

"Call me Edna, please," Rothmann interrupted, forcing a smile. "No reason for us to be so formal."

"I appreciate your concern...Edna, but I must resolve a very personal matter. It's something I must do alone. It's just that it takes a little time."

Rothmann reflected on her previous conversations with Jenni. The editor was convinced Jenni was having troubles with a man, her husband, probably, or a lover. *What a waste*, the senior editor thought. *A gorgeous woman like this throwing herself at some hairy, slobbering beast and getting nothing but sorrow in return.* She felt she could comfort Jenni and show her a path of deliverance through her temporary crisis. She was convinced that whatever was troubling Jenni could be resolved through tenderness and sympathy.

She had to try. If only she could subtly find a weakness in Jenni's mantle, a way to penetrate the facade and convince her there was an alternative. She must be careful in her pursuit. She must not breach the acknowledged rules that constitute charges of sexual harassment. So far she had been getting nowhere with Jenni. But she believed there must be a weakness, vulnerability in this troubled woman. Perhaps the opening had come in the form of this leave of absence. Perhaps, Rothmann thought, this was the opportunity she had been seeking.

"The door is open, Jenni," Rothmann persisted. "Anytime. I offer the invitation with an open heart as well as an open door."

"Thank you, Edna. That's very good of you," Jenni responded and left the senior editor's office.

\* \* \*

That evening the ringing phone shattered the stillness of Jenni's small apartment like the rattling of a machine gun, making her jump in her seat. She lifted the receiver and placed it to her ear.

"Hello," she said briskly.

"Jenni," Edna Rothman's husky female voice said, "it's Rothmann here."

"Yes, Edna?"

"Please let me see you...and talk to you." Rothmann said beseechingly. "I'm sure there is something I can do to help you before it is too late."

"You want to see me?"

"Yes."

"But, Edna, really, I don't need help."

"I believe I can assist you, Jenni. It wouldn't be out of my way to come to your apartment."

"No! Not my place! No!"

"Jenni, I'm only trying to be...your friend."

"But you can't come here."

"How can we talk then?"

"I don't know..."

"I don't understand. Why can't I see you ... to resolve any difficulties?"

"No. You just can't come here."

"It's him, isn't it? He's the problem, your husband. I knew it. That bastard is ruining your life!" Rothmann spat the words out.

"Please, Edna," Jenni said. "I can't see you now. Give me a few days."

Rothmann was silent for a moment as if contemplating what course of action to take.

"I want you to pull out of this predicament, Jenni," Rothmann said. "I've taken a personal interest in your welfare. I want you to rid yourself of this beast who is hurting you. Once and for all."

"Beast?" Jenni murmured. "Why did you choose that word?"

"Because he is evil. Isn't he?" Rothmann said.

"Yes," Jenni said, her voice exhaling the word in a gush of air.

"I knew it! It never changes," Rothmann said. "Don't you see that, Jenni? All men are evil."

"What?"

"They have no hold on us. Why this mad allegiance to them? Why do women insist that we must have them in order to complete our lives?"

Jenni said nothing.

"Look what this man is doing to you," Rothmann continued. "Has he made your life better since you've known him?"

God no, Jenni thought. But, at this point, she wasn't contemplating Ed Butler's involvement. Edna Rothmann was speaking of Ed and her marital conflict. She knew nothing of the true problem in Jenni's life. The blond assassin had turned it into confusion and chaos. She believed that he somehow possessed her subconscious. He might even know where she lives. He could be nearby at this moment. Rothmann could be placed in a dangerous situation if she showed up here, she thought.

"I don't mean to preach to you," Rothmann said. "I know I am. But please consider what I am saying and take it purely as it is intended...in your best interest, Jenni. Get rid of him. Get him out of your life before he ruins it."

"I wish it were that simple."

"If he can do this to you, hurt you like this, then getting rid of him should be simple."

"It's not. You don't understand. It has nothing to do with Ed."

"You think I don't understand, Jenni. The trouble is," Rothman said softly, "I understand only too well."

"No, you don't, Edna," she said, her thoughts on the assassin. "He's not like other men. He's different."

"They all are. But he's the same as all of them. Believe me."

"But he is. He truly is different."

"How? In what way?"

"He...he makes unusual things happen. Bad things. He's hurt people."

"What?" Rothmann exclaimed in startled disbelief. "What in the name of God are you saying? You're involved with a brute? I'll call the police."

"No. Please don't do anything irrational. It's not like you think, Edna. That's what I've been trying to tell you. He's dangerous. But you can't get involved."

"Has he threatened you, Jenni?" Rothmann was incredulous. "Is that what's troubling you?"

'Yes," Jenni said, her voice quavering. "That's it. I'm afraid."

"Come home with me tonight then," Rothmann said in an outpouring of compassion. "I'll take care of you. I'll protect you. I promise."

Jenni gulped back a sob. In her own way, Jenni thought, Rothmann does care. She was a good woman at heart. "No, Edna," she said. "I don't want to put you in harm's way."

She gently laid the phone in its cradle and chopped off Rothmann's words. Better this way, she thought.

\* \* \*

"Here's what we are going to do," Clayton Bancock told Gordon Aldrich. "We'll place Limbo into a program with no specific target. We let his subconscious take us where we cannot go. We will let him pick his own target in his dream. But he will be programmed to kill whomever he finds buried in his dream. She will most likely be the one we seek."

Aldrich scowled at the comment. "Why?"

"I believe he will go to her, whoever she is. We have to discover the identity of this woman."

Now Gordon Aldrich once again fought with his conscience as he was summoned to participate in yet another murder. The safety of his wife and daughter weighed against the murder of innocents. Torn as he was, Aldrich could not sacrifice his own family for the life of someone he did not know, regardless of her guilt or innocence.

Limbo was placed into the *DREAMS* experimental lab, drugged and induced into REM sleep. Reluctantly Gordon Aldrich supervised as three research assistants programmed him to kill in a dream whomever he encountered. He sat before the main console of the system that controlled the DREAMS project and watched words and symbols flash on the face of the monitor. He had become indifferent now to their meaning, wiping from his mind the ultimate result they would produce.

From inside the glass-encased sleep room Limbo's mind traveled to where he desired...to where Jenni slept.

Unknown to Clayton Bancock, Gordon Aldrich or any of DREAMS' personnel, Elymas had planned to ride along in Limbo's dream. He didn't believe Limbo would snuff the girl. But he certainly would. In the confines of his own private penthouse apartment, without the aid of equipment hook-ups, Elymas's body drifted in space, six feet above his bed in an unconscious state. In his own dream he traveled with Limbo on the astral plane. He was, after all, without the aid of any accoutrements, truly the *"Dream Master of the Mind."*

\* \* \*

Jenni knew there was no way to stop him. He was coming to her and she was incapable of resisting. It was useless to try even if she had the will. She had somehow entered his dimension in her dreams and he had entered hers. There was no escape.

She lay in the dark of her small apartment, the hazy, ethereal lights of the street heightening the dreamlike state into which she had drifted. She planned a dream to bring him into it.

She was asleep. The dream came swiftly. Through the fog of her mind she knew he was near. She could feel his presence. Her eyes searched the darkness, seeking his form. Was this really a dream? Had she actually have dreamed about being asleep in her own room?

Fear clutched her throat. He stood there just inside the front door, the dim light casting him into half shadow. He appeared ghostlike, unreal. But she knew he was real enough to fear, and she knew he had come to consummate what had begun in her dreams.

Silently, he moved across the room and stood beside her bed. His body was silhouetted by the dim streetlights as he bent over her and she saw that he was naked. How did he get in the apartment?

His hands touched her. She recoiled, sensing an electric surge in her body. Was it fear alone? She didn't try to escape. She didn't cry out. Fear had silenced her voice.

"I have come to your dreams," he whispered. "I am the one you have been seeking."

No! She silently screamed. This is not what I wanted. He is going to rape me. I won't indulge him. I can't.

She felt his hands tearing at the thin material of her pajamas. He caught it at the breast and ripped downward, rending it to shreds. Her naked flesh was exposed to him and she felt the simultaneous thrill of fear and sexual arousal. He bent his head toward her and she could feel his hot breath on her breasts. She felt the sweet, delicious pain as he drew her left nipple roughly into his mouth.

Fear kept her immobile. Fear of death. The image of two dead people lying on the sidewalk still filled her brain and she was frozen in place. Once before in her dream, he had thrown her from her bedroom window. Was that about to happen again? Was this again only a dream? Was the fear she felt only a sensation brought on by her subconscious?

He fell on top of her, his hands peeling away the last remnants of her garments as he mauled her body.

Was this to be her death? Was it at hand? She had feared him from the first moment she had seen him. She knew he was capable of bringing death. Yet, she did not fight or cry out. She capitulated. There was no fight in her. He worked at her voraciously, animal-like in intensity. Sexual pleasure mixed with fear. Was this, then, the ultimate sensation for which people strived?

Her eyes adjusted to the lack of light in her bedroom and stared at his face, a mask of mocking pleasure. She turned away and, in the black room, she saw movement in a corner by the closet door. There was someone else in the room, buried deeply within the shadows, a dark foreboding shape, an ominous specter. Was it the image of death; death itself? Had death come for her in visible form?

No. It was a man, dressed so darkly he was ghostlike, barely noticeable. But his eyes betrayed him. They glowed bright red in the blackness.

Elymas, the demon in black, hugged the darkness. He watched in fascination as Limbo raped the woman he sought, if only in a dream. Then, suddenly, his voyeurism was interrupted by a knock at the apartment door and a weak voice spoke. The dark demon reached over and quietly turned the knob and let the door creak open.

\* \* \*

There was a small, neighborhood bar on the street where Jenni lived, not far from her apartment house. Edna Rothmann went there and had a quick martini before she felt calmed. She sensed something terribly wrong in Jenni Butler's tone. There was a ring of fabrication in the way she had been brushed off by Jenni who seemed to be in more danger than she let on. Rothman believed she needed to be rescued. The poor girl was alone, trapped by this lunatic husband who dominated her.

Rothmann downed another drink to fortify her determination and stepped from the bar. She walked to Jenni's apartment, glancing at her watch. It was later than she thought, nearly eleven o'clock. The inner door to the building was locked. Rothmann found Jenni's mailbox and was about to ring the bell. There was a speaker beside the row of boxes. She would have to announce herself. Her finger hesitated over the buzzer. She realized that Jenni would only reject her again as she had on the phone. Rothmann knew she had to confront Jenni face to face and make her listen to reason.

The senior editor stood in the foyer, uncertain of her next move. She was about to give up when she suddenly got a second wave of determination as, through the glass foyer door, she spotted an elderly man coming down the stairs. Rothmann fumbled for something in her jacket pockets, pretending she was searching for her supposedly misplaced keys as the man opened the door to let himself out. Rothmann stepped through the door before the old man let it shut behind him.

"Thanks," she said, slipping past him. "Can't find my keys."

The old man glanced at her warily and continued to the street.

Rothmann took the stairs two at a time. Why was she hurrying, she wondered? Was time running out? Or was it a sense of foreboding danger she felt? She slowed down on the third floor and got her breathing under control. When she got to Jenni's door she knocked quickly without giving herself time to reconsider. There was no response. She knocked again, harder.

Come on. Open up, Jenni, she thought. I'm not backing down. Her hand reached out and touched the doorknob. It was cold to the touch. She turned it, surprised to discover that it was unlocked. She pushed the door open and stepped into the apartment. She let it close softly behind her.

The small apartment was dark. All the lights were out.

"Jenni," Rothmann called out softly. "Jenni, are you here?"

She stepped farther into the room.

But she was no longer in Jenni's apartment. Instead, she had entered a gently rocking cable car on The Roosevelt Island Tram moving up over the streets of Manhattan. The tramcar moved along cables parallel to the Queensboro Bridge. It was headed out towards Roosevelt Island in the middle of the East River.

"What the hell is this?" she swore, her body charged with apprehension. She thought the drinks she had in her system were playing tricks with her mind.

There was no one else in the tramcar but herself and a man sitting in shadows in the corner opposite her. Outside the car, rain beat on the windows. A flash of lightning shot across the sky and the crackling sound that accompanied it heightened Rothmann's trepidation.

The man in the car did not answer. The car gently swayed as it steadily climbed away from Manhattan.

"What the hell is going on? Where am I? Where's Jenni?" Rothmann demanded, trying to keep hysteria out of her voice. "How did I get here? What kind of trick is this?"

The man stood and turned to face her. He was tall, dressed completely in black, suit, shirt, tie, all black. His hair was jet-black, combed straight back and glistening with raindrops. He stepped towards her. Fear shot through her body as his face was revealed in a flash of lightning. Even his dead eyes were jet-black with a sutble burning red in the center. He flashed a menacing smile.

Rothmann mustered her courage. "Where's Jenni?"

"Jenni is occupied right now with a friend of mine," came the answer. "You've entered her dream. Too bad for you!"

There was a tremor in her voice. "Who are you?" she cried.

"Why, I am the master of dreams," Elymas answered whimsically, taking another step closer to her. "I will make your dreams come true."

"Don't you come near me!" Rothmann cried, her open right hand jutting out in front of her, the index finger pointing at him. "Don't take another step."

He threw back his head and let out a short burst of laughter. Then he began to undo his shirt, slipping it out of his trousers and unbuttoning it slowly and deliberately.

Rothmann backed against the door. She looked around the car frantically for a weapon, for something to defend herself against this menace. The car was empty, stripped clean. Looking out the window she saw they had moved out over the waters of the East River.

"What kind of crazy nightmare is this?" she screamed. "Did I pass out? How can this be?"

Elymas stepped out of his trousers and Rothmann saw his conspicuous erection pointing at her like some huge, ugly, vulgar weapon.

She screamed as he reached out for her, his hands gripping her shoulders and ripping her blouse from her body in one wrenching motion. In an instant, she was bare to the waist. Her blouse and bra hung in shreds around her hips. She instinctively threw her hands over her breasts. His fist cracked across her mouth and knocked her to the floor.

Rothmann was screaming and crying simultaneously. She was stunned by the indifferent brutality of this creature. His eyes gleamed, now turning green, reptilian. His unblinking stare chilled her. The most degrading, appalling horror she could conceive was about to happen to her. She was going to be beaten and raped by an arrogant, gloating monster.

He reached down, took a handful of hair in one hand and began choking her with the other. He was far too strong for her and she could not fight him off. He flung her from him and stepped back, his hands poised on his hips, mocking her, daring her to move. She dragged herself to her feet and stood up.

"You can't get away with this," she managed to say through swollen, bloody lips.

"You should get a little ice for those bruised lips," he scorned.

He came closer and stood over her, as if to size her up. He reached down and roughly tore her skirt and underwear from her body, revealing the smooth skin of her shaved pubis. Rothmann was sick and ashamed that she should be exposed like this, her secret sexual sensitivities flagrantly violated.

His mocking laughter ripped the air, tearing at the shreds of her sanity. He savagely put one hand on her chest to hold her down while he forced her legs apart with the other. She was too weak to resist. He mounted her and drove into her with unbelievable force. She nearly fainted from the tremendous pain and shock. She hadn't let a man enter her in more than twenty years. She screamed in terror as the tram car climbed to the pinnacle of the cable line.

In a flash of rage and pain, Rothmann found the strength she needed and got a knee up between his arms and shoved him away from her with all her might.

Elymas, the demon, smiled cynically as he purposely stumbled backwards to see what she would do.

Rothmann struggled to her feet and moved to the door. Her hand found the latch. She slid the door open. A burst of wind and rain flooded the car.

"Don't touch me again!" she cried, tears and blood streaking her face. "Don't touch me, you bastard, or so help me God I'll jump."

He laughed and stepped defiantly toward her.

She glanced down at the river and the island below. A wide abyss yawned beneath her. Thunder rolled like kettledrums and she flinched at the sound. The demon reached out and clutched at her throat. Rothmann let go of the door and stepped out into the void. She did not panic. She knew she had to be dreaming. There was no other explanation for what was happening to her.

Somehow, she had gotten trapped in a nightmare. She would wake up before hitting the black water below.

No one ever dies in a dream, she thought.

# Chapter Twenty-One

"What the hell is going on?" Clayton Bancock cried aloud at Gordon Aldrich and the research team.

The men had worked frantically to find where the foul-up had originated. They checked back, searching for a programmed error. Gordon Aldrich stood up and faced Bancock.

"I haven't the slightest idea," he said calmly.

"Damn it," Bancock swore. "What caused this turn of events? Limbo was programmed to kill the woman. The same as before. He was not supposed to rape her. And who is that other woman who entered the room? And what the hell happened to her? She was there for an instant and then she was gone."

Elymas had not appeared in the dream; at least not to their eyes.

"I can't tell you because I truly don't know," Aldrich insisted.

"Call it off," Bancock ordered. "Until we find out what is going wrong. Three hits already and only one success. This doesn't make sense. Why isn't Limbo responding to the program as planned? Why didn't he kill her?"

"Maybe he likes her?" Aldrich said facetiously. Aware that Bancock was not amused, he quickly added, "Remember, this is an experimental program. We don't know for sure how the killer is going to react or what is buried in his subconscious."

"He is supposed to obey the commands given to him, is he not?" Bancock said.

The program was shut down. Aldrich turned to Bancock. "Limbo is not fully under our control. His subconscious might not permit him to kill someone he doesn't want to harm."

"I don't buy it," Bancock fired back.

"We're into an area we know little about. Apparently we haven't perfected the system yet."

"You're the goddamn expert, Aldrich. This is too important to still have bugs. Fix it!"

Aldrich didn't respond. It was useless to argue. He would have to analyze the program and find out just where the DREAMS assassination project had failed. It would, of course, have to start with Limbo. He was the key, the link to the subconscious of each target. If there were weaknesses, they had to be in Limbo's ability to bypass the system.

"This must be done," Bancock said. "You have no choice."

Aldrich knew he meant that as a threat.

After Bancock left the room, Aldrich ran the disk again. In the attempt to assassinate Charlie Washburn, the female figure in the background was hardly discernible, vague, obscured by shadow and distance. But in this new disk Limbo had become intimate with her; so intimate that her face was close and clearly defined through the photo implant apparatus linked to Limbo's brain.

\* \* \*

When Aldrich first saw the face of the girl in the dream he thought she looked familiar to him, someone he knew or had met somewhere. The thought persisted. He did not let Bancock know what he felt. He showed no reaction or emotion when the CIA man was near him and they watched the disk together. But, now, alone, he played the disk over and stared at her face. Where had she come from? What was her connection to the *DREAM* experiment? This was the second time she had appeared. Was she able to travel on the astral level on command and know when and where to interfere?

Finally, it came to him.

This woman had come to him over a dozen years ago when he was at Boston and was in the rudimentary stages of development of the DREAMS project. It wasn't called that then. It was his baby, invented by him, developed by him on money from grants. He held the rights to the system. The project was instituted to correct sleep disorders, namely, dysfunctional dreams, nightmares. The function, at that time, was to regulate dreams so that they did not become nightmares. But a frightening scenario kicked in during REM sleep. A process was introduced into her subconscious, like the more sophisticated version infused in Limbo's, it could mix the dream with pleasant thoughts.

Had these subconscious memories become linked, thought Aldrich? Were the two subjects communicating on the astral plane? Were there others also involved whom he had treated?

Back then the girl had suffered from sleeping disorders that

141

plunged her subconscious into erotic juggernauts. She claimed she controlled these as lucid dreaming. She was a rare case. Few could create and control a dream in REM stage from beginning to end. But then, she was losing control of her planned dreams and sought assistance in stopping the onslaught. Aldrich's concept, "thought implants," were devised to halt unnecessary subconscious resurgence of unwanted nightmares. The project, at the time, was the infancy of a child yet to grow.

He hadn't seen the woman since then. She had walked away from the experiment and never returned. Aldrich and his staff tried to contact her but she never returned their calls. And soon after that she disappeared; either moved, changed her name or got married. Aldrich gave up trying to find her.

Now she would be just as hard to find, he thought. Even living close by in New York it would be almost impossible for him to locate her and warn her that her life was in danger. He had no phone, was not allowed out of his room other than to work on DREAMS experiments. The girl had obviously saved Charlie Washburn's life. Without her intercession, the presidential candidate would surely have been killed.

For all his misgivings, Aldrich believed there had to be a way out of his predicament. He now feared for any life that might be terminated, terrorist or otherwise. The people running DREAMS, he determined, were no better than the terrorists who killed so many. Bancock had made him a reluctant accomplice by holding his family hostage. Perhaps she, being free, could inform the authorities and end these attempts at murder. And the nightmare was heightened when he considered that Bancock had other ways of finding her.

Then there was the second woman who had entered the target's apartment at the end of the visual. Johnnie Limbo had been distracted and had turned as she entered the room. His brain implant had picked up her image and placed it on the screen. A dark shadow seemed to flow over her and she disappeared in an instant. Who was she? How did she play out in this unauthorized scenario? Was she a figment of Limbo's or the girl's imagination in the dream or was she reality? Because she was visible on screen, Aldrich assumed that Bancock had also seen her. Had the dreams crossed the line into reality? What in heaven's name was going on?

\* \* \*

Bancock visited Johnnie Limbo in his room. Limbo knew the ex-CIA officer's patience was at an end. The strain showed on the grim expression of his mouth and the set of his jaw.

"How did you bypass the programmed hit?" Bancock demanded.

Limbo kept his cool. "I don't know what you're talking about," he replied.

"Enough of the bullshit, Limbo." Bancock dropped a disk in the machine and Jenni's dream came on the TV set. "What do you call this?"

"Looks like a hot scene to me," the hit man quipped.

"Don't be a smart ass. How did you manage to create a dream in this girl's subconscious that was not programmed?"

"I didn't know that I had."

"Did you create this dream?"

Limbo was cynical. "I don't think so. I thought you did."

The disk ended at the point that Bancock had ordered it shut down. But it had recorded enough of the episode to see Edna Rothmann enter the dream.

"Who was the other woman and how did she get into this dream?" Bancock insisted.

"How the hell would I know? You made this dream with all your gadgets. You guys sent me in and you pulled me out."

"This was not what you were programmed for. Somehow, you bypassed her death. You found her. You got to her. We didn't. You knew how to reach her. We still don't know where she lives. You found her in your subconscious mind. You apparently live in there with her. You're fighting this, Limbo."

"If you say so. I'm telling you I don't know her. You guys are fucking around with my brain. How the hell do I know this isn't your fault; a problem that you created."

"Why didn't you kill her? You should have wiped her out without a pause. And yet, you didn't. You fought the program and somehow got involved in a sexual fantasy. I think you're too fond of this girl, Limbo. I think she's on your mind too much. She has now shown up in two targeted hits; buried in your subconscious."

Limbo said nothing. He had nothing to offer.

"What happened to that second woman who entered the apartment? You obviously brought her into this dream too. She wasn't programmed to appear. Who is she? Where is she? What happened to her?"

"I don't know, damn it!" Limbo exploded. "Get the fuck out of here! Leave me be!"

"You created that fantasy as well as the rape of the first girl, didn't you?" Bancock persisted.

"I must have if you say so."

"What else can you do?" Bancock demanded. "Can you choose any method of death you please in a dream? Can you read people's minds?"

"They're your dreams. Not mine. I've got nothing to do with it. I am what you have made me into. You've got it all figured out. Why are you asking me?"

"Did you know all along that you could do this?"

"I'm under your power, Bancock," Limbo answered. "Whatever I do is your making. Whatever happened, you caused it. You created this system. You created me. I'm a fucking freak. And I'm sick of this shit. Tell your boss I want to talk to him."

Bancock was stunned. "Who are you talking about?" he said. "What do you mean?"

"You know fucking well who I'm talking about. Tell Elymas I want to see him. Tell him I want out. I'm through with this goddamn game."

Bancock couldn't believe what he heard. This punk knows about Elymas. How was this possible? The mysterious "Master of Dreams," as he called himself, kept his identity private. Then it occurred to the CIA castoff that it was Elymas who had insisted on bringing Limbo to DREAMS in the first place. What was the relationship between these two? And how would it concern him?

"I don't know what you're talking about," Bancock managed.

"You're full of it, CIA-man!" Limbo shot back. "You know damn well who I'm talking about. Tell him I want out."

Bancock abruptly turned and exited the door that his two henchmen stood guarding.

Limbo smiled. "Got you where you live, didn't I, Bancock?" he called after him.

# Dreams

\* \* \*

When Jenni awoke it was still dark in the apartment. She sat up quickly, the memory of the night gripping at her mind. She got out of bed, turned on the lights and searched the apartment. She was alone. The front door and all the windows were locked. Had he actually been here? It must have been a dream. Had she imagined it all; another dream that seemed real?

She realized suddenly that she was completely naked. The bed covers were ruffled but still intact. Had she slept on top of the bed all night? At the side of the bed, on the floor, were the torn remnants of her pajamas, mute testimony, she thought, to the energy expended in the fantasy. Was it truly that, a fantasy? Had she torn the garments from her body herself? She walked to the bathroom and felt the soreness between her legs. It hurt slightly when she walked, a mild pain as if her skin had been rubbed raw.

Could she have done this to herself? She noticed red marks on her right breast in the mirror. She stepped closer to the glass and examined them. There was definite redness around the pink corona of her nipple. The spot was slightly sore, as if someone had bitten her there.

She remembered with a thrilling and frightening excitement, the truth she had been trying to suppress. Had *he* come to her again in dreams, dominated her and used her to satisfy his savage sexual desires? She shook with fright and watched her flesh break into bumps. Were her dreams now so real that she might have mutilated herself?

What else could this mean? She had definitely not created this dream, even in its slightest form. Apparently, she thought, he can project himself into her subconscious. Was she now to be his prisoner on the astral level?

She strained her mind to bring events into focus. She could recall only fragments of the ordeal, fleeting images and sensations. She had obviously slept. She checked the alarm clock by the bed. It was nearly midnight. Two hours had passed since she had fallen asleep. What else had she dreamed? Did she actually hear Edna Rothmann's cries for help or was that also a vague memory of a dream. Had she fallen asleep with thoughts of Rothmann running through her mind? She must have also dreamed of her.

145

# Chapter Twenty-Two

Laura Whitney took a subway to Varick Street in lower Manhattan. She was scheduled to meet with the printer of her forthcoming coffee-table book entitled "My Art." Generally, she took the subway to destinations in the city that were not out of the way. She felt it was easier to jump on a subway train than getting a cab in Manhattan at mid-afternoon on a business day. Besides which, she liked to walk from the station through the streets.

The book was designed to feature thirty-five of her paintings, oils and watercolors. The front cover would show her dramatic painting of city lights at night that she was struggling to finish. The cover would be printed separately at a later date. Laura loved the design of the book and today she was scheduled to sign off on final proofs of the interior pages at the printer. But Laura was prepared to demand a surprise addition to both the printer and the publisher. The book's editor and the production manager were scheduled to meet her there. She knew they would not like what she proposed.

Under her arm Laura carried a 14" x 20" oil painting wrapped in plastic bubble-wrap and brown paper. The subject was a head-and-shoulder portrait of Elymas, the demon, depicted precisely as she remembered him. Ever since the corneal procedure that replaced both her corneas with those of the deceased medium, Vera Lancaster, Laura's eyes were like a camera shutter that registered exact lasting images in her brain. These images were retained and brought into her consciousness when she desired. Once again, tormented by Elymas's recent apparent appearance, she had painted a grim picture of his face. Only his eyes troubled her. Were they black, red, green? As she remembered, they seemed to change. She decided to paint the pupils completely black.

Her objective was to place the painting at the end pages of the book along with a summary of Elymas, explaining him and his crimes. I will expose the bastard, she vowed. Let as many people as possible know about him, who he is, what he is. She determined that, if her book sold well, people would become interested and create a buzz big enough to reveal his presence. It was her way of sending a wanted poster to all readers she could reach. The demon must have more enemies at large than just Spendler and her. She thought of the quote from John Donne's poem—"No man is an island." It must apply here. Someone, somewhere, was aware of Elymas's presence among them. Knowing the evil he had inflicted on society there must be many who felt as she did. Perhaps combined these victims might flush him out; stop him.

Laura was horrified that she might have seen Elymas on the street while lunching with Carl Spendler. The thought of him alive was more disturbing now than in the past. Belief that he had been destroyed at the séance conducted by her and Spendler was shattered. Elymas had revealed himself in demonic form at that séance. And there, the spirit of the medium, Vera Lancaster, came into actuality. It was the spiritual power in her angelic body that destroyed the monster; or so they believed at the time.

Laura was met at the printer's office and escorted to the plant conference room. Here she was shown color proofs of the paintings that were to appear in the book. It was close to noontime when the parties involved had reached agreement on all paintings selected for printing. It was then that Laura peeled the wrapping from the painting she brought with her and laid it on the table, face up.

"What is this?" asked the publisher's representative, the art director of Laura's book.

"I want this painting included in my book," said Laura. "It can be at the very end."

"Well, this is sudden," said the art director.

"And highly irregular at this stage of the process," said the printer's production manager.

"I don't think this is a valid request," said the publisher's art director.

"We have our printing signatures already laid out," said the production manager. "We have no room. Every page is accounted for."

"Drop something else," Laura insisted.

"But everything is approved and assigned in position," said the art director. "This is an unusual and unreasonable request, Ms. Whitney. Given the late stage of the process. We are ready to go to press."

"That's right," the production manager said. "We don't have the time or space. We have a schedule involved here."

"I insist on producing this picture along with this statement," Laura said as she handed a typewritten page to the editor who glanced over the copy quickly, an indulgent frown on her face.

"I can't approve this without checking with my senior editor," said the art director.

"Then get on it, Laura said. "I'm not backing down."

"This copy," the art director raised the typewritten page, "has no bearing on the interior of the book. It seems to be a message or warning."

"It is exactly that," said Laura. "Most specifically, a warning."

"What is the purpose of this portrait? Who is this person?"

"You may believe this or not," Laura said. "This man is evil incarnate. He is a consort of Satan. He is from hell."

"You cannot be serious," said the art director incredulously. "Is he a character you've added to the book?"

"No. My book is not fiction and he is not fictitious. He is real life. And I am deadly serious," Laura answered, becoming adamant. "He has committed countless murders and is amongst us now to continue his assault on humanity. He must be stopped. We have to find him. My painting is the only way to identify him. We must put an end to him."

"I don't know what to say," the art director said. "I am stunned. We may be treading on libel here. This would put an enormous cog in the procedure. I would think this would have to be cleared with our lawyers."

The door to the conference room opened and David Grant, the president of the printing firm entered.

"How's it going?" he asked. "Sorry I'm a little late." He shook hands with the art director and with Laura. "How are you, Laura? Everything to your liking?"

"We've hit a snag," said Harry McKay, the printer's production manager.

"And that is?"

"Ms. Whitney wants to insert a painting and text on a separate page. We are locked in. We don't have the room. It would mean a shift of signatures to accommodate the space."

"Nothing we can do?" asked Grant.

"Oh, we can do it but it means reworking."

"May I offer a suggestion?" David Grant said, speaking to Laura. "If you insist on this painting being in the book, perhaps we can print it as a separate page and insert it in the book. This way we retain the format we have established. No time lost. As a separate page the portrait can be placed into the book in the front or the back."

The art director looked to Laura. "What do you think?" he asked, realizing this got his company off the hook. As a separate printed piece, their name would not be connected to the repercussions that might arise.

"Fine," Laura answered. This, she thought, might work better for her purpose. The flyers, as loose pages could be printed separately and even handed out to people individually. They wouldn't have to buy the expensive book to see Elymas and know about him. "Yes," she said. "Sounds good. Do it right away."

"How many do we print?' asked Harry McKay.

"Make it the same number run as the book," said Laura. "And print me an extra two thousand."

"May I see the painting" David Grant asked.

Laura reached down where the painting had been placed by her side, leaning against a corner of the conference table. She slipped it out of the wrapping and handed it to David Grant.

He turned it face up and almost collapsed, his eyes open wide and staring. There, before him, was an incredible likeness of the demon, Elymas, whom he had vowed to kill. He could never forget that this was the demonic man whose face appeared on the secret website as the ideological symbolic head of a cult who promoted murder.

David Grant sat down, his face pale and drawn. He was devastated. His chest had constricted as if the force of a charging linebacker had slammed him.

"Is anything wrong, boss?" Harry MacKay said. "You don't look good."

"This man..." Grant said, grimly staring at Laura. "Who is he? How do you know him?"

"He is evil," she responded. "A murdering demon. What does it matter how I know him?"

"I know him," Grant said.

"What?" exclaimed Laura. "What are you saying? You know him!"

David Grant rose to his feet. "Please," he said. "I would like to speak to Ms. Whitney privately. Would everyone please leave us alone for a few minutes? Thank you." Turning to Laura he said, "Please come with me to my office."

Once there he closed the door and sat at his desk. He placed the painting of Elymas on top of the desk and gestured for Laura to take a seat opposite him.

"Now, tell me," he said. "How do you know this man?"

"I could ask you the same question," she responded, her voice teeming with anticipation.

"All right," Grant said. "I'll start. This monster ran a secret society that exhorted and applauded the murder of innocent people. He ran a cryptic website that posted photos of victims and actually praised the murderers."

Laura wrung her hands. "It sounds like we're talking about the same madman."

"One of his serial murder cohorts murdered the woman I was going to marry. Struck her down brutally and mercilessly."

"Oh Mr. Grant, I am so sorry," Laura said. "I didn't mean to pry."

"It's all right, Laura. How did you come to get his likeness down so perfectly? This is exactly the man I saw."

"I'll have to recount from the beginning."

"Please."

"A few years ago I was blinded in a freak lightning storm."

"Good lord," Grant said. "Now I'm bringing back bad memories."

"You can imagine how that was for an artist; to lose one's sight," Laura said calmly.

"I can't begin to imagine."

"Well, it was devastating. After living in blindness for a while, I was informed that I might receive a corneal transplant to restore my sight. The human body does not reject the cornea, any cornea. It doesn't matter the donor. I consented to the operation and I got my sight back. Better than ever. I no longer needed glasses."

"I dread to ask whose corneas you received," Grant said.

"It's not what you think," Laura smiled. "I don't have *his* corneas. But I went through a period of turmoil. Strange occurrences happened in my life, deaths that should not have happened. A suicide. A murder. My husband and I were determined to find the cause of malevolence that surrounded me since the transplants. We discovered the donor was a medium named Vera Lancaster who had lived in Maine."

"A medium? You mean like séances? Contacting the dead?"

"Exactly. In her case she brought this man, this demon, Elymas into existence at a séance. God knows where he came from. Vera Lancaster died of a heart attack. Fortunately, or unfortunately, I was the recipient of her corneas shortly after her death."

"What did this demon, this Elymas, have to do with you?"

"He disrupted my life. To this day I don't know why. I believe it had to do with attaching himself to his conjurer. He is capable of infinite evil. I am sure he has brought harm to many people. In my life, he was a horror."

"What do you hope to accomplish by printing his portrait?" Grant asked.

"I want as many people as possible to see and know him; what he has done and what he may still do."

"Sort of a wanted poster."

"Yes. Exactly."

David Grant pondered a moment letting his chin rest on both hands. "I am going to pick up the cost for your painting of this fiend."

"That's not necessary, Mr. Grant," Laura said.

"It is, Laura," Grant answered. "I intend to print a hell of a lot more than your order. I am going to spread your poster of him all across America. I have clients in advertising, marketing, direct-mail. We'll flush this bastard out. We'll get him."

"I don't know what to say," Laura said. "I never expected this kind of help. The fantastic coincident involved here may set off a tidal wave of retribution. I'm sure there are many other victims of this fiend who will join us."

"I hope so," Grant said. He got up, reached across his desk and shook hands with Laura. "Keep in touch," he said.

\* \* \*

Laura left the painting with David Grant and headed for home. She got in an uptown subway car just as the doors were closing. It was lunchtime and not too crowded. She released a sigh as she found a seat. Laura's eyes wandered the car unobtrusively as she pondered the idea of doing a large oil painting of the people seated opposite her; a young Hispanic man obviously in love, cuddling with his young sweetheart; an elderly woman with years of memories revealed in her smile and glazed eyes; a construction worker with a bandaged hand; a few men dressed in suits; female office workers; a messenger carrying a large flat package, and, opposite her, near the doors, sat a man reading a magazine that he held high enough to cover his face. Her eyes suddenly focused on the front cover of the magazine. The masthead, in a large dignified serif typeface said *Lady*. Below the masthead the entire cover was filled with the face of a man. Laura was immediately stunned by confusion and fright.

She clutched her throat and gasped!

The front cover of the magazine was an exact full-page color reproduction of her painting that she had just delivered to the printer. It was the face of Elymas, the demon.

How could this be???

How could her painting be reproduced on this magazine cover within an hour? Impossible! No one had ever seen it before she showed it today at the printing plant.

The train pulled into a station. The man stood up. He was dressed entirely in black. He dropped the magazine to his side, turned, smiled at Laura and stepped from the car.

Fear slammed her like the blow of a hammer.

God help me, she thought!

It is Elymas himself!

She jumped from her seat and sprang for the open doors before they closed. On the seat where he sat Laura spotted the magazine that the demon had left behind. She grabbed it and vaulted onto the platform as the doors slid shut behind her.

She had been heading north to her studio on Twenty-Third Street but stepped off the train onto the platform at West 4th Street. Elymas turned toward the exit gates. Laura plunged ahead after him. Don't let him get away. He's not looking back. He hadn't seen me get off after him. She watched him climb the stairs to the street. She followed after him. At the street level he headed east.

The demon went into the streets of Greenwich Village with Laura trailing close behind. She kept back just far enough, using the pedestrian traffic as cover, so that he wouldn't see her. It was a weekday afternoon and the streets were filled with both tourists and residents. She followed him into jammed pedestrian traffic that congregated around vendors who lined the sidewalks.

She watched Elymas turn a corner on Spring Street and finally join a group of sightseers milling at the entrance of an art gallery. The demon penetrated the throng. The people, young and old, absorbed him into their midst as they flowed into the gallery like so many grains of sand in an hourglass. How strange, thought Laura.

The sidewalk emptied and she was able to see the theme of the display window of the gallery. Two large and very familiar paintings adorned the facade. A sign above them proclaimed a message in large bold type—RECENT WORKS BY LAURA WHITNEY.

She stopped dead in her tracks. Of course, this was an art gallery in which she did exhibit some of her work. Since Vernon Hale, the gallery owner who had previously represented her, committed suicide, she had used other sources.

She followed the people through the entrance. The crowd miraculously parted as she walked through, each person turning to face Laura. Her sight was drawn to the walls of the gallery. They were filled with her paintings. Paintings she had completed and paintings that were still in her mind. How was this possible? Had Elymas created an illusion? How could he know what was in her mind? The observers stepped aside as if Laura were a wedge driven between them, creating an open path to Elymas.

There he was, alone, separated from the horde, standing with his back to her. Then, suddenly he spun around to face her, his black suit jacket spread open, his right arm extended outward, a finger pointing at Laura. No. He was pointing at something behind her. A broad smile sliced his evil face, and he broke into laughter.

She gasped and turned to see what was beyond her.

Raging flames shot up at the entrance wall. Elymas had somehow triggered an incendiary combustion. Massive flames devoured the walls engulfing the interior in smoke and fire. The flames spread quickly, consuming everything in the way, people, furniture, paintings. Laura watched, in absolute horror, as her beloved paintings burned, and packs of innocent lives ended in frightful agony.

Laura screamed and awoke.

She was in bed at her apartment in the Murray Hill section of Manhattan. It was nighttime. Frank, her husband, lying beside her, sat up.

He placed a hand on her shoulder. "Laura," he cried. "Are you all right?"

"Frank! God almighty!" she sobbed. "A nightmare. Terrible dream."

"Calm down, honey," he implored. "Relax."

"Yes. Okay," she said, snapping on the table lamp next to her. She got out of bed.

"Where are you going?" Frank asked.

"Some water. I need a drink of water."

"Stay there," he said. "I'll get it. You just relax."

Frank went to the kitchen as Laura sat back on the bed. Something colorful resting on the end table under the lamp got her attention. Her breath stifled in her throat.

She reached down and picked up the magazine she had lifted from the seat of the subway car...*in her dream!*

On the cover was the reproduction of the painting she had just delivered to the printing plant, the portrait of Elymas, the deadly demon.

How did this magazine get here? Where did it come from?

Frank heard her gasp and returned quickly with the water.

"Is anything wrong?" he asked.

"Frank, this is frightening," she said. "I can't figure this out." She showed him the magazine cover.

Frank took it from her and flipped through the interior pages. It was filled with completely blank pages.

"What the hell is this?" Frank said. "Some kind of sick joke?"

"No, Frank. No joke. Something really strange. This was part of my dream. Elymas was on the subway with this magazine in my dream."

"But how did it get here?"

"That's the problem," Laura affirmed tenuously. "I don't know. But how could it get printed on the cover of *Lady* when I just handed the painting to the printer only today. And they do not print *Lady Magazine.*"

"Laura, this has to be a single copy mock-up of the cover

154

wrapped blank paper. It's a hoax."

"But, Frank, this was a dream. I saw this magazine in a dream. How did it get here in our bedroom?"

"A true puzzle, I'll grant you that," Frank replied. "Let's check it out in the morning. We'll call the magazine and see if they know anything about it. But try to get some rest now."

They lay back in bed in the dark. Laura stayed awake. She knew she had dreamed it all, the train, people in the gallery, the explosion. But was it just a dream? Was the subway ride part of the dream? No! It couldn't be. She definitely was on the subway train. She came home by subway. She remembered the rest of the day. She was home, took care of some paperwork and had dinner with Frank. And she didn't remember ever having the fake magazine at all during that time. She recalled clearly the details of the day up until she fell asleep.

She remembered that Carl Splender had told her about the nightmare he had about the marathon runners and the reality connected to it.

It had been a dream. Entirely. It had to be.

# Chapter Twenty-Three

Jenni Butler called Rothmann's office. She was told Rothmann had not reported for work.

"Is she sick?" she asked the senior editor's secretary.

"She hasn't called in," she was told.

Jenni was sinking in a sea of fear and confusion. She sat alone in her apartment feeling overwhelmed and helpless. Rothmann was right when she proclaimed an evil had come into her life, an evil so powerful and strange she dare not imagine what it truly was. Inhuman? Her will to resist had weakened. She thought perhaps this was what the threshold of madness was. Perhaps she had already gone mad from the strain of last year's events. Perhaps the blond man was a product of her delusions and really did not have substance. Wasn't that what Spendler believed?

She wondered if she would still have a job at *Lady*. She knew she could no longer concentrate on the trivialities of editing magazine articles. After the talk with Rothmann about her attitude she knew she would be walking on eggshells with any more time off. And her phone conversation last night had sort of settled her dismissal. Rothmann would not tolerate her continued absenteeism or her abrupt refusal of help.

What to do?

Her only recourse, she resolved, was to find solace with Carl Spendler. He understood her dilemma. Only he could help.

\* \* \*

Carl Spendler picked up Jenni in front of her apartment. They drove through Manhattan, over the Henry Hudson Bridge, to the Riverdale section of The Bronx where DREAMS was located. The old Victorian residence appeared welcoming to Jenni. DREAMS. A suitable name for a clinic involved in dream therapy, she thought. At first she was adverse to the idea of restriction in a private room and subjection to observation while she slept. But Dr. Spendler assured her it was not at all confining, that she would be staying in a studio apartment and that she would have freedom to wander about the facility except for the restricted fourth floor. He was satisfied the therapy would work. He had faith in the organization, convincing her that, in the few short years he had dealt with DREAMS, he had relatively good results.

"Big place," Jenni noted, surmising the size of the four story ornate Victorian structure. The front gate was unlocked to receive them.

"It certainly is," said Spendler. "It occupies about two square acres and the rear of the property butts almost to the river. No streets cut through the property, so it is entirely private."

"How do the patients manage to sleep with that railroad running along the river?" Jenni asked, noting that a train had just passed along the riverbank at the base of the sloping hill to the rear of the building.

"I'm not sure, but you don't really hear much outside sound now that you mention it. Perhaps the walls are soundproof. After all, they do deal in sleep."

"Makes sense," Jenni said. "It just seems like the most unlikely place to study dreams. You'd think they'd have settled somewhere more isolated. Out in the deep woods, say, completely away from the city. Have you been here many times before?"

"No. Not really. A few times with patients. The foundation itself is not that old. Maybe only ten years if that. The building, of course, is a lot older."

"And you trust them?" Jenni said.

"Well, yes. I've had no reason not to. I've had excellent results with the clients I've referred here." Spendler was totally unaware of the recent duplicity of the organization.

At the entrance Jenni noted the DREAMS' medallion.

"What does that symbol signify?" she asked.

"Not sure," Spendler answered. "I can only surmise it is their trademark. Your guess is as good as mine as to its meaning."

A tall man, dressed in white, came through the huge oak front doors. He held out his hand to Spendler.

"Dr. Spendler, nice to meet you again," Dr. Harvey Spivak said, extending his hand to Spendler.

Spendler shook the hand and introduced Jenni.

"We'll take good care of you here," Spivak said. "Come inside and let's get set up."

Mike Walsh

As they passed through the front door Jenni noted that the video cameras poised over both doors followed them as they entered.

"You will be assigned to a private room," Dr. Spivak told Jenni after the necessary papers were processed. "Most likely your stay with us will be no more than a week."

"How can you do that?" Jenni asked.

"Ah..." said Dr. Spivak, smiling wryly, "it's all in the knowing. If we divulged the secrets of our success, we might give competitors the advantage. But here is what I can divulge. You will be escorted to a private lab where our research is conducted. When you are sleep-induced. Here you will sleep comfortably while we track your dreams. After a limited period we should be able to decipher the cause of your nightmares. Dream research will probe your nightmares and, by specific therapy, we will be able to pinpoint the cause of these dreams. This information will be passed on to Dr. Spendler, in this case, to deal with the problem head on, so to speak."

"Sounds simple," Jenni said. "Like pulling a tooth."

Dr. Spivak laughed. "Not quite. The subconscious buries, as memories, everything we encounter in life. Probing the subconscious is a colossal task. But here at DREAMS we have streamlined the process. No pain. Novocain of the brain, in essence. And easy recovery."

Of course, Spivak thought, she will never know the true clandestine purpose of DREAMS' existence. The priority members of management served dual functions earning a lot more money they might have otherwise earned. Loyalty to the unknown source of the foundation's funding enhanced by the prospect of wealth. Jenni would be one of the many patients who visit for general therapy that kept DREAMS legitimate. The foundation must stay legal to exist.

"We'll have to fill out all the proper paperwork and we'll get you situated." Dr. Spivak said.

"Tell me," Jenni asked, "what do the initials *D R E A M S* stand for?"

"Why, I thought you knew, Dr. Spendler. They are 'Dream Research Encompassing Alternative Memory Surveillance'," Dr. Spivak lied.

"I'll be damned," Spendler said.

158

* * *

Jenni was pleasantly surprised when she was escorted to her room in the facility. It was larger and better furnished than she had supposed. In her mind, she envisioned a typical hospital room, bed, bathroom, monitoring devices, and a couple of chairs. But not so. It was more like a two-room suite in a good hotel. The cost and payments had been explained to her and it was not prohibitive. One week would not break her. She was still covered by Ed's group insurance. And, she was still employed.

She thought about Ed. He was supposed to sell the better of their two cars, the Mercedes. Some money would come from that. Could she depend on him? But the money was a moot point, as she would be back to work in a week.

She sat in an armchair and contemplated her plight. What could they truly accomplish here, she wondered. She thought their conclusion might be no different than Carl Spendler's. She wondered how DREAMS' therapy compared to his sessions with her. Would they have group discussions and would she be expected to relate to others what she had experienced? Could she speak freely with strangers of her sexual fantasies? She doubted it.

Dr. Spivak had mentioned a room where she would sleep while her dreams were monitored. What kind of technology would they use? Could they induce dreaming? Was it going to be comparable to the short sessions she had had back in Boston when she had let her sexual fantasies and lucid dreaming get out of hand. There she had undergone only a few weeks of strictly private sessions. Whatever they had foisted back then had worked temporarily. Months later she had returned to lucid fantasies.

Then she thought, this was happening to her because of Ed. Damn! None of it might have occurred if Ed had been faithful to her.

Should she have agreed to this therapy, she wondered. Or should she have gone to the FBI with the information about the attempted assassination of Charlie Washburn? Most likely they would have been condescending and sent her packing. A dream! No proof! Just a stupid dream! She would sound like a lunatic and would come under constant observation...if not more.

As she looked around the room, she realized that there was no telephone. At first she thought that seemed odd. For that matter, there was no television or radio either; no distractions in the room. The only accouterment was an electric clock on an end table. She was allowed to bring with her an overnight case with a few changes of clothes and a shoulder bag with some basics. She had no visitors or contact, for that matter, with anyone for the remainder of the entire day. By evening a meal was delivered to her room without ceremony. She tried to eek information from the service attendant; to no avail. He merely delivered the meal and left.

Hours later she attempted to idle away the time by climbing into bed with a paperback novel she had brought with her.

It was morning before someone came for her. An attendant dressed in white, entered the room with a wheelchair.

"Time to go," he informed her.

"Where are we going?" she asked.

"You have to be interviewed," said the impassive man. "I don't know the procedure. I just deliver you to the reception room."

She had donned casual clothes, slacks and a blouse, as she was told. The attendant sat her in the wheelchair. The ride through the myriad corridors increased the fuzziness of her perception and she wasn't sure just where she was situated in the building. In her clouded mind the sensation of dread was prevalent during the jaunt to their destination. She had to fight for control. The fear of drifting into a dream beyond her command now loomed in her consciousness like a menacing force. Get a hold on it, she screamed in her mind. Open your eyes! Stay awake! Observe everything around you. Remember what is happening. Why? Why?

The wheelchair stopped in front of an elevator. While she waited, she glanced around, surveying her environment. She presumed she was on the second or third floor. She turned to her left. On one side was a wall of four elevators. Directly opposite them was a wall of glass. Behind that glass wall stood two men, talking. One, dressed in white, had his back to her. The other faced her. All the indigenous personnel she had seen trafficking the long straight corridor seemed to be dressed in white uniforms, except the man who faced her beyond the glass wall. Oddly out of place in this pristine white atmosphere, his attire was in total contrast to the personnel surrounding him. It was completely black–black suit, shirt, tie, and black hair. And piercing black pupils that looked directly at her. He smiled softly as if acknowledging acquaintance. An uncontrollable chill of apprehension passed through her like a jolt of electricity.

The other man, in white, with blond hair, turned to see who it was over his shoulder that drew the attention of the man in black. As his face turned, fully revealing itself to her, she gasped in terror and almost choked on her on breath.

No! This couldn't be!

It was the blond assassin from her dreams! Here in a dream research center!

Was she dreaming now? Had she fallen asleep and was only imagining this scenario? She tried to rise from the chair but a strong hand held her in place. The elevator doors opened and she was wheeled in.

Come on elevator, her mind screamed. Get me the hell out of here!

In the elevator, she was turned to face front just as the doors closed. She watched the blond assassin excitedly ran to his dark companion while his hand danced in the air, a finger pointing directly at her.

# Chapter Twenty-Four

The elevator doors slid shut. Jenni watched Limbo and Elymas disappear behind them. She sat in the wheelchair fighting back panic. Should she get up? Should she wait until the doors opened at their destination? The elevator was descending. Wait, she thought. At least she was getting closer to ground level. How to escape when the doors opened? The wheelchair faced front, the attendant behind her. Apparently, he suspected nothing. Yet his right hand rested on her shoulder.

There were three other institution personnel with them on the oversized elevator. She braced herself to move when the floor monitor hit the main level. But which way to run when she bolted out of the elevator? If she went the wrong way, she might be trapped somewhere unable to find her way out. If she remained, they would have her at their mercy. She had no alternative. She must break away.

The doors opened. There were people waiting. The attendant behind her took his hand off her shoulder and placed it on the back of the wheelchair to guide it. Jenni planted her feet on the floor, stood quickly and charged. Three people parted as she bolted through them. The man with the wheelchair was taken by surprise and was momentarily interrupted by the confused group waiting to enter the elevator.

Jenni started to her right. She was in a corridor that she considered to be at the back of the building. There were no windows or exit doors. Run, her mind screamed. Run for your life!

The corridor curved to the right. She sprinted down it. Thank God, she thought, she was dressed in street clothes. She was not dressed in one of those barebacked nightgowns you saw in hospitals. But, then, this was not a hospital, was it? She was wearing a pair of low-cut white sneakers that gripped the shiny tiled floor as she ran.

Ahead, she saw a door opening as an attendant was stepping through it, carrying plastic bags of garbage. She ran towards it. She now heard hurried footsteps pounding behind her and people shouting. She got to the door, grabbed it and hurried through. She was outside in a concrete courtyard surrounded by a four-foot high chain link fence. The garbage handler looked askance at her and turned back to his task. She fled by him and grabbed the top bar of the fence in both hands and catapulted it in one swift motion.

Ahead of her was a sharply declining grassy hill that ended four hundred yards later at a stand of overgrown deciduous trees. Beyond the trees the Harlem River sliced between her and Manhattan. The cluster of trees ended abruptly at a perimeter of railroad tracks that ran along the river.

She ran desperately, barely avoiding tumbling down the hill. Three men pursued her, all in white garb. She crashed through the stand of trees, fighting her way through the overgrowth. She glanced back. She could make out the features of faces now. Were they gaining?

She pushed harder. The railroad tracks suddenly appeared before her. A train whistle blew. She could see a freight train turning a bend about one hundred yards away. To her right, about a mile away, she spotted a low bridge that crossed the river and to the left she could see the much higher Henry Hudson Bridge, over which she had crossed when driven here by Carl Spendler. If she could cross the tracks just before the train arrived, she might gain a minute or two and make it to the smaller bridge. Her pursuers might not guess which way she had gone if their vision was blocked by the train.

She waited as the train drew closer. Just before it got to her she bolted across the tracks ahead of it. Once on the other side of the train she raced toward the low bridge to her right. This, she believed, was The Spuyten Duyvil Bridge, which handled vehicle and passenger thoroughfare from Manhattan. The bridge was a swing bridge that opened at water level.

She picked up the pace, running alongside the freight train, which was to her right, blocking off the view of her pursuers. The entrance to the bridge loomed about a hundred yards ahead as the caboose, signifying the end of the train, passed her. She glanced back.

Damn it! Her trackers had guessed she would head to the low bridge. They were not far behind. Could she make it? And even if she did, could she outrun them across it? Now, it was her only route to freedom. Perhaps she would encounter people on the bridge who might help her. She had to try.

Finally, she broke onto the bridge just as the entry gates dropped, notifying travelers that the bridge was about to swing open to let a boat pass through. Jenni ducked under the gate onto the moving section and headed towards its center. She realized, after making the move, that she might have trapped herself. There was nowhere for her to go as the middle section of the bridge swung open to create lanes for boats to pass. In the meantime her pursuers had caught up to her and stood waiting by the gate.

Jenni moved to the bridge railing. Directly ahead of her, in the river, a boat was coming towards the bridge. It was a tourist boat, one that circled Manhattan Island, loaded with sightseers. It was still a few hundred yards away as the bridge continued to swing open.

Jenni decided swiftly. She judged the surface of the bridge on which she stood was no more than fifteen feet above the water. She ran to the end of the section as it pointed upriver. To her left she saw the men who were chasing her standing at the non-moving section that was attached to the land. She climbed over the guardrail, poised for an instant, and dove into the shockingly cold Harlem River.

She surfaced and sliced through the water towards the oncoming tourist boat. She could see people on the deck jumping and screaming, pointing at her. She reached the boat that had slowed to a stop in mere minutes. Tourists had collected on the side where she swam, causing the boat to lean a bit. A lifesaver was thrown to her and she was hauled to the deck.

Saved. How lucky she was, she thought as towels were wrapped around her. As the sightseeing boat entered the Hudson River, she glanced back at the deck of the closing bridge. Her trackers were watching her from behind the guardrail. She lifted her right hand to her mouth and blew a kiss to them, not caring whether they saw her or not. She was on her way to downtown Manhattan by way of the Hudson River.

# Chapter Twenty-Five

Jenni realized she could not stay in her apartment now that Elymas knew who she was and where she lived. Was he truly part of the DREAMS organization or had she imagined seeing him there? Could he, like her, be a patient? No! He must be connected to them. They had chased her. Why? What was DREAMS? The papers she had filled out at the DREAMS research center contained her address and phone number. She must get away and think things out. She needed a plan of action.

The problem existed though; she would run out of funds if she didn't work. But she couldn't return to her apartment or work. They knew about her job at *Lady*. And she could not muster the discipline required to perform properly. She would be fired even if she showed up at the office. She could only imagine what Edna Rothmann thought of her now.

She could last a while on the money she had in the checking account. There was at least eight thousand dollars available until the money came from the sale of the house in Connecticut. Thank God, she thought, she had not changed clothes in the DREAMS clinic. She still had her water-soaked wallet in the back pocket of her jeans. At least she would be able to tap some money quickly from the first ATM machine she found.

She did not return to her apartment. She had only a few dollars and some change in her pocket. By the time the tourist boat had docked at mid-Manhattan an hour had passed. She was certain the people who were after her were already watching her apartment. Her clothes were almost dry by the time she departed the boat on foot. As she walked through the vertical valleys of Manhattan she had never felt more alone, more helpless and more vulnerable. Where to go? Somewhere out of New York? If only someone would listen to her and believe her. If only the police would help. But they could not identify the blond man and they would never accept her story of a dream killer. And would they believe that DREAMS might somehow be involved?

Where to go? Who to turn to?

She thought immediately of her sister when she referenced going to the police. Lottie's husband, Bill, was a cop, a detective, in fact. Lottie had suggested that Jenni come out to her house and spend a few days with her. Perhaps Bill Chambers was the temporary relief she sought. But she decided against heaping the burden of her woes on Lottie so quickly.

And suddenly it became obvious to her. There was only one person who might help her now, the same person who had deposited her into the hands of DREAMS, Carl Spendler. Surely he didn't know of Elymas's presence there. Or did he?

Before she made the phone call she weighed her decision. Supposed Spendler was somehow involved with the people at DREAMS. After all, it was on his suggestion that she sign in at the facility. But this premise did not make sense. Why would a man like Carl Spendler be tied to assassins?

She stifled her lesser of fears and made the call.

Spendler answered on two rings.

"Spendler here," he said.

"Dr. Spendler, this is Jenni Butler," she said, keeping her voice calm.

Spendler sounded startled. "Miss Butler? What can I do for you?"

"Dr. Spendler, may I come to see you?"

"See me at DREAMS? Isn't that where you are?"

"No. I am not there. I would like to come to you."

"You're not at the clinic? What happened?"

"I'll tell you when I see you. This is imperative. I believe my life is in danger."

Spendler was silent. Had I made a mistake, Jenni thought.

"I'm on my way out. But come over right away."

Jenni took the subway uptown to Spendler's office. He met her at the door and ushered her into his private office.

"My God," he said incredulously upon seeing her, "what happened?"

Jenni quickly explained the situation in detail and how it related to the man whom she had seen the murderer in two dreams and who dominated her nightmares.

"Are you absolutely sure your life has been threatened?" Spendler asked.

"Am I certain? Yes! I was chased by two men and had to jump into the river to escape. Yes, my life was threatened."

"I'm trying to be devil's advocate, Jenni. I'm not challenging your assumption."

"This was no assumption, Dr. Spendler. The killer in my nightmares saw me. He was there. I was running for my life. He pointed to me and I was seriously chased. No doubt about it."

Spendler pondered a moment. Then he said, "I don't understand this at all. The DREAMS organization is a dream therapy clinic. It's been in operation for a number of years. I have sent patients there with positive results. How could this be? What is going on there?"

"I don't know. But I can't believe it's any good."

"Jenni, let me get this right. You are telling me that you believe DREAMS to be somehow responsible for the assassination of that terrorist and the attempt on the life of Charlie Washburn. Is that about right?"

"Absolutely right. And they know that I am aware of what they are trying to do. They are hellbent on annihilating me."

Spendler got up from his desk and walked across the room to a table where he had heated coffee. He poured a cup and handed it to Jenni.

"Thanks," she said grateful for the hot liquid.

"Tell me what happened after I left you at DREAMS," Spendler said, eager to learn the facts.

Jenni explained rapidly how she had seen the blond man and his strange cohort, how she had escaped while being chased, how she had dived from the Sputyn Dyvil Bridge and swam to the tourist boat.

"My God, Jenni," Spendler said. "You'll pardon my saying but you are a piece of work. Getting away like you did."

Jenni smiled. "No, I don't mind you saying it," she said.

Spendler paused a moment, trying to reconcile something Jenni had said that rattled his brain.

"Tell me a little more about this other man you say was with the guy who dominates your dreams," he said.

Jenni carefully described the brief encounter she had with Elymas and Johnnie Limbo. "I got only a brief glimpse of him, but it was an image that you don't forget."

As she described him Spendler felt the chill in his blood. Dear

God, he thought. It's Elymas. He could visualize him clearly by her frightening detailed description. Was the demon here once again? How did he show up in an institute like DREAMS?

"First thing we've got to do is get you some dry clothing and a place to stay," he calmly stated, trying to hide the anxiety in his voice.

"Well obviously I can't go to my apartment."

Spendler thought a moment and then said, "My place. It's got plenty of room to spare."

Jenni agreed. She really had no choice. Once they arrived at Spendler's house Jenni stepped into a hot shower after leaving her still damp clothes for Spendler to attend to. Within minutes she joined him in the second floor kitchen wrapped in an oversized blue bathrobe. Spendler was busy whipping up a Spanish omelet.

"Are you hungry?" he asked. "Omelet okay?"

"Certainly," Jenni answered. "Thank you for your help, Dr. Spendler."

"No problem," Spendler responded. "And call me Carl."

After their meal Spendler said, "What do you expect we should do about this situation?"

"I don't know," Jenni answered. "I guess we tell the police."

"That and maybe the FBI since you believe there was an attempt on the life of a presidential candidate."

"That'll suit me fine."

"Good. I know an FBI field agent named Farrell. We'll call him in the morning."

"My brother-in-law is a police detective," Jenni said. "He was with me when the blond killer murdered two people. He is aware of what's going on."

"Fine," Spendler said. Suddenly becoming pensive he added, "Jenni, I want you to know sincerely that I had no idea whatsoever that there was any reason for you to be threatened by the people at DREAMS. I knew them strictly as a clinic for dream therapy. I had no idea of what you claim is happening there. I still find it hard to believe."

"You don't have to apologize, Carl," Jenni assured him. "I trust you implicitly."

The ringing doorbell downstairs startled both of them. Spendler went to one of the windows at the front of the house and looked down. There on the front steps stood Jillian, Spendler's current galpal.

"It's Jillian," he said to Jenni, "the woman I've been seeing."

"I'll get lost," Jenni said. "Can I hide upstairs?"

"Don't worry. Stay right here. I'll let her in."

"Will she be a problem?"

"I doubt it."

"But you'll have to explain me, won't you?"

"Probably, to a degree."

"I don't think anyone should know the circumstances of why I'm here right now."

It didn't matter what Jenni thought. Jillian had let herself in and was standing in the archway of the dining room that opened to the kitchen.

"Well, hello!" Jillian said, an obvious ring of disdain in her voice. "What have we got going on here?"

"Hello Jillian," Spendler said, rising and coming towards her, his arms open in an obvious posture of embrace.

Jillian held her left arm straight out in front of her, her palm outstretched, and halted Spendler's advance. "And she's in your bathrobe yet," she stated. "Nothing on underneath I'll bet."

"Jill," Spendler said, "this is not at all what you think. Jenni is a patient."

"I'll bet," Jillian snapped. "She looks kind of *impatient* to me."

"Damn it, Jill," Spendler countered. "This is no way to behave. There's no reason for..."

"Go to hell, Carl!" Jillian grunted, turned on her heel and stomped down the stairs and out of the house.

"Well, I'll be damned," Spendler murmured. "Can you beat that?"

Jenni got to her feet. "I'm so sorry, Dr. Spendler," she exclaimed. "I've caused you too much trouble already."

"No. You haven't. And it's Carl. Remember?"

"All right, then. Carl."

"You need dry clothes," Spendler said. "Do you mind wearing something of Jillian's?" Spendler pointed over his shoulder. "The girl who just left. She's about your size. Just 'til we buy you new duds."

Jenni smiled. "Right now I guess I don't have a choice."

169

Mike Walsh

\* \* \*

"Really, Dr. Spendler," Jenni said in response to his offer to let her bunk here at his building. "I don't want to impose on your hospitality. One night I'll agree to, but to bunk in..."

"Well, you certainly can't go to your apartment, considering what you told me."

"I'll try to get my sister, Lottie to make room at her place."

"Let's think this situation through," Spendler offered. "If your life is in danger the best thing is to contact the police and get you out of harm's way. You might bring danger to your sister's family. Here you'd be safe for the time being."

"I don't know," Jenni said. "Lottie's husband is a police detective. I'm sure I'd be safe with him."

"Nonsense," he retorted. "Why bring danger to them. This is a lot of house for one man. There are private bedrooms and baths here. You can take your pick."

"Really..." she started to object again.

"It's settled," Spendler said. "Help yourself to Jillian's clothes while you're here. You appear to be about the same size. I don't think I'll be seeing her again."

"Now you see," Jenni said. "I'm causing trouble already."

"No. Not really. Jillian and I had nothing more than a physical relationship. We got together once in a while and...Hell, I'm embarrassing you."

It was settled for the time being. Spendler called Detective Hodges, who had worked with Spendler on investigations in the past. He mentioned Bill Chambers and his relation to Jenni Butler.

"The police will meet us tomorrow," Spendler told Jenni. "They will investigate your claims about DREAMS."

\* \* \*

Lottie Chambers' thoughts about dinner were cut short by the ringing phone. She jumped slightly, a reflex action from her marriage to a police officer. During that time, she had never stopped worrying about Bill's safety. She knew he was experienced enough to handle practically any situation he got into, but there was always

170

the unexpected. Through Bill's experiences, she became aware of the malice in humanity she never thought possible. She picked up the phone. It was Jenni.

"What's wrong?" Lottie asked.

"I've got to talk to Bill," Jenni said. She sounded anxious. "Maybe he can help me."

"Of course," Lottie said. "What is it?"

'It's that murderer I told you about. I've seen him again."

"You have?"

"Oh God, Lottie, he knows where I live." Her words ran together.

"Calm down, Jenni, please. Where are you now?"

"In Manhattan. But I can't go home. I'm afraid to go back to the apartment."

"Have you gone to the police?"

"Not yet. That's why I need Bill."

"He's in the city," Lottie said." He's leaving in about an hour. I'll call him and have him pick you up. Where are you now?"

"I'm staying at Dr. Spendler's house right now," Jenni said. "He's my psychotherapist." She gave him the address.

"Bill's not far from there. Give me the phone number. I'll have him call you."

"I'm staying here tonight," Jenni said. "I'll be safe here."

"Are you sure?" her sister responded. "The kids are away. You can stay here."

"I'll be alright here. Just let me talk to Bill."

Jenni gave her Spendler's number.

When Lottie hung up the phone she pondered her sister's predicament. She wondered how much of Jenni's past practices were now affecting her life. She would know soon enough, she thought.

\* \* \*

Bill Chambers was a remarkably easy going individual. Because of the nature of his work he adapted a straightforward and uncomplicated point of view towards his personal life. He simply didn't let things get to him. He saw so much violence as a New York City homicide detective that he patterned his personal life in direct contrast to his professional one.

He did not mind, as Lottie suggested, that having Jenni camp at their house until her troubles passed would disrupt the days of pure pleasure he had planned to spend with Lottie. It sounded as though Lottie's sister was in serious trouble.

In the morning he found a parking spot one block from Carl Spendler's westside brownstone, an major accomplishment by New York City standards. Spendler answered the front door.

"Are you Carl Spendler?" Bill Chambers asked.

"Yes. Bill Chambers, I presume?" Spendler responded, reaching out and shaking hands with Bill.

Spendler ushered him into the house where Jenni stood in the foyer. Remarkably, she did not seem as distraught as he had expected. She was dressed in a skirt and blouse, hair dried and coiffed and makeup applied (all belonging to Jillian), looking calm and in control. Yet Lottie had painted her as being in a state of agitated flux.

"Thanks for taking the time to come, Bill," she said. "I'm sorry to trouble you."

"It's okay, Jenni. I don't mind. I'm a cop. It's my job."

The group entered the drawing room and sat opposite each other, Jenni and Spendler on a couch and Bill Chambers in an armchair opposite them. Chambers wondered if the relationship between these two extended beyond doctor and patient.

Jenni explained briefly the events leading to the present circumstances. Chambers listened and jotted down some notes on a small pad.

"You know, Jenni, we're talking some major crimes here. But without evidence you're bucking the tide."

\* \* \*

Jenni and Carl Spendler joined a team of police officers led by Bill Chambers. The group drove to the DREAMS building in Riverdale. Bill Chambers had brought the matter to the authorities and a warrant was procured to enter and search the premises.

Dr. Spivak was aghast that the police had a reason to investigate the facility.

"Ms. Butler was checked in yesterday, yes, as she asserts," he

172

said when asked about Jenni's brief visit. "She was an in-patient undergoing a brief stay for dream therapy."

"Why did she leave so abruptly?"

"I don't know," Dr. Spivak answered.

The investigating detective handed Dr. Spivak the composite drawing that had been assembled that morning at Bill Chambers precinct in Manhattan.

"Do you recognize this man?" the detective asked.

Dr. Spivak, of course, immediately recognized Johnnie Limbo as a part of the team conducting secret government research experiments on the top floor. He and a handful of key personnel had been sworn to secrecy. He wondered if it came to this would the federal government edict override local authority. He didn't even blink.

"No," Spivak lied.

"You're lying," Jenni affirmed. "He was here yesterday. I saw him."

"How dare you accuse me of lying," Spivak said. "I don't know every patient personally. Perhaps he is a patient. Perhaps he is here. But I don't know him," Spivak continued. "I recognize Ms. Butler of course because she came here only yesterday and caused such a disturbance."

"Your people chased me!" Jenni cried.

"Of course we chased you. We were afraid you would harm yourself. Why did you run?"

"I ran because I saw that man who is trying to kill me," she burst out.

"Detective," Spivak said, "Ms. Butler was admitted as a patient suffering from delusions induced by dream malfunctions. We had go get her safely away from the railroad tracks and the river. I was told she jumped from the Stypen Divel Bridge."

"You bastard," Jenni cried. "I was running for my life."

Dr. Spivak rolled his eyes with disdain and glanced at the questioning detective who handed the doctor a search warrant. "We will see for ourselves," he said. "Floor by floor."

Bill Chambers took Jenni's hand. He guided her alongside the detective in charge and his entourage of two uniformed officers.

"Let them do their job," Bill Chambers said.

"I doubt we will find anything." Jenni said. "They think I'm a blundering kook."

After hours of search they uncovered nothing. Records did not show Limbo as a patient. He was not visible even on the top floor. When asked what the lab on the fourth floor was used for they were told as research. The police team was given access and found nothing incriminating.

As they left, the detective in charge said privately to Bill Chambers, "Sorry, Bill, there's nothing here. I would find out more about these 'delusions' the doc mentioned."

\* \* \*

"Now, Jenni, you will be staying with Lottie and me." It was a question rather than statement, given the seemingly obvious scenario into which Bill Chambers had stumbled.

Jenni hesitated and Spendler offered, "Jenni can stay here. I've plenty of room."

"I'm concerned with her safety," Chambers said. "At my house I can protect her. I am on vacation for two weeks."

"What about the kids?" Jenni asked.

"They're spending the week at my parents on Long Island. They have a swimming pool. Kids would stay there all summer if we let them. And when I'm not at home I can have the house watched."

"What's best for Jenni is what counts," Spendler said. "So it's settled."

"Now, can we get you some stuff from your apartment?" Chambers asked Jenni. "Money, clothes, paper work; things you'll need."

"Absolutely," she responded, knowing she must go there.

"We'll go together," Bill Chambers said. "We'll take just what you need. I'd love to see that bastard show up at your place."

"Call me when you're settled," Spendler told Jenni. "I need to know you're safe."

Jenni smiled and surprising even herself threw both arms around Spendler in a gratifying hug. "I will," she said earnestly. "Promise."

As they entered her apartment Jenni's heart hammered in her chest even though Bill Chambers was right beside her. Chambers went in first and quickly searched the premises. It was empty; apparently no one had broken in.

Jenni took a suitcase and loaded it. On the way out she got all the cash she had in the apartment, her checkbook and credit cards and dropped them in her handbag. The way she felt, she might never come back. She wanted to clear out right away.

Back in the car Bill picked up the conversation. "Tell me about this guy, Jenni," he said. "The guy who is stalking you."

It was as if he had pressed a release button. Jenni poured out her bizarre experience so quickly the words came in a flood. Bill knew the crux of her situation because of discussions with Lottie. She talked a lot about her sister lately because she worried about her. Jenni dropped the bomb when they entered the Midtown Tunnel. She believed that she was privy to a vision of Charlie Washburn dying by the hand of an assassin.

"Are you serious, Jenni? Assassination?" Chambers said. "I don't want to sound discouraging, but a dream is damn slim evidence to go on."

"I realize that, Bill. I believe something terrible is happening that must be stopped. Someone should investigate. Shouldn't we bring this matter to the FBI?"

"I'll follow it up for you, Jenni. I promise."

"You believe me, don't you?" she asked.

"Yes, of course," was the prompt reply. "Tell me more about this guy who is threatening you. What makes you think he's following you?"

"Bill, this entire situation is so bizarre. It's like fantasy has become reality. Did Lottie mention anything about me going to a sanitarium for dream therapy?"

"Vaguely; only that you were seeing a therapist. That would be Spendler, I guess. She didn't mention a sanatorium."

"What happened to me today is exactly what makes me believe this is not fueled by a dream but some outside element."

"What do you mean?"

"Carl Spendler delivered me this morning to a place across from the very top of Manhattan facing The Harlem River. It is called DREAMS. It's a sanitarium specializing in dream therapy. I was to stay one week to help end my problems." Jenni paused, thinking of how to phrase her ordeal in the simplest terms.

"What happened?" Bill Chambers urged.

"I was put in a wheelchair to be delivered to a therapy lab. As I was on the elevator on the third floor, before the doors closed, I saw *him*."

"Who?"

"The killer. The one you saw kill those two people a year ago on the street in Manhattan. The guy in my dreams. He is the same one who tried to kill Charles Washburn."

"Are you serious?" Bill Chambers asked, his voice incredulous.

"Yes. I'm deadly serious."

"Jenni, he's a known murderer. That's a fact. You and I are witnesses. Now we have something to respond to. Was he a patient there?"

"No. I don't think so. He might be. Although he was dressed the same as other people who worked there."

"Regardless. I've got to call this in."

"There's more."

"What?"

"I fled. I was frightened. So I ran when the elevator doors opened. I bolted and ran. I was chased by two men."

"Him included?"

"I don't know. I kept ahead of them. I made it to the river and onto a small low bridge. I dove in the river and swam to a sight-seeing boat."

Incredulous, Bill Chambers thought and smiled. "You got away by jumping from a bridge, into, that would be The Harlem River, and swimming to a boat?"

"And I can't go back to my apartment. They must know where I live."

Chambers was silent for a moment; then he asked, "Do you trust this guy Spendler? After all, he delivered you to this place."

"I considered that at first. But I don't think Carl Spendler has a dishonest bone in his body. He wants to call the FBI."

"He's right," Chambers said. "They'll have to look at this business about Washburn."

They got off the Long Island Expressway at Woodhaven Boulevard. Lottie's house was not far from here, Jenni recalled. What will Lottie think of all this, she thought? Is she really pleased with letting me camp at her house? Will she believe me?

The car turned off the boulevard and wandered through a series of streets lined with similar two-story houses on small city lots.

Many heavy old trees formed a canopy on Lottie's street. Lottie was standing on the front steps of the house as the car pulled into the driveway. She felt better already as soon as she saw the smile on her sister's face. It was sincere.

The women embraced, their arms locked around one another.

"I'm so glad you came," Lottie said. "It was the best thing for you to do."

"I'm glad I'm here too, Lottie," Jenni said. "I feel a lot safer now." The thought occurred that she might also have brought danger here along with a sense of security.

# Chapter Twenty-Six

That evening Bill Chambers took Jenni and Lottie to an Italian restaurant for dinner. He knew the owners, two brothers, since high school. The brothers were overly exuberant and gathered around the table in an impromptu display of gaiety. Nearly ten minutes elapsed before the laughing and backslapping subsided.

Jenni ate an excellent meal with a true hunger. Her plate was cleaned while Lottie and Bill were still eating. She felt guilty that she was finished so soon. "I didn't realize how hungry I was," she said. "I hadn't eaten since early yesterday."

Lottie smiled, a thin veneer over her hidden sense of worry for Jenni. Once her sister had described her plight to Lottie, she thought Jenni might be in more trouble than she had imagined.

As Bill Chambers finished his meal he looked directly into Jenni's eyes. "Jenni," he said softly, "I've called your claim into headquarters that this killer is at the sanatorium. But you will have to go there with the police to identify him."

"I don't understand, Bill," she said.

"Well, it's not going to be easy to convince someone that an assassin is gunning for Charles Washburn based on your dream. We might be able to get him on the murder of two people last year. And you're the only eyewitness who can identify him."

"Perhaps we should warn Washburn," Jenni said.

"Warn him that someone is planning to assassinate him?"

"Well — yes," she answered.

"Don't you think he might already be aware of that if what you claim is true? I'm sure he knows there are people out there who want him dead. I could name a few politicians who might."

"But the blond man I saw in the dream *is* going to kill him."

"He's part of something bigger than those one or two murders of incidental people. I'm sure of it. They might have been experiments leading up to Washburn's death."

"How can you be so sure?"

"Because this assassin killed the terrorist, Asim. I was in that dream. I saw him kill *that* man. And my vision occurred exactly at the time of his death. The circumstances were the same in both cases, Asim and Washburn. Both dreams were similar."

"Jenni," Chambers said. "Do you realize you're suggesting a conspiracy? Who do you suspect is behind all this?"

"I wish I knew the answer to that," Jenni replied. "Then I'd know what these deaths mean. I'd know how to stop them. Don't you see, Bill? The fact that this killer is physically present at a place called DREAMS makes it seem not so far-fetched for him to be in my dreams. Is it at all plausible that this place has the technology to enter people's dreams?" She paused, caught her breath and then said, "Oh dear God, what the hell am I saying?"

Lottie interrupted. She had not spoken as Bill queried Jenni. "For God's sake, Bill," she finally said, "you sound like you're grilling Jenni. She's been through hell."

Chambers backed off. "I'm sorry," he said. "It's just the nature of my business. You tend to follow a pattern of reaction. What I'm trying to say is that we really don't have enough evidence to offer a conspiracy theory. A dream or two just won't cut it."

"But Bill," Lottie said, "Jenni said she saw the terrorist killed in one dream and next morning he was dead. And the same thing happened with Charlie Washburn. The same killer in both cases. Isn't that a common link?"

"It might be," Chambers said. "But Asim reportedly died of a heart attack and Charlie Washburn didn't die."

"That's because, in the dream involving him, I screamed and interrupted the killer," Jenni said.

"And, don't forget, he broke into Jenni's apartment," Lottie said.

"Listen," Chambers said to his wife. "I don't want to sound cynical, but I've got to play devil's advocate here. Why didn't he kill Jenni when he could? Hell, if he was in her apartment, talk about opportunity. If he intended to kill her, then he would have done it that night."

"But he raped her instead!" Lottie screamed.

Bill turned to Jenni. "Was he actually there, Jenni? Did he actually rape you, Jenni? Are you sure? Or was this also just a dream?"

Jenni paused to contemplate before she answered. "I'm not sure," she said. Then she added, "I'm really confused. I wondered

179

why he didn't kill me. It worries me. There is something strange about him. It's tied to the dreams...to dreams in general. He has some kind of ability...maybe...like hypnosis. He was in my apartment. At least I thought he was. It was real yet it seemed like a dream. But I was powerless to fight him."

"Can you be sure it *wasn't* a dream?" Bill Chambers asked.

"There was a dream involved. There had to be. He seems to be able to manipulate dreams into reality. There was a sexual assault. The next morning I examined myself. I was physically mauled. There is no doubt."

A man sitting at the bar directly behind them momentarily diverted Bill Chambers' attention from Jenni. He was looking at the table, at Jenni specifically, and, as he caught Chambers' eyes on him, he jerked his head sharply away. He was turned three quarters of the way around on the stool to observe Jenni and he had to spin around to face the bar. The motion was obvious. Chambers decided to keep an eye on him. Tall, lean. He had the grim look of a professional. Chambers was not sure where to place him, CIA, FBI, the Mob, the Military. He didn't have the look of a cop. Chambers made him as the smooth, dangerous type; a typical hit man.

"Tell you what, Jenni," Chambers said, "I'll take you into the city tomorrow and arrange for you to look at some mug shots. You might get lucky and pick this guy out. In the meantime I'll get a warrant to visit this place in Riverdale."

"I've been through that mug-shot process last year," Jenni said. "I came up with nothing. I couldn't find him."

"We'll look at more faces. I'll have them reconstruct his face from your description. When we get a sketch together we'll circulate it. Someone may recognize him. It's worth the effort."

"Is that the best thing to do?" Lottie asked.

"Honey," Bill Chambers answered, "it's a start. There isn't a hell of a lot we can do right now other than identify this guy. That's half the battle. Unless we get lucky and he is still at DREAMS. At least then we'll know who we're dealing with."

"I'm ready to do anything," Jenni said.

Later, as they left the restaurant, and Bill Chambers said goodnight to the owners, he noticed that the tall man was no longer at the bar.

*Dreams*

\* \* \*

A car had been following them from the restaurant. As Bill Chambers eased his SUV into the driveway of his house, he realized the car that had been in his rearview mirror slipped by him and glided down the street. He didn't say anything to the girls. They got out of the car and let themselves into the house as he watched them. He took his time to make sure the car was gone. There was no mistake. They had been followed.

Now Chambers no longer doubted Jenni. Someone had her spotted and had trailed her to his house. And, since the man in the bar did not fit the description of the killer Jenni had described, Chambers now believed her about a conspiracy. Her explanation could be an inability of hers to adequately describe what had happened. He couldn't explain why she saw murders when she dreamt, but he knew there were people who had such premonitions. Even the police used psychics to help solve murders. And he wasn't about to deny what he didn't understand. Maybe Jenni had some ability to tap into someone else's thoughts. Lottie had talked about Jenni in terms of her mysterious knack to fashion fantasies into dreams. Chambers had always dismissed such talk as frivolity. Now he wasn't so sure.

Whatever Jenni had seen or experienced apparently interested someone else; enough to track her here.

He had a moment's trepidation as a car similar to the one that had followed them came down the street. But it was not the same one. He took his hand off the butt of his pistol and buttoned his jacket. When they were inside the house Lottie made coffee while Jenni sat at the kitchen table. Chambers lifted a cigarette out of his jacket pocket and lit it. As he blew the smoke into the air Lottie turned to him.

"Bill," she said, "you're smoking again. And you look...worried."

He doused the cigarette. "I was just thinking about Jenni's dreams. And the killer. You know, Jenni, if we contact Charlie Washburn and explain your premonitions to him you're going to be descended on by many people, including the FBI. You'll be opening yourself to unbelievable assaults by the government."

"I understand," Jenni said.

181

"I can't guarantee what will happen," Chambers said. "But you're not going to be able to dodge it. They'll probably take you into custody for surveillance and questioning. It might even be for your own safety."

"Then you do believe me," Jenni said, relieved.

"Yes. I believe you."

\* \* \*

Bancock's personal team of strong-arm men, Raymond and Foster were assigned to follow Jenni and kill her, but only if there were absolutely no witnesses.

The two men trailed Jenni Butler and the Chambers to an Italian restaurant where Raymond realized he made a mistake by getting too close to Jenni. Chambers spotted him and he knew it. Now he would have to take all three of them out. If he hit the girl alone there was the possibility that she had already revealed what she knew to Chambers. Raymond knew he had to hit them when they least expected it. He might have to get rid of the bodies. But first things first.

\* \* \*

Bill Chambers lay in bed with his 9mm pistol on the night table where he could quickly reach it. Lottie slept fitfully, turning during the night, as the fears she felt emerged from her subconscious. Chambers did not sleep. He couldn't. The fact was, that they were followed home from the restaurant bothered his cop instincts. He quietly got out of bed, took the pistol with him and went downstairs to the living room. He sat in the dark in a sofa that gave him the best vantage point. His back was to a windowless wall and he faced the part of the house on the driveway side. If this hitman were going to strike at the house tonight, he would have to come in the front or back doors or one of the windows on the main floor. It was a fairly large house and there were many windows. Chambers had positioned himself midway between the front and rear of the house. To get inside the hitman would have to pass in front of any of the windows that Chambers could see from his position. The only weak spot was the kitchen to the rear. The dining room walls blocked his view to the rear of the house. But if the intruder entered that way he would still have to pass Chambers to get upstairs.

After only one-half hour of waiting he saw someone pass by the living room window heading for the rear of the house. There was a screened porch at that end which joined the kitchen and dining room. The man would have to break in through the porch door first and then through the kitchen door. Then he would have to pass through those two rooms directly into Chambers' path.

Chambers had the advantage over the intruder. He knew the layout of the house in the dark. He heard the first soft noises of crackling glass and then the kitchen door opening. There was the sound of a slight squeak he meant to fix but never had. The bastard would never make it through the living room. As the man's form filled the living room entrance Chambers yelled loudly enough to wake everyone in the house.

"Freeze! Police!" he yelled.

The man opened fired in Chambers' direction. The shots made no noise coming through the chamber of a silencer and tore into the wall behind him. He was crouched low enough for them to have passed harmlessly by.

Chambers thought the sound of his gun exploding twice as the bullets ripped through the intruder's body would awaken the women sleeping upstairs and scare the hell out of them. The intruder crashed back into the kitchen, spun completely around and crumpled to one knee. He tried to raise his arm but failed as Chambers fired again. He was dead. There was no doubt about it.

Behind him, Bill Chambers heard a crashing sound in the driveway and he turned in the direction. A second man was running by the window. Chambers aimed his gun to fire and thought better of it. If he missed, the bullet might carry across the driveway into his neighbor's house. The distance between houses in a Queens street was not that wide. He bolted to the front door exiting it in time to see a running shape disappear around the corner and out of sight. He went back into the house.

Lottie called from the head of the stairs.

"Bill! My God, Bill! What's happening?" she shouted.

"It's okay, Lottie," he called back to her. "Don't come down. Everything's under control."

"What happened?" she called out. "There were shots fired."

"Someone broke into the house. I shot him."

Lottie descended the steps. "Are you all right, Bill?" Fear for her husband's safety made her disregard his order to remain upstairs.

"He's dead," Chambers said. "I didn't want you to see him."

The body of the dead man lay half in and out of the dining room entrance. His hand still clenched the pistol.

"Was he a burglar?" Lottie asked, her voice cracking with fear.

"No. I think he was here to kill Jenni. And maybe us too. I doubt if he planned to leave any witnesses.

"You knew he was coming, didn't you, Bill?" Lottie said.

"He followed us from the restaurant. I can't be sure but there may be another one. I want you to go upstairs. Get the thirty-eight out of the closet. Take the safety off and wait for me. If anyone else but me comes up, shoot him."

"Okay, Bill," Lottie said.

"What's happened?" Jenni asked. "Is it him?" She was standing on the landing, her hands clenched at her mouth in fright.

"No. I don't think so," Lottie said. "Bill wants us out of the way. It's all right now, Jenni." Lottie explained what had happened.

"Oh, God, what have I done?" Jenni sobbed. "What have I done by coming here? What trouble have I caused?"

"You saved your life by coming here," Lottie said. "Come with me." She guided Jenni to her bedroom, got the gun from the drawer and the two women sat on the bed, waiting.

Downstairs Chambers made a phone call to the nearest police precinct, identified himself and related the circumstances. He hung up the phone and waited. Through the living room windows he could see his neighbor's lights go on. If there were a second man outside, he would not be coming in. Within minutes of his call Chambers heard the wail of a police siren.

# Chapter Twenty-Seven

Bill Manning entered Charlie Washburn's office.

"The woman from *the* dream is here," he announced. "She's got an FBI escort with her."

"Send her in, Bill," Washburn said.

Three well-groomed men entered the room with a woman behind them. The first man introduced himself and the others, then stepped aside and revealed Jenni.

Charlie Washburn was stunned. There was no mistaking her as the woman in her dream. Short brown hair, alert eyes, heart shaped face. He would have known her anywhere.

"Come right in, Miss Butler," he said. "Sit down, please."

"Thank you for seeing me, Mr. Washburn," Jenni said. She moved to a chair opposite Charlie Washburn. The presidential candidate never took his eyes off Jenni. Two FBI men took seats on a couch against the wall while the third remained standing.

"I can't believe this," Charlie Washburn said. "You are exactly the woman from my dream. I'm glad you got in touch with me. I want to hear your story."

This morning the FBI had contacted Washburn relating the bizarre story of a woman who claimed she could identify a man who is planning to kill him. Washburn didn't put much credence in the tale, but when he learned that the woman claimed to have seen an assassination attempt on his life in a dream, he insisted that Jenni be brought to him immediately.

Jenni was lifted by special helicopter from New York City to Washington D.C. and, within a few hours of the time Bill Chambers had ushered in the FBI, she was personally confronting the man she hoped to save from death. The investigators had heard too many weird tales of death and mayhem and were not impressed with her story. She would have been written off as merely another in a string of crank claims during an election year had it not been that her tale was reinforced by the assassin whom Bill Chambers had terminated. This circumstance gave the story credibility.

"Mr. Washburn," Jenni said, "I think this man is going to make

# Mike Walsh

another attempt on your life." Jenni took a drawing from one of the FBI men and handed it to Charlie Washburn. It was a composite drawing of Limbo that she had helped the police compile.

Charlie Washburn glanced down at the face on the white surface. "Yes! Damn it!" he exclaimed. "This is the man who tried to kill me in that dream. No doubt about it. He was going to shoot me. It was your scream the broke it up. You woke me."

Jenni related her connection to Limbo, beginning with the deaths of the two people on the city street. She told the congressman of the dreams that tormented her, in which Limbo tried to kill her, and, finally, the dream in which she witnessed the terrorist's death, its timing and circumstances. And finally the coincidence in the structure of the latest assassination attempt on Charlie Washburn.

"Sounds farfetched," Washburn said. "The idea that it is possible to kill someone during sleep."

Jenni said, "I didn't know if you would believe me."

"What do you gentlemen think?" the presidential candidate spoke to the FBI agents.

Walter Farrell, the standing FBI man, spoke. "Here's what we believe. The man is a contract hit man. Through Ms. Butler we were able to trace the couple he killed a year ago. The victim was a mob official who fell out of favor and she was his mistress. Ms. Butler saw this man commit those murders," He pointed to the sketch. The New York Police could not identify him. Would you believe he has no criminal record? Yesterday, we ran a complete check on him based on Ms. Butler's description. His name is John Collins. We don't know if that is his real name. He is supposedly a plumbing supply salesman. At least that's what we found. But we can't find a company that employs him. There is a man who fits the profile though. He uses the name Johnnie Limbo. We don't have anything on him. Like a phantom. He specializes in assassinations. He is a contract hit man. We know of him and how he makes a living. But he has been very elusive. He is apparently very good at staying under the radar. There was never any description of him; nor fingerprints. We never could nail him. This might be that man."

"Who is he working for now?" Charlie Washburn asked. "Surely he can't have put this operation together himself."

"We don't know," agent Farrell said. "Could be anything; a terrorist group, religious fanatics. It runs the gamut. He could even

186

be working for a private party, one person.

"Who hates me that much to want me killed?" Washburn said.

"I don't mean to be antagonistic," the agent said, "but popular as your defense disarmament movement might be, there are almost as many people who would like to see it disappear."

'I'm aware of all that," Washburn said. "Be specific."

"It seems logical...those who would profit from an unusual arms buildup; those who want to see America build a very strong, overwhelming arms budget, including those countries who align with us on the arms buildup. How easy to control the country when that is in the hands of the wrong people. It goes on, Mr. Washburn. You see the problem?"

"Yes. I know it won't be easy to find out who is behind this conspiracy, if it is that. Now, what about Ms. Butler's allegation that there is a connection to the assassin and her dreams? Explain how she was able to be in my dream at the same time and see exactly what I saw so vividly. It's like I had watched a movie."

"I must admit I don't have much faith in parapsychology," agent Farrell said. "The Russians were into it much more than we are. PSI, telekinesis, thought transference."

"What do you mean?" Charlie Washburn said. He had heard that there was a military budget for experimental research in such an unexplored area, but he felt he had apparently underestimated its possibilities as a valid force.

"I understand there is a small budget," Farrell said. "But we haven't had much success in that area. Maybe the problem is that no one has faith in the potential of using paranormal psychology as a weapon. It's vague. It apparently doesn't work."

"Maybe it *does* work," Charlie Washburn said. "You seem to know a lot about the subject."

"I checked up on it," Farrell said.

"What about my dreams of this man?" Jenni interjected. "How would they fit in?"

"I'm not sure," Farrell said, "but this is fascinating. There is a theory that dreams can be manipulated through the subconscious, programmed on one end to influence a targeted subject on the other. Done while the subject is asleep."

"Is it possible? Could someone actually die while sleeping because it was intended?" Washburn asked.

Agent Farrell replied, "People die in their sleep all the time. From what I can gather, most people who die while sleeping die from heart failure during the REM phase of sleep. That's when we dream."

"Then it is possible!" Charlie Washburn exclaimed. "If someone could send this man Limbo to kill me while I dreamt then he might have succeeded. And let me assure you, I was scared. I believe if Ms. Butler had not saved me, I might have died of a heart attack. If this is what we're up against then there is no way for me or Ms. Butler to be safe from future attack."

"Just one thing," agent Farrell said. "It seems to me that whoever is planning this would have to know where you are at the time in order to attack you."

"You're not suggesting that we go into hiding?" Washburn said.

The agent did not respond.

"I have a campaign to wage," Charlie Washburn pronounced. "I can't go incognito. It's impossible. I'll have to take my chances."

"There's a good chance, now that we're on to them," the FBI agent said, "that they will not try to hit you again. It's Ms. Butler who would be the logical person to eliminate. She knows too much about this Limbo character."

"We all do now," Charlie Washburn said.

"We don't know yet who he's working for," Farrell said, but in his mind he had already determined there had to be a connection between dream assassination and the organization named DREAMS that specialized in dream therapy. And Ms. Butler claimed she saw Limbo there. "If this thing is as big as we're making it out to be, then Limbo might not be around for long. In fact, he might already have been eliminated or is in hiding."

"I could name a couple of people who would like to see me dead," Charlie Washburn said. "This theory you mentioned about the possibility of manipulating a person through his subconscious while he dreams ... whose theory was it? Who originated the concept? Is there a patent issued such technology?"

"That we don't know," Farrell said. "But we'll stay on it. Every bit of information helps."

"We've got to follow this through," Washburn said. "Ms. Butler may just have uncovered something important. Think of the consequences if this is used as a weapon and is in the wrong hands."

"We've got to protect her first. Get her out of harm's way."

"Would you be willing to let the FBI take care of you?" Charlie Washburn asked Jenni.

'Yes. Certainly." Jenni answered. "That's why I'm here. I'm afraid to face this alone."

"We don't want to gamble with Ms. Butler's life," Farrell said. "We know Limbo is dangerous and will definitely commit murder. We've got to find him."

"All right then," Charlie Washburn said, "let's get the wheels rolling."

# Chapter Twenty-Eight

Renowned artist, Laura Whitney, at her appearance before TV cameras, felt a sense of trepidation that lingered all morning. She felt TV was not her forte; especially a live show that was seen by millions. The show followed the midday news and competed with the glut of soap operas on other major stations. Her publisher suggested she make an appearance to plug her coffee table book that showcased many of her paintings.

When she finally got the call to come on stage, she mustered her courage and walked onto the set as positively as she could. She wondered if the applause was for her personally or merely a formality the audience afforded all guests.

The hostess, Maureen Glenn, greeted her with a handshake and a broad smile.

"Welcome, Ms. Whitney."

"Thank you," Laura answered, hoping her nervousness did not show in her voice. The hostess indicated for her to sit. The stage was set like a living room. Laura sat on the couch beside Maureen.

"This is such an honor," the hostess said. "I've admired your work for so long."

"Why thank you. I hope you don't mean since you were a child."

The audience broke into mild laughter.

"I have a few of your prints in my home," said Maureen. "I especially love your *Broadway Snow Storm*."

"Thank you."

The hostess held up Laura's book to the camera. Prominently, on the cover, was a full color reproduction of her masterpiece, "*City lights*."

More applause, only louder this time. Laura blushed. Was this approval for her or the painting? She wasn't used to this kind of reception. Viewers in a gallery talked to her individually as she passed between them, rarely as a group, and never with such a large audience as this.

"Tell me," said Maureen, putting the book on a table in front of them, "when did you start painting?"

"I was about ten," Laura answered, shyly at first. "I started with watercolors. Oils came in my teens when I learned how to handle them."

"Was it difficult for you or did it come naturally? I know there are people who have an affinity for art and seem to know as second nature what they want to produce."

"It wasn't that way at first. I loved art. I loved to draw. But, like any craft, you have to learn it. I studied. Practiced."

"Your work is just marvelous. Forceful. If I may say so, dynamic and colorful."

Laura smiled coyly.

"Tell me, Ms. Whitney..."

"Please. Call me Laura."

"Laura, then. You went through a terrible period in your life a few years back. Can you tell our audience of your ordeal with blindness?"

Laura knew this question was coming. She hoped her voice wouldn't quake. She was prepared. "It was over three years ago. They say the odds of being hit by lighting are very, very rare..."

"Were you actually struck by lightning?"

"No. But close enough. My husband and I were having dinner at a waterfront restaurant in The Hamptons one summer night when a sudden storm came up. A lightning bolt hit the window where we were sitting and the flying small debris hit me in the face. Broke my glasses and cut both my corneas. Blinded me."

"Oh! How terrible for you, of all people, an artist," the hostess said.

"Yes. Definitely. I couldn't believe such a thing could happen to me. I was blinded for a while. Almost a year, then I got a corneal transplant."

"How does that work?"

"Works fine now," quipped Laura, smiling. The audience responded with a spurt of mild laughter.

"I'm sorry, Laura," the hostess said. "I didn't mean to sound facetious."

Laura continued. "I understand. I don't know the technicalities but, from what I understand, the damaged corneas were cut out and the new, healthy ones from a recently deceased donor were placed precisely in the same area."

"Has your eyesight been affected by the new corneas?"

"Absolutely," Laura was feeling more comfortable now. Soon she would be able to make her special announcement. "I wore glasses before the accident. After the operation I didn't need glasses at all. My new eyes were so good I saw colors and images beyond what I ever experienced before."

"What do you mean?"

"Before I had to build a painting step by step, from concept to sketches to studies. Work it up. Either paint from life or take photographs. I needed models. After the operation, the concepts for paintings, vivid colors and images swirled in my mind. I could see finished paintings when I closed my eyes by merely imaging what I wanted."

"That must be fantastic."

"It is. If I see something I like, that I believe would make a good painting, I can retain that image instantly in my subconscious and bring it into my conscious mind when I like. And I see it as a painting. Now all I have to do is duplicate it on canvas."

"Miracle eyes," Maureen Glenn said, not realizing she had originated a phrase that defined Laura's situation exactly.

"Miracle eyes," repeated Laura. "Could be."

"Was the donor a young person?" asked the hostess.

"Not at all. From what I learned she was middle-aged."

"Was she also an artist?"

"No. She was a medium."

"A medium," Maureen was fascinated. "You mean like a psychic?"

"Exactly."

"This is unusual," said the hostess. "Did she communicate with the dead?"

"I suppose."

"Who was this person?"

"Her name is unimportant," Laura answered, hesitant to proceed with such intimacy, but knowing she must not let this opportunity pass to warn the viewers. "The point here is what caused her death."

"I don't understand," said Maureen.

Now for the shocker, thought Laura. "The medium died

conducting a séance. She and a few of her friends conjured a spirit and brought it into existence."

Maureen Glenn sat dumbfounded. She said nothing.

"This spirit," continued Laura, "was not benevolent. It was an evil spirit, a demon, bringing destruction with it."

"Are you serious?" asked the hostess, not sure if she should change the subject, yet reluctant to dismiss the shock value of what Laura was asserting. "Are you saying here that this medium actually contacted an evil devil from death?"

"I don't know about death," Laura said. "This demon is among us; present in reality."

A collective sigh was heard from the audience.

"His name is Elymas," Laura continued. "He caused the medium's death and has murdered a number of people since."

Now the audience gasped.

"How is it that the public didn't hear of this creature and these murders?" Maureen's tone suddenly exhibited skepticism.

"You've heard of them. They have been in the news. No one has connected the killings to this creature."

"I feel strange asking this," continued Maureen, "but, being that you inherited this woman's eyes, has the fact that she was a medium affected you in regard to this...demon?"

"As a matter of fact," said Laura, her confidence now asserted, "it certainly has." She lifted her book from the table and opened it to one of the last pages. She lifted the loose printed page with the full color image of Elymas that David Grant had printed for her and held it up to the camera.

"Can you focus on this print?" she asked.

The camera zoomed in on the printed sheet Laura held open. It was the frontal painting of Elymas' face. Her "miracle eyes" had recorded the grim portrait exactly. A face that had been unknown was now seen on television by millions of people.

"This person," said Laura, "is alive. He walks among us. He is not human. He is from hell, a disciple of the devil. He is here to kill, destroy, to spread evil...beware of him... look for him everywhere..."

Maureen Glenn, incredulous, interrupted Laura. "Surely, Laura, you can't be serious..."

"Of course I'm serious!" Laura shot back. "His name is Elymas.

Mike Walsh

We must stop him! We must...!"

Suddenly Laura dropped the print and stood up. Her face went white. Her eyes bulged. She raised her right hand and pointed at the audience.

"Oh! Mother of God!" she cried loudly. "Look! There! In the audience! He is here! He is sitting right there! God help us!"

Heads turned to where spectators believed Laura had indicated. Pandemonium broke out. People got out their seats. In the back some left the studio. Practically everyone was standing trying to see whom it was Laura had singled out.

"Where is he?" cried Maureen Glenn. "I don't see him."

"There! Right in the center! A few rows back! He's laughing at us."

"He's not there," insisted Maureen, having picked up the print and holding it in front of her. "I don't see him."

But Laura saw him. Elymas sat right where she pointed. He was smiling at her and he winked. The entire audience saw instead, in that seat, only an elderly woman who looked docile enough to whip out her knitting.

And then she was gone. Vanished. POOF!

# Chapter Twenty-Nine

Gordon Aldrich had discovered something new about the DREAMS project. You never know what will develop until it does.

The drug "ingylorim," in the body of a person with uncommon abilities, like Johnnie Limbo, not only allowed him to accept commands to kill on the subconscious level but also enabled him to transcend the commands. Once Limbo had been programmed to kill, the drug tripped a reaction that enhanced his own abilities. Limbo was able to release the deepest, most secret fears in the subconscious of the targeted victim while in the dream. It seemed that when Limbo entered the dream of the victim those hidden fears were revealed to him. Limbo knew this and constructed those dreams, the same way he was able to manipulate people and objects.

He placed a visual replica of the victims' worst nightmares in their minds. This, in reality, is what killed them. The terror they faced in those dreams was too great to cope with and they died of fright; of heart failure.

It was a mystery to Aldrich. He could not explain why it happened. Limbo was disobeying the data he was programmed to obey. He was deciding who should die and how. The bastard was having fun. He determined not to kill the girl in the dream, but he attempted to kill other people who were not included in the plan. The program apparently not only had bugs in it but it served as a vehicle for Limbo to create his own sexual fantasies as well.

Limbo was an enigma. Aldrich had no way of knowing that Elymas was the unknown force that formed Johnnie Limbo's ability to perform within the dream he had been programmed to invade.

Aldrich had now come face to face with yet another dilemma. He was torn with visions of his wife and daughter locked away somewhere in fear for their lives.

How could he function? The strain was so great at times he thought he would come apart. He imagined his hands around Bancock's filthy throat as he choked the life out of him.

If only it would do any good. Kill him. Upset the operation by destroying the leader. Would that act free his family? This was his only concern. Harnessing Limbo's ability for his own purpose must take a back seat until he found a way to take a stand.

\* \* \*

Bancock met Henry Montgomery in the screening room. The senator was concerned with Bancock's inability to control the situation. Each time he spoke to him there seemed to be a new problem, encompassing more people at every turn. It was getting out of hand. Montgomery was beginning to doubt his decision of selecting Bancock as the man to share his grand goals.

"I don't understand why Limbo is fighting a programmed kill," Bancock said. "He was to eliminate this girl, Jenni Butler. But he didn't kill her. Instead, he did something strange. He bypassed our system and created his own dream involving the girl."

"How?" Montgomery asked.

"Damned if I know."

"Can we resolve these problems?" Montgomery did not disguise his disdain with the events stalling the project. His eyes pierced as his brows dipped.

"We've got the research team on it now," Bancock said.

"Why don't we just dispose of Limbo and start over with a new killer?" Montgomery said. "There must be a ready supply of them."

"Kill Limbo?" Bancock questioned. "I've considered it. But we need him."

"Why? What makes him so special?"

"That's just it. He is special. Our 'dream killer' must have psi abilities, the mentality of a psychopath, and the willingness to work with us. It isn't easy to find the combination."

"So what we have is a Frankenstein monster instead."

"Yeah. Sort of."

"All right," Montgomery said. "He can bypass the computer input. Somehow he does it. But so far he can't escape the system, right? He still kills the people *we* program him to kill."

"Yes. Except for the girl. And he creates his own nightmares for his victims. It's almost as if we have unleashed a demon that was buried in his subconscious."

"Can we anticipate what else he may be capable of doing? We don't want any surprises that can hurt us."

"So far he alters the commands. We don't know what he might do in the dream until it happens."

"Where is the girl now?" Montgomery said.

"We missed her. She got to the FBI. Our man, Raymond, was killed. The cop shot him. And I'm sure they can identify him"

Dammit!" Montgomery swore. "We can't afford this now. She'll blow the whole thing wide open."

"They won't believe her. Who would? Killing someone in his dreams? Impossible science fiction."

"What about Raymond's body, the guy the cop killed in his house?" Montgomery asked. "They'll trace him to us."

"Not to us. We'll cover it. The body has already disappeared. The police report will also disappear."

"But, since we had two men there at the cop's house to kill her, they know someone is after her. If they couple her wild story with the fact that someone is really out to kill her, they'll add credence to it."

"Raymond could have been a burglar," Bancock said. "There's no reason to connect him to us. They don't have enough to go on."

"What about the cop and his wife?"

"They'll have to die. An accident. Happens all the time."

"My God, Bancock, what do we have to do, kill everyone in her life?" Montgomery said.

"Could be the only choice we have. We definitely have to eliminate anyone who could slow us down. We are committed. We can't let a few puny lives stand in our way."

"I hadn't planned on this. Knock off a few minor people who are standing in our way ...OK. But we're creating an epidemic of death. We're bringing attention to ourselves. How can we cover these deaths?"

"A few coincidental deaths, that's all they are," Bancock said. "There's no tracible weapon and a crazy story about dreams that kill from a woman who has been seeing a psychotherapist. I don't think the FBI will get very far."

"But hitting Charlie Washburn along with these deaths, it's pushing it. The FBI won't buy accidents. Especially since she's already told them how Washburn was going to die."

"What can they prove? There is no way to connect DREAMS to the deaths. Imagine them trying to prove that people who died of heart attacks were murdered."

"But the FBI won't give up."

"We're into it now, senator," Bancock said. "We can't back out. Is that what you want?"

"No. Of course not! But..."

"There's no way out?" Bancock assured him. "Whether we kill them or not, the dilemma is the same."

"Who else is involved in her life who might have listened to her? Family? Friends?"

"No kids. She's divorced. We're checking on her husband but she hasn't lived with him for over a year."

"You've got her disks?"

"Yes. Her only relatives are her ex husband, her sister and her cop husband."

"You're right of course," Montgomery said. "There is no going back. We have to finish what we started."

# Chapter Twenty-Nine

Deep in the interior of Maine, three automobiles pulled up to a house in a small clearing near a lake. Jenni Butler, Bill and Lottie Chambers, their two children and three FBI agents emerged from the cars. The men carried luggage and equipment to the cabin as the two women walked beside them.

The cabin was a two-story building about two hundred yards from the edge of the lake. The lake was over a mile across. The cabin was constructed primarily of hand-hewn logs. The large open room on the main floor was planned around a stone fireplace. There was a kitchen and a bath on the lower floor and two bedrooms and a bath on the second floor. The staircase to the second floor led to a balcony that overlooked the main room below.

It was primarily a hunting lodge that the FBI used on occasion for a variety of purposes. Right now its function was a temporary hideaway for the five people under the "Witness Protection Program" who had the distinction of playing key roles in the strange plot to assassinate Charlie Washburn. The three FBI agents were there to provide security. The three witnesses were to stay incognito until agent Farrell and the FBI unraveled the mystery and determined it was safe for them to come out of hiding. Lottie and Bill Chambers' two children had also been taken into custody as a precaution and were under government protection. Luckily, since the month was July, they would not be missed in school.

Jenni could make out shapes of houses on the other side of the lake and small sailing craft dotted the blue-gray water. What have I gotten Lottie and Bill into, she thought as she entered the cabin. If I had gone directly to the FBI or to Charlie Washburn, I wouldn't have involved Lottie and her family. Now, look at the mess I've created. Their lives are in danger because of me.

Jenni wondered what the people in the few houses around the perimeter of the lake thought of the activity here at the cabin she was assigned to. None of the other houses were close enough to determine just what was going on. There were many acres between each and dense trees cut one off from the other. Perfect seclusion.

199

They settled in and unpacked the bags. Jenni was assigned a bedroom at the end of the balcony; Lottie and Bill got the room next to her with the kids next door to them. The FBI men were at the other end of the balcony. All told there were five bedrooms.

As Jenni unpacked her bags she wondered who owned the cabin. Was it someone's place that the FBI rented for special situations or did the government own it? How safe were they here? It was fully outfitted with oversized early-American furniture which Jenni noticed showed signs of wear as she placed the clothing she brought in a bureau drawer. Who else used this drawer, she wondered.

How long they would be forced to remain here? She had heard stories of witnesses whose lives were threatened having to completely change their identities and relocate to a new state; start a new life. She hoped that wouldn't be the case with her and Lottie. At least she had no attachments, no children, no husband. She could do it. What would happen to Lottie's children if the FBI couldn't put an end to the terror that stalked them? Would they have to become a completely different family in a different part of the country?

The only consolation she felt was that the FBI had taken over and it was out of her hands. She felt, at least, temporarily relieved. The fear and desperation had been replaced, though, by a new sensation, guilt. She had clearly brought this situation upon them all. She wondered what they were thinking in their room next door. Did they hate her for what she had gotten them involved in?

Lottie and Bill came into her room. She had left the door open and Bill stood in the doorway while Lottie spoke.

"Let's go downstairs and whip up some food, Jenni," she said. "Agent Farrell said there is plenty to eat."

Jenni focused on her sister's eyes, not knowing what to say. The feeling of guilt welled within her and manifested itself in a sudden flood of emotion. She burst into tears.

"Oh, God, Lottie...," she cried, her head slumping into her hands.

Lottie went to Jenni, who was sitting on the edge of the bed, and threw her arms around her sister's shoulders. She pressed hard in a gesture of sympathy. "Don't cry, Jenni," Lottie pleaded. "Please don't."

"Look what I caused ...," Jenni sobbed. "Look at the trouble I've brought to you and Bill. And the children. How can we explain what is happening to them? They must be frightened out of their minds."

"Thank God they are old enough to talk to. I explained the situation to them before we left New York. They think that they are being watched over because of Bill's work. It will turn out all right in the end."

She turned to Chambers. 'Isn't that so, Bill?" she said.

"Of course," Chambers replied.

Jenni lifted her head and looked into her sister's eyes. "I feel so guilty, Lottie. I don't know what would have happened if you hadn't helped me.

"Let's not even talk about it," Lottie said.

\* \* \*

Downstairs, agent Farrell and the two women cooked dinner in the kitchen while the others watched the news on television.

Farrell came into the great room carrying trays of food. He laid it on the large, round table in the center of the room. The men sat down to eat as the women joined them.

"I'm going to leave tomorrow," Farrell said. "I've got to keep on the case. Hudson and Mosher here will stay with you. You won't have to worry."

"Can I get a gun?" Bill Chambers said. "I'd feel more comfortable with one. Your people took mine back in Washington."

"Sure," Farrell said. "It'll be all right. I'd rather you had one. More fire power, so to speak."

They ate. Throughout the remainder of the meal not much was said, although Farrell knew he would have to inform Jenni that Edna Rothmann had been found dead in the alleyway of Jenni's apartment building. She had died under the oddest circumstance. She had either jumped or had been pushed to her death. Her death again was connected to Jenni Butler. Farrell had no doubts now about the possibility of a conspiracy involving a strange new weapon that killed on command allowing the victims no escape. Someone was eliminating anyone who might have been close to Jenni Butler; anyone to whom she might have told her unbelievable tale. Did that include him, he wondered. He was never good at relating to tragedy or grief. He always felt awkward.

He waited until everyone had eaten before he spoke.

"Jenni, I have something difficult to tell you. You're going to know eventually."

"What is it?" Jenni asked.

"There has been a death related, we believe, to the 'dream' assassin."

"Who?" Jenni said. "Tell me."

"It's Edna Rothmann ... "

"Edna!" Jenni exclaimed. "Oh God! No!"

How else could he handle this, Farrell thought. There was no way of being subtle. "I'm afraid so," he said.

Jenni began to cry. The tears came in uncontrollable layers. Lottie tried to console her. "It's not your fault, Jenni," she said. "They caused this, whoever they are. Don't ... "

Jenni leapt from her chair and ran up the long flight of stairs to her room. Lottie followed her.

"I'm sorry," Farrell said. "I didn't know how else to tell her. It would have come back to her through the papers, TV."

"How did she die?" Bill Chambers asked. "Are you sure she was a victim of this madness?"

"Yes," Farrell said, "we're sure." He related the circumstances by which she had died. "Edna Rothmann fell from Jenni's apartment window. She was found dead in the alley."

"My God!" Chambers said. "There's no way to fight this thing, whatever it is. If they choose to kill you while you sleep what chance do you have to protect yourself?"

"It looks slim," Farrell answered.

"What the hell good are guns against it? We can't go to sleep is the problem. That is when we're attacked."

"We have only one advantage," Farrell said.

"What's that?" Chambers said.

"They don't know where we are."

* * *

FBI agent Walter Farrell found many facts he suspected in the files the central bank of computers provided him. The military was apparently into research studies in parapsychology but nothing about dream research connected to assassination showed up. There were one or two files that were classified top secret and these had piqued his interest. Funds had drastically increased for this research in the last few years. Some studies were listed by name but the top-secret files did not have code names. Farrell didn't even speculate as to their aims.

How much of the research in the area of parapsychology resembled the dream killing Jenni Butler had witnessed, he wondered. Did the military know about assassination through dreams? Were they into it, to use as a weapon?

Farrell needed a link to the experiments that were being conducted in secret. He needed information from those in the loop. Who, he thought, might be aware of a program as apparently advanced as the one they had stumbled upon?

Appropriations came to mind. He had skimmed through the many names of people involved in promoting the programs and raising funds. Many names. But one came to the fore—Senator Henry Montgomery, head of the Appropriations Committee. Montgomery was the link. Logically, he would know more than any of the others about the subject. Farrell didn't deceive himself that Montgomery would provide information about secret activities. What he hoped to get was information about terrorist groups involved in the same experiments.

Would Montgomery cooperate?

\* \* \*

Senator Henry Montgomery was worried. How much did FBI agent Farrell know? Was he here to see me because I appear to be the logical person to pump for information, or does he know of my involvement in the DREAM project?

"It's a damn conspiracy," Farrell said to Montgomery. "I'm sure of that. There are many people I can think of who would want to see Charlie Washburn dead. I'm sure you know many yourself."

"Including that madman who supposedly took a shot at him," Montgomery said. "As he claimed."

"Yes. I'm aware that there are lone assassins as well."

"I don't know what I can tell you that you don't know already," Montgomery said. "I find it remarkable that you believe such a project is in existence; people dying in dreams by a programmed assassin. Sifi technology. Sounds highly improbable to me. I know there have been some attempts to experiment with parapsychology but I don't think anything ever came of it."

"Remarkable or not, I believe it is in operation right now. I wouldn't even attempt to tell you how, but much has happened to confirm my beliefs." Farrell had related to Senator Montgomery some of the incidents leading up to his involvement in the investigation and the meeting between Charlie Washburn and Jenni Butler. He mentioned just enough of the facts to arouse Montgomery's curiosity, but he was careful not to mention the names and locations of the witnesses. Farrell had to keep a closed lid until the investigation was resolved. By the same token, he did not expect the senator to be overly generous with what information he possessed. The best that Farrell could hope for was a lead, a direction to probe.

"Assuming that you're right," the senator said, "and, let's say for the sake of argument, a terrorist group does have such a weapon. What can I do for you?"

"I know you are involved with appropriation for many projects. The study of parapsychology as possible military weapons is one of them, I'm sure. I don't expect you to leak any military secrets, but I hoped you might be able to point me in the right direction. I'm in the dark, operating blind. I need to know, aside from the obvious who you think might have the capability of initiating a technical breakthrough like this."

"Who is most obvious, Mr. Farrell?"

"I would think Russia or China, of course."

"You may have just answered your own question," Montgomery said.

"How do you mean?"

"I can't think of anyone who has the budget or the research capabilities to put such a project into operation other than perhaps Russia. Their scientists have pumped more time and energy into these studies than we have. Funds are not easy to come by here. Most of my constituents put damned little faith in such unproved science."

"But Russia or China are not the logical choices to want to eliminate Charlie Washburn. Wouldn't they want someone on the disarm ticket in the White House. Makes it a whole lot easier for them."

"Perhaps," Montgomery said. "That remains to be seen. Of course, by taking a crack at Washburn the blame would be laid at the feet of the right wing in America. Clever propaganda stunt on the part of the left if it is merely fiction."

"All right," Farrell said. "I won't debate the point. Assume we rule out Russia and China. Who else might have developed such a process?"

"Could be any number of countries whom China or Russia financed and aided in developing such a system. How could we know? If what the Butler woman says is true and it actually happened, it could be launched from almost anywhere in the world."

"Could it be limitless in range?"

"I don't know," Montgomery lied. " But why not? You're describing a weapon that has nothing to do with distance and geography. For example, the Butler woman claims she saw the terrorist, Asim killed in a dream. And he died in Cuba. You're talking about instant death with no restrictions."

"You're right," Farrell said. "Wherever they are operating, they can strike from anywhere. How do you stop them?"

"If this is truly operational," Montgomery said. "I can't think of any way."

"What about this DREAMS organization in New York?" Farrell said. "Does that ring a bell?"

"Who?" Montgomery asked. "I'm not aware of such a project."

No, thought agent Farrell. Really? Yet I know of it.

* * *

Had agent Farrell known that the DREAM killer was linked to a military experimental group of the CIA he would not have felt that the witnesses' position was secure at all. Once Jenni and the Chambers family came under the protection of a Federal agency, and Clayton Bancock knew this, it was no difficult task to pluck their whereabouts out of the machinery of secrecy.

The myriad connections from one bureau of government to another overlapped to the extent that a well-connected executive had little trouble finding what he wanted to know. By putting out probes,

Mike Walsh

a query or two in the right places, to the right people, and pertinent facts, if not direct answers, fell into place. Bancock knew, at the outset, that the FBI would hide the witnesses at some out-of-the-way place. It came as no complete surprise that the hiding place was a lakeside cabin in Maine that he, himself, had used as a hideout in the past. It was dubbed house number i2. They still used the same code number. Bancock would have thought by now they would have changed it.

The FBI agent in charge of the case was Walter Farrell, a man Bancock knew. He was one of the more experienced agents. How much did he know, Bancock wondered. Had he surmised by now that the assassination attempts came from a military experimental group outside the government? He doubted that Farrell would be as privy to the top secrecy of the DREAM program as readily as Bancock was to the whereabouts of the witnesses. But a clever guy like Farrell, you never know. He might get on to them. He had cracked big cases in the past.

The lab was secretly online again. Johnnie Limbo was brought into the role of DREAMS assassin once more. As he slept he was set up to kill Jenni Butler.

"This time I want no failures," Bancock told Gordon Aldrich as the target program was arranged. "This girl dies and I'm holding you responsible."

"I'm not sure that he will kill her," Aldrich said. "You know that. How can you hold me responsible?"

"I expect you to work the problem out. He must obey the commands he is given. What good is this program if the assassin we chose won't cooperate?"

"I don't know what is wrong," Aldrich insisted. "It's in his subconscious. It doesn't matter to him where she physically hides. He knows how to penetrate her subconscious. He can enter her dreams no matter where she hides."

"Use more drugs. Anything. Just make it work! We can't start over now," Bancock said. "This woman must die immediately."

"Where does it end?" Aldrich sighed.

"That is not your concern. Just get it going."

# Chapter Thirty

Upstairs in the lake cabin Jenni slept restlessly...and dreamed. In the dream she lay on the bow of a twin-engine Chris-Craft motorboat, baking in the mid-July sun. She was clad in a bikini, a towel stretched out under her body as protection from the hot surface of the deck. The movement of the water rocked the boat with gentle sensual motions that lulled her into a half-sleep.

There was movement beside her. She opened her eyes and squinted at the man standing there. He was wearing jeans, cut off just above the knees. He was tall, over six feet, lean, deeply tanned and his color accentuated his golden hair. She knew him immediately.

She didn't move, as if frozen by fear and anticipation. He knelt beside her. His hands reached down and gently glided over her body, urging her to arousal. I'm dreaming, Jenni thought. This is a dream. I'm in bed and this is a dream. She wanted it to end, to wake up, but she only moaned with constrained pleasure.

In the next room Lottie awoke to the sounds of activity that apparently were coming from the room in which Jenni slept. She got up and on the edge of the bed while she contemplated the cause of the disturbance. It sounded like the noise of an engine running.

She reached over to wake Bill, but decided against disturbing him when she saw how deeply he slept. She quietly slipped from the room and carefully walked along the balcony to the source of the disturbance.

\* \* \*

Limbo's arms lifted Jenni easily from the deck and carried her into the cabin of the craft. Gently, he deposited her on a bunk bed, his hands all the while creating their magic with her senses. His long fingers probed the source of her pleasure.

Was this really a dream, she thought?

She was afraid to move, afraid to resist him.

He could kill me now, just as he might have the last time. Why didn't he?

Mike Walsh

His hands continued their pleasurable plying of her flesh. Strangely, she was on the verge of fighting him. It would be the beginning of the enmity that had grown within her psyche.

Suddenly, in the midst of her struggle, her body stiffened. The cabin door opened and Lottie stood in the frame. Jenni turned and saw the exclamation of shock on her sister's face.

* * *

Lottie approached the bedroom door. Jenni should have been sleeping inside but instead, Lottie heard the sounds that awakened her. She put her ear closer to the door. The sound was identifiable. It was the purring engine of a boat. She could even pick up the distinct sounds of water slapping against the beam.

Did Jenni have a television set turned on? But, she recalled, there was none in the room. Puzzled and concerned, Lottie turned the knob and pushed the door open. Instead of a dark room, which she expected, bright sunlight exploded in her eyes. She had entered a world she did not recognize. It was the cabin of a boat. Through the windows she saw the bow of a vessel as it sliced through blue water. Jenni was immersed in a struggle with a man who held her down on the deck of the small boat. He appeared to be violently attacking Jenni in sexual contact.

"My God, Jenni!" Lottie cried out. "What...?"

The man with Jenni turned to confront Lottie. His eyes widened and stared directly into hers. She felt a sudden, terrible fear as those eyes penetrated her soul. For an instant she considered fleeing the room and run back to Bill. But she felt immediate concern for Jenni. Her hand left the doorknob and she came farther into the room.

"What is this?" she cried out, a tremor of fear clutching at her throat, making it difficult for her to get out the words. "Stop!"

Jenni squirmed out from under Johnnie Limbo, terrified for Lottie.

"Lottie!" she screamed. 'Good Lord!' Lottie! Get out of here! Quick! Get out of the room before it is too late!"

"Jenni," Lottie persisted. "What is this man doing here?"

Jenni jumped off the bed and stood before Lottie. She thrust her arm at the door and pointed a finger.

"Get out, Lottie!" she cried. "Get out quick! You're in my nightmare!"

208

\* \* \*

Bill Chambers awoke from the muted noises in the next room. He reached out his right arm to touch Lottie, a reflex reaction of habit, and recoiled when he did not make contact. He sensed danger and sat up immediately. He reached over and slipped the Glock pistol from its holster. He moved across the room swiftly and silently without turning on the lights.

Where was Lottie? Had she gone to Jenni? Were the girls merely talking loudly next-door? He didn't think it was that simple. There was a strange sound like a motor running. He thought at first that it might be the burner kicking over but he wasn't sure if the building had one. He slipped into a pair of pants and put his sockless feet into shoes.

He edged the door open and slipped onto the balcony. The light on the landing was burning. Lottie must have turned it on. He felt relieved. He wondered if he should wake the FBI agents before he checked Jenni's room. Chambers put the pistol in his side pocket and kept his hand on it.

That odd motor noise grew louder as he neared the bedroom door. He opened it slowly and stood in stunned shock at the scene that confronted him. Lottie was struggling with a man on the edge of a boat deck. He fit exactly the description of the man Jenni Butler said was the "dream assassin." What the hell was this? What had he stumbled into? Was the a nightmare?

Limbo was trying to push Lottie overboard into the water as the boat plowed through it. Jenni, clad in a bathing suit, was pulling at Limbo, trying to break his grip on Lottie.

Chambers cried out. "Freeze, you sonofabitch! Take your fucking hands off her!"

He lifted the pistol and started across the rocking boat. Limbo heard him shout and was momentarily distracted. He turned and watched Chambers enter the dream. He smiled.

Bill Chambers entered the room and charged into his own private hell. He was no longer on the deck of the boat.

\* \* \*

Mike Walsh

"It's all screwed up. What should we do?" Aldrich asked Clayton Bancock. "Should I abort and bring Limbo back?"

"No," Bancock said. "How long will he sleep?"

"Hard to say. Five, six hours unless I wake him."

"If you keep him programmed to the Butler girl and keep him hooked into the system, will he continue to stalk her?"

"Yes. I suppose so. As long as she sleeps."

"All right. Stay with it. I want her and her friends out of the way now. No going back."

Aldrich looked directly into Bancock's eyes. "Why don't you give it up?" he said boldly. "They're on to you. Maybe they don't have your name or the DREAM program yet, but they will. The FBI won't let up now. That's why they're protecting Jenni Butler. You can't go on killing people and believing no one will realize how they died. Your targets are growing in number. You can't kill them all."

Bancock scowled. "Just do what you're told and keep your opinions to yourself," he snapped.

"Can't you see it's coming down around you?" Aldrich persisted.

Bancock fumed. Aldrich had spoken the words he had thought himself. But he was committed and believed these temporary setbacks could be overcome.

"Listen, Aldrich," he said icily, "this thing is bigger than you or anyone can imagine. We are dealing with the perfect covert weapon. We're talking about power. The lives of one person or a dozen are insignificant to the DREAM program. Do you understand that?"

"You intend to kill them all if necessary?"

"You're beginning to see the light."

Aldrich was outraged. "Who the hell do you think you are?" he snapped.

"I am in charge and don't you forget it!" Bancock shot back.

Aldrich turned away from Bancock. He looked into the laboratory room where Johnnie Limbo slept. Bancock's two research stooges stood silently by his Limbo's side, monitoring the equipment. Aldrich understood only too well Bancock's implications. His life and those of his wife and daughter were forfeit. Bancock would not let any one of them live. Once Aldrich was deemed no longer necessary, he would simply have them all killed. It was that simple. They were the insignificant people Bancock mentioned.

210

Aldrich heard Bancock leave the room as the door shut behind him. He didn't turn around. He kept his eyes on Limbo. So this psychopathic killer was the ultimate killing weapon, he thought. What a sham his superb personal concept had become. His eyes wandered to the two research assistants in the lab. Killers, just like Bancock. How could men of science knowingly become part of a project like this?

Then he thought of his own situation. He wondered if those men were caught in a similar predicament. Were their families also threatened? He could ask them, but he dared not take the chance. More than likely they were Bancock's handpicked henchmen like all of the people who worked at DREAMS.

He knew he would have to do something. He couldn't exist in life as a murderer. But what alternatives did he have? He would wreck the machinery and throw the project off track. He could kill Limbo. But in both cases the powers at the top would rebuild the machinery and get another hit man. In the meantime, he would not have eliminated the danger to himself and his family.

There had to be a way out.

\* \* \*

Lottie struggled with Limbo but he was too strong for her. She glanced back at the expanse of water behind her and her legs quivered. The racing motions of the boat made her head spin. Jenni was trying desperately to loosen the his hold on Lottie. She struck him with clenched fists but he didn't relent. He backed Lottie to the edge of the deck. Her feet bumped against the low railing. He dragged Jenni with him.

"Go for a swim," he said as he pushed Lottie over the side.

She hit the cold water hard and was quickly pulled away from the boat. Fear swelled in her and she began to panic. She froze and started to sink. As she went under she saw Jenni leap from the boat.

Jenni broke turned away from Limbo and dove over the side seconds after Lottie went overboard. When she came up she was about fifty feet from her friend. She struck out quickly with a strong, even stroke. She was fighting time. Lottie could not swim and the fear of water would cause panic. Jenni saw her friend's arm flailing in the air as she struggled to stay afloat.

Oh, God! Don't let me be too late! Don't fight it, Lottie. Relax. Please. I'm coming. Harder! She pumped long, smooth strokes and took even, timed breaths. Not much farther. Faster. Get there in time.

She broke stride for an instant to get her bearings.

Oh, no! Lottie was not in sight. She had gone under.

Jenni dove down to find her. She didn't see her. She swam below the surface till her lungs nearly burst. When she came up for air she bumped right into Lottie. She had been near the surface when Jenni had dived below her. She grabbed her friend and pulled her close. Lottie was still tense and struggling.

"Relax," Jenni said. "Lottie. It's Jenni. I've got you. Relax and let me swim."

Lottie stopped struggling almost immediately at the sound of Jenni's voice. Jenni got her left arm around Toni's neck and lifted her chin. She began swimming. At first she had no sense of direction. She glanced around. There was a shoreline behind. She turned slowly, swimming in that direction. Land looked about three or four hundred yards away. She was a strong swimmer, but she wondered if she could make the distance while hauling Lottie. Lifesaving was not one of the things in life you practice.

She had to make it.

Lottie's splashing dragged on her. She kept an even sidestroke with her right arm while she held Lottie with her left. Her lungs burned and she sucked for air.

It was a long way yet. It seemed as if she hadn't moved at all from where she had started.

Dear God, are we going to die like this? In a dream. Would they really die or would she wake up just before the end?

She could feel her arms tiring. Cramps were next. They would surely drown if she got cramps now. She hefted Lottie higher under her arm to make sure she kept her head out of the water. Her sister's eyes opened. So far she was alive and conscious. Jenni hoped she could keep up the pace.

The pain came suddenly, in her right arm. It was sharp, surely a muscle spasm. She jerked it back and shook it, trying to loosen it to get rid of the pain. She had to tread water, but gave up the attempt quickly as she started to sink with Toni's weight pulling her down. She had to keep moving.

*Dreams*

She grimaced and struck out for the shoreline with determined resolve. Land seemed only a distant mirage. Was she getting any closer or was the land also an illusion, like the dream?

She was tiring. Hauling Lottie was quickly draining her energy. It always looked so easy when someone is pulled in from the water by a lifeguard. Jenni had never done it before and was afraid she wouldn't make it to shore.

She propped up Lottie's head again and continued her struggle. Think about other things, she thought. Don't think of the pain.

She forced thoughts into her mind. Ed Butler. Damn it all. Did she still love him? She thought of her parents and their unusual strictness. She wondered if they ever loved her. The death of Edna Rothmann jumped into her thoughts. My fault. All my fault. The guilt would remain.

No, she thought. It was not her fault, not her guilt. It was Limbo the murderer and the murderers who gave him impetus who were to blame. Not her. She was a victim. As much a victim as were Rothmann, Lottie and Bill.

She suddenly lost her rhythm and slipped underwater for an instant, Lottie's weight bearing down on her.

Oh God, she thought, I'm not going to make it. Don't panic.

She broke the surface and gulped air. When she recovered, she slipped back into a steady motion toward the shoreline and the cabin, which was now visible. She could make it out distinctly in the morning light. There was the dock on the beach and the speedboat alongside.

"A little longer, Lottie," she said aloud. "Just a little more and we'll be there."

Keep your eye on the dock, she told herself. Aim for it. Soon she would be able to touch bottom as she neared the beach.

Her heart pounded in her chest. Her right arm felt like it didn't belong to her body. It wasn't responding to her commands. It should have ascended and descended into the water three times more rapidly than it did.

But the house, boat and dock did look closer. Yes. She was make headway. Easy, girl. Easy does it.

There was movement on the dock. Someone was walking to the end. A human shape. A man.

"Help!" she screamed. Again. Louder. "Help! Help me!"

He came to the edge of the dock. She could see him clearly now. Was it one of the two FBI agents left behind to protect them?

Then she knew who it was! She recognized Johnnie Limbo. The golden hair was unmistakable. How could he be here? This was reality. He had been in her dream. Only in her dream. And he was behind them on the boat.

The truth became obvious.

She was still in the nightmare. The sense of reality, of being immersed in water was beyond question. The fear of death was so imminent she felt her heart might burst. She truly had believed she was actually in the water fighting for her life.

With the dream killer here it meant she was dreaming. The dream had not ended. It was a personal nightmare created by the killer specifically for Lottie. Somehow he knew about Lottie's fear of water. He was trying to kill her.

As long as he was here, in this dream, it would not end until both she and Lottie were dead.

"You bastard!" Jenni cried into the wind. "You rotten bastard! I'll get you! I'll survive and I'll get you!"

# Chapter Thirty-One

As Chambers charged into the bedroom he stumbled over a chair and landed on his knees on the unfamiliar, rough, hard surface of concrete.

The blond man was gone...vanished. Chambers was no longer in the cabin of a boat or in the bedroom. He was down on all fours in all too familiar surroundings.

A reality to horrible to imagine! Bill Chambers remembered. It happened a long time ago, when he was still a rookie cop. He had chased three punks who held up a liquor store in the South Bronx. They had killed the owner and had raced down the street just as he arrived at the scene. He had let his emotions supersede his training and had plunged into the darkness of an alley after them without waiting for backup.

The alley led to a network of corridors, almost a maze, typical of tenements in the area, and he had lost the stick-up men by taking a wrong turn. He realized he had placed himself in a bad position. He was lost and he was on their turf.

Suddenly, he was surrounded by many threatening hoodlums. By reflex, he aimed his revolver and fired. He took one down and the pistol misfired. When he thought he would be killed, two police officers had come into the alley in time to assist him. A squad car had also answered the alarm. He wondered often what his chances might have been if he hadn't been assisted by the two armed patrolmen that night.

But that was then...this was now!

He was in the alley where he narrowly escaped death at the hands of the three hoodlums he had been chasing so long ago.

Impossible, his mind screamed. It's an illusion.

He leaned against a brick wall and lifted himself to his feet. The surface of the wall was rough and hard against his hand. It felt real. The concrete under him had the firm, sturdy feel of reality. But this couldn't truly be happening.

He stood up and anxiously glanced around. It was nighttime, just like before. The alley was dark, lit only by the lights from apartment windows above. It was the same as he remembered it. He believed he was at the end of a cross alley shaped like the letter "H." If he recalled correctly, he should be able to easily find his way out of this labyrinth.

And then what would happen? Would he wake up?

He tried to think himself awake. It didn't work. Was he trapped in a dream that he would have to play through to the end? He had to get out of this trap and back to the girls. They were in harm's way and he was their only salvation.

He moved cautiously forward in the dim light. The nightmare had always ended as he was being savagely beaten. He would wake up frantic, in a cold sweat. But this was different. He was aware this was a dream. It had to be.

He turned a corner. He could go to the right or the left. As he recalled, he only had to keep making a series of left turns and he would end up on the street. Where would that street be? He was walking faster now, feeling the fear rising within his body. He turned the corner to the left and confronted the first of the punks. He was at the end of the alley blocking him. A length of chain dangled from his right hand.

You could not die in a dream, Chambers told himself. You always wake up before the end.

He turned back the way he had come. He saw two other punks blocking the exit at the end of this blind passage. The nightmare was following the script, his script. He was going to have to fight his way out.

The third passageway led to a blind alley. There was no exit. The hoodlums waited at the end of the alley for him to come to them. The other hoodlum was charging through the narrow passage behind him. Their purpose was to trap him between them, but Chambers could hear him coming fast. He had to time his response just right.

As he neared the two men he aimed his revolver at the shapes and fired. Two shots and the gun jammed just like before. He didn't think he hit either one. They stayed where they were and waited for him.

Chambers saw the lone thug's shadow grow larger. When he felt the punk was about to turn the corner, he stepped out and kicked him square in the groin with all the strength he could muster. Chambers caught him totally by surprise and connected dead on target. The young hoodlum fell backwards clutching his midsection, letting the chain fall from his hand as he hit the ground. Chambers stepped over him and gathered the chain into his own hands.

He raced down the alley towards where he thought the entrance to be. With one thug down, he might be free to escape. He glanced back at the fallen hoodlum. He was not moving.

A left turn. He was facing another corridor. At the end he could see a bare brick wall. Again, the alley turned to the left. Chambers raced around the corner and confronted still another long, dark corridor. Did they end?

He was running around in circles.

He could hear the crash of footsteps behind him. The two thugs were racing after him. At the next corner he swung to the right, hoping his pursuers would assume he would only turn left. It worked. When they got to the turn they instinctively went left. As the last one rounded the corner Chambers stepped out and struck quickly. With a strength that surprised even him, he brought the chain down across the back of the hoodlum's head. The punk collapsed and rolled against the wall.

Two down.

Chambers knew he was not going to find his way out of the maze easily. First he would have to deal with the last assailant, and then he had to worry about how to get back to Lottie and Jenni.

He broke into a sprint, heading back in the direction he had come. The third robber had stopped to check the condition of his fallen companion. He saw Chambers and, in an instant, he was running again.

At least the odds were better, Chambers thought. One on one. Just you and me now. And we both have weapons. Even ball game.

He passed the intersection where he had dropped the first adversary who was still on his knees, clutching his groin. He turned as he heard Chambers charging him and raised his hand to ward off the chain that Chambers ripped across his featureless face. This time he wouldn't get up.

Chambers stopped to listen for the inevitable sound of footfalls. The alley was silent. There was a deadly tension hanging in the air. The hunter was stalking his prey. Chambers was lost in this terrain. He could not be aggressive. He didn't know the turf and his opponent did.

He moved cautiously, his eyes darting to every shadow. When he defeated the third adversary, he would have time to think. He tried to clear his mind for the battle to come.

But the terrifying thoughts would not go away. He was living out a nightmare, his own personal nightmare. He forced his thoughts to Lottie. She was in a dream that took place somewhere on water. Her personal nightmare was that of drowning. He had seen the boat and Lottie struggling with the killer. And he could not help her. How much time did he have to get back and save her? And how would he get back?

Ahead of Chambers was a brick wall. Another dead end. He could turn only right or left. Was he back where he had started? He approached the intersection with extreme care, listening for the slightest sound. The hazy light from either junction revealed no motion.

His fear was a living thing, an overwhelming terror. He knew how this nightmare might end; with his death. He always woke from this familiar, dreaded nightmare in a cold sweat, realizing that only the act of waking had saved him each time. Would he awaken from this realistic dream?

He stepped closer to the intersection of the two alleys. He could not bring himself to cross. What if he just stayed here and waited? Maybe he would wake up.

Suddenly, from behind, strong arms slipped a chain over his head. He reacted quickly and drove his left hand up between his throat and the chain, keeping it from strangling him.

The pain in his wrist was fierce. He reached back and tried desperately to get his right hand on his attacker. If he could gain purchase, he might be able to catapult this thug over his shoulder. He had done it in similar situations. But the thug who had him in his grip was surprisingly strong. He kept his head back, out of reach, while he increased the pressure on the chain. Chambers' left wrist would crack from the strain. Then he would be at his antagonist's mercy.

He lifted his right leg and placed his foot flat against the brick wall facing him. His leg was at an angle, his knee bent so that he was close to the wall. He pushed with all his strength and caught the thug off balance. They both fell swiftly backwards against the opposite wall. The punk was going all the way down. He had no chance to regain his balance. His head crashed against the opposite wall. A hard snap sounded like the crack of a hammer on wood.

The thug's grip slackened and the chain fell away from Chambers' throat. He rolled off his assailant and quickly got to his feet. The bastard was out cold. Chambers bent down closer to see his face. There were no definable features. It was a face in a dream.

Chambers backed away. His wrist was numb with pain. He kept it high and close to his body. The three thugs were demolished. All he had to do now was find his way back to reality.

But first he would have to penetrate this maze of alleys.

He headed to the right; back to where he believed he had started. After two turns he was in a small courtyard, not unlike what he remembered from his duty as a rookie in the Bronx. Above him were the windows of the tenement apartments, their shades drawn to keep out prying eyes. Clotheslines were strung across the courtyard, connecting windows from opposite walls to one another. They created a crisscross web against the surface of the night sky.

To his immediate left were stairs that led to the first-floor landing. There was a hallway and an entrance to the street. He knew the buildings he was looking at no longer existed. In their place now stood only piles of rubble. Yet how could this be so real?

He started up the stairs, feeling that soon the nightmare must end. Suddenly, the metal door above him burst open and two more chain-wielding hoodlums leaped in front of him, blocking his way to the hallway and safety.

More of them! He turned to go back the way he had come. There was another hoodlum coming from the alley entrance behind him. He had to face another three thugs. He felt he wouldn't make it this time.

He wasn't going to escape this dream alive. Death in a dream. Jenni was right. Dreams could kill.

Was he going to have to face three more hoodlums, and another three until they inevitably killed him?

\* \* \*

Two things happened which gave FBI agent Farrell a direction to move his investigation.

First, the man Bill Chambers shot dead in his home was identified as a killer who was known by the CIA. It seems the hit

219

man had followed Jenni Butler and the Chambers family to their home. This didn't necessarily mean that the agency was responsible for the attempt on their lives. The man Chambers killed might not have been sent to his house to eliminate them. He could have merely been gathering information.

Secondly, after his session with Senator Montgomery, agent Farrell realized that, without having been told her name, Montgomery referred to her as "the Butler woman". He knew Jenni's name. The senator was somehow connected to the DREAM project that was also now in prime suspicion as the base of operations. How else could he have known Jenni Butler's name?

The senator, because of his super national defense posture, did have a logical reason to want the presidential candidate dead. Washburn proposed the exact opposite of what Montgomery stood for. Was the DREAMS project a secret organization privately funded or was it one of the "top secret" parapsychology research programs conducted by the military? Was it possible that it was a government project that was being misused by some people with their own personal agenda?

Farrell got the wheels in motion. He was lucky enough to have stumbled onto Senator Montgomery as a prime suspect and was convinced he was the link to a conspiracy. He assigned a tail to watch the senator around the clock. Farrell wanted Montgomery to lead him to the originating point of the project. He wanted him to make the simple mistake of panicking.

Charlie Washburn was in Dallas at the moment. Farrell called him at his hotel and was put through immediately.

"Yes, Mr. Farrell," the presidential candidate said, "what have you to report?"

"I think I've found our link to the dream killer," he said.

"Who is it?"

"How well do you know Senator Henry Montgomery?"

"Personally, not at all. But he is well known to me because of his constant attacks on my platform. You must be aware of his staunch backing of an extraordinary military defense budget?"

"Yes."

"He's one of many strong opponents to the disarm movement." He paused, realizing Farrell's implication. "What exactly are you suggesting, Mr. Farrell?"

"I think Senator Montgomery is one of the men behind the plot to kill you."

"You're not serious."

"I'm afraid so. I don't want to accuse him yet. I want proof. I'm following up on him. I think that some members of the CIA may be involved too. But I'm not sure."

"I can't believe that Montgomery or anyone on the opposing side would go this far. Kill me! Why?"

"I don't know yet. It has to do with the military industrial complex syndrome. Apparently there are secret projects in the realm of parapsychology being conducted and the CIA may be involved. The man Bill Chambers killed was linked to the CIA. He was one of their hired hit men. He got careless."

"Was he going to kill the Chambers couple and Jenni Butler?"

"I'm not sure about that, but it's a reasonable assumption."

"What do you want me to do?"

'Keep a low profile for awhile."

"I can't do that. I'm running a heavy schedule."

"I shouldn't have asked. I want you to keep what we have discussed strictly between us while I pursue the investigation. One question. How trustworthy are the members of your staff' Some of them already know about the dream assassination attempt and Jenni Butler."

"I trust everyone of them. But how can I be certain of their loyalty? I would not have suspected that Henry Montgomery would try to kill me."

"How about Bill Manning? Is he loyal and in your camp?"

"No question."

"All right. Let as few people as possible know what is happening. Lives can be in danger with a slip of the lip. If you can keep it to just Manning that would be best."

"I'll do whatever you say to safeguard the lives of those three people," Charlie Washburn said. "How safe are they?"

"I believed they were completely protected," Farrell answered, a troubled look on his face. "I even doubted Jenni Butler's story at first. But now, I'm not so sure."

"What can you do?"

"I'll have to move them again."

"It's impossible to accept that there are people like this in our government. I suppose we can thank God for men like you. Thanks for everything you're doing," the candidate said.

"It's my job," Farrell said simply. "I'll keep in touch."

No sooner had Farrell hung up than the phone rang. It was one of the agents in house no. 82 in Maine.

"Farrell, all hell's broken loose here," the agent said. "You'd better get right up here!"

"What's happened?"

"They've disappeared. The people we were guarding."

"Disappeared! Gone. All three."

"How? Was there a struggle?"

"No struggle. When they didn't come down from their rooms this morning we checked and they were gone. Both cars are still here and all the clothing they brought is intact."

"They might be in the woods somewhere. Hurt. Call the local police. Get a search party going. But give them as little information as possible. I'll be there as quickly as I can."

"Right."

# Chapter Thirty-Two

Gordon Aldrich watched in amazement as the dream images Johnnie Limbo created flashed in sequence on the screen in the lab rooms. Bancock, beside him, watched in equal astonishment.

"This is incredible," Bancock exclaimed. "Limbo is going to kill them all, anyone who interferes with him. What a weapon we have created."

"A Frankenstein monster, you mean," Aldrich said. Bancock is no more than a power-sick lunatic, he thought, letting no one come between him and his aims. The DREAMS project had no current relation to its origins. It had not been intended as a weapon for murder. Bancock and people like him had seen it's potential as a covert military messenger of death from the start. Aldrich felt that, since he had capitulated, he had become no better than the men who used it for their own malevolent purposes.

Even worse, he knew better. Not only did he give them his discovery to use as an instrument of murder, but he was now an accessory to murder.

I've become a pawn and a murderer, he thought. I'd rather die than go on like this. What good am I doing my family? Where will this madness end?

The dramas on the screen unfolded, mixing together and overlapping as the mind of Limbo transmitted them. Jenni struggled in the water to save her friend while Chambers battled for his life against a stream of delinquent hoodlums.

"It's taking too long," Bancock said, standing beside Aldrich. "We've got to control him. Get it over with."

"How? What would you suggest?" Aldrich was sarcastic.

"I'd suggest," Bancock responded belligerently, "that you adjust your input. Make the commands more forceful."

"How about a time limit?"

"Good," Bancock said. "Do it. Make it one hour."

"If he doesn't comply, what then?"

"How the hell should I know? You're the damn expert. Just make it work."

"Limbo has been sleeping for two hours. I'll give him one more hour."

"Fine."

On the wall near the door a red light flashed and lit up Clayton Bancock's name. It was a signal notifying him that a call had come in for him on his private "clean" line.

"I've got to leave," Bancock said. "Enter the limit and demand that Limbo kill these people within that limit."

The phone call was from Senator Montgomery. He sounded rattled. "We've got real troubles," he told Bancock. "Farrell of the FBI came to see me. He's getting too close. I think he knows more than he let on."

"Damn," Bancock said. "I didn't expect this so quickly. What did he say/"

"He wanted to know if I could give him any idea of who might have come so far in developing paranormal weapons. Terrorists. The like."

"What did you tell him?"

"The same as you would have. China. Russia. Let him run around in circles for a while."

"How did he get to you?" Bancock wanted to know.

"It's no secret that I'm in favor of strong defense spending. He figured that I would be a good source to guide him."

"I know this guy Farrell," Bancock said. "He's a smart bastard. If he's on to you, he'll dog you. From here on be damned careful. Don't come here anymore. I don't want you leading them to us. Call me on this phone only if you feel it's necessary."

"How will I know what's happening? How will I know if you've taken care of the witnesses?"

"Don't worry. I'll handle it from here," Bancock said. "Just keep a low profile until this cools. We'll get Washburn later."

"Maybe we ought to scrap his assassination for now," Montgomery said. "I'm not so sure this is the right time. They're too close to us."

"You're not thinking of backing out, are you, Senator?" Bancock said. "Remember, this scheme was yours. You're not thinking of hanging me out to fry?"

"No. Of course not," Montgomery answered defensively. "I just think we may have taken on too big a bite."

"Listen to me," Bancock asserted. "The witnesses, all of them, must die. We can't allow them to live. That includes Washburn and FBI agent Farrell if we have to."

"You can't be serious. We can't declare war on the FBI."

"Senator, you, of all people, knows the importance of the DREAMS project. This one damned woman who interrupted our attempts has caused us more trouble than all the stages of development over the last six years. Her involvement is snowballing into a full investigation. We can't afford this to go any further."

"I suppose you're right," Montgomery said reluctantly.

"You know I am. Now do what I say and stop worrying."

\* \* \*

Gordon Aldrich gave new instructions to the underlings. The two research assistants stayed nearby as if guarding Johnnie Limbo, watching him, their roles more as wardens than scientists. Aldrich entered the code to alter instructions in the memory banks of the systems.

DREAM KILL — AMENDMENT TO ORDER

The letters showed up on the monitor.

ABORT ORDER TO KILL JENNI BUTLER — *DO NOT* TERMINATE JENNI BUTLER.

Jenni Butler would not die tonight. The dream would end. Limbo would remain sleeping for another few hours. The drugs would keep him under for at least that long. Aldrich waited. He was certain his counter order was effective.

ORDER CONFIRMED...came the response on the monitor.

Aldrich relaxed and watched the two assistants for any signs that they suspected what had happened. Could they know what he was doing? They were busy monitoring Limbo's life functions and glanced at him only perfunctorily. They didn't seem to care what Aldrich was doing.

Who was there to question what he did? Wasn't he in charge? Only Bancock superseded his orders; and he was gone.

It was three AM. He believed Bancock was asleep somewhere in the building. He entered the coordinates for DREAMS headquarters. He stared at the words on the monitor. Then he punched in the words that would change his life.

Mike Walsh

NEW TARGET: CLAYTON BANCOCK: KILL
IMMEDIATE
He renounced Bancock's power over him once and for all.

* * *

Jenni couldn't keep Lottie above the water much longer. Thank
God she was conscious and finally relaxed, Jenni thought. She'd
never have gotten this far if she had to drag a struggling body. What
a terrible way to die, she thought, knowing it is not a true death. If
only there was a way to wake up, to come out of the nightmare
normally.

Ahead were the shoreline and the dock. Johnnie Limbo was
standing on its end, his expression mocking. She was close enough
to see him clearly. Mocking me, she thought. Watching me die and
enjoying it.

Then, suddenly, there was activity around the house and on the
beach. Two police cars had pulled up to the house and uniformed
men piled out of the cars. She spotted the two FBI men who were
assigned to guard her as they joined the police. The contingent
spread out on the property and some of the men disappeared into the
woods behind the house. The two FBI men came down the dock.

Jenni screamed as loud as she could but she knew they couldn't
hear her because the overhead roar of a police helicopter that was
descending on the beach muffled her screams.

Johnnie Limbo was no longer at the end of the dock. He was
gone. Instantly. Vanished. Poof!

Had the dream ended?

Just as suddenly she and Lottie were no longer in the water.
They were back in the bedroom of the lodge, on the floor. Jenni
lifted her sister's head. She was weak, but her eyes smiled at Jenni.
Thank God, she thought. She was waking up. Thank God.

* * *

Bill Chambers, still fighting for his life in his own personal
nightmare, decided the two hoodlums on the stairs behind him
presented a greater problem than the one below. If he charged into
the two above him, they would surely defeat him. At least if he took

226

out the lone thug behind him, he might get lost once again in the corridors of the alleys. There he would have a better chance to last longer. But he had to get back to Lottie ... and quickly. He was afraid that even if he stopped these three there would be three more and three more, until the nightmare ended with him dead.

He turned and charged with a raging ferocity. His opponent underestimated Chambers' will to survive and he stood his ground. Chambers hit him hard and fast. The element of surprise worked. He stumbled over the fallen hoodlum and fell flat on the piles of rubble around him. He got to his knees expecting the other two thugs to charge him. But there were no hoodlums confronting him. The tenement houses were suddenly gone. The alleys were gone. No courtyard, no alleyways, no rubble.

The images of his memory grew vague and faded completely. In their place was the bedroom in the lodge in Maine. On the floor before him Jenni sat with Lottie's head cradled in her arms.

Chambers fell to his knees by their sides.

"Is she alive?" he asked desperately.

"Yes," Jenni said. "She'll be all right."

Lottie raised her head at the sound of her husband's voice. She smiled at him weakly.

\* \* \*

In all the years of dealing and double-dealing Clayton Bancock had never seen his best plans fall apart so quickly. He had faced many a crisis before that, at the time, seemed complicated enough to bring down his network of illegal transactions. But he had always possessed the guile and ability to solve the problems that seemed damning. After all, it was exactly a lifetime of scheming that both created the dilemmas and solved them.

But the DREAMS project was an anomaly. It was not like illegal arms sales through the private sector; it was not like assisting pro-terrorist governments with mercenary advisors; it was not like profits from technological advances passed on to the enemies of the capitalist system which made them possible. The DREAMS project was difficult to control. The men he had to rely on were not of his ilk, he felt; mere employees, whose loyalties would turn to the next paycheck. They were men like Aldrich, who believed only in their work; those fanatical geniuses whose ambitions related only seeing their work somehow produced.

Aldrich was difficult to handle. Men like him always were. Inevitably, they had to be coerced, tortured and ultimately disposed of. Their uses were limited only to the development of unique programs.

But that was only part of it. The DREAMS project obviously could not depend solely on the subconscious mind of psychopaths like Johnnie Limbo. When a complication arose it seemed to compound. And Bancock didn't have the answers to solve them. He was forced to allow Aldrich to work them out. How long would Aldrich hold out before he caved in and broke?

And now, as Bancock finished the phone call with Senator Montgomery, he was convinced that with him he had merely another spineless backslider to deal with. Politicians, Bancock thought, are all cut from the same cloth. Not a one with the courage of his convictions, not a one who wouldn't turn and run. He hated them all, the left and the right. They changed their beliefs as the pressures of the polls dictated. He would feel no compunction about eliminating Montgomery if the circumstance presented itself.

But, for the moment, the problem of the witnesses had to be put on hold. First, deal with the FBI. And after that lay off the assassinations for a while, maybe until after the election.

After a warm, refreshing shower, in his pajamas, he poured himself a Jack Daniels and lit a welcome cigar. He was in his small apartment in the top floor of his Long Island mansion. He sat down and turned on the television to watch the news and catch up on the current affairs in the nation.

Bancock's apartment was relatively small, living room, kitchen, bath, dining room, bedroom and study. So, when he heard a sound of movement behind him, it was startling. He spun around, expecting to see one of his staff who had gotten into his locked apartment without authorization. What he saw made his heart beat faster.

Johnnie Limbo stood before him.

"What the hell!" Bancock exclaimed. "What are you doing here, you son of a bitch? You don't belong here?"

"I'm in your dream, Bancock."

"What are you babbling about? I'm not sleeping. Besides, I

228

didn't authorize you to be anywhere except where I command. Now get the hell out of here."

"You don't understand, Bancock," Limbo insisted. "You are sleeping! Take a look at your ashtray. Your cigar is burnt halfway down and it is out. If you are awake you'd be smoking it."

Bancock checked the ashtray by his elbow. The cigar had burned out. How could this be? He didn't remember putting the cigar down. He didn't remember smoking it.

"What the hell...?"

"I'm going to enjoy this, Bancock," Limbo said. " I'm here to kill you and you're going to die."

Bancock got to his feet. Fear shot through his body like a bolt of electricity.

Johnnie Limbo reached into his coat and brought out a Glock pistol endowed with a silencer and leveled it at Bancock's heart.

Oh God! No!

Bancock's heart gave out and his life ended in an instant without Johnnie Limbo having fired one shot.

\* \* \*

Gordon Aldrich knew he was free of Clayton Bancock and that the project was dead when the FBI agents invaded the headquarters in Northvale. When Aldrich realized what had happened, he knew he had made a terrible mistake in eliminating Bancock. The Feds were closing in and, if he had only waited, he might not have had to kill Bancock. Now, he had become what he abhorred, a murderer.

Damn it, he thought, he was already indirectly a murder. Bancock had forced him to use his process to kill and now, when it might not be necessary, he had murdered without being forced to do so.

So what, he thought. Damn them all! If he hadn't put an end to Bancock the madman might have continued to kill innocent people without regard in some other endeavor. Perhaps even Aldrich's own loved ones. He convinced himself that he had made the right decision. Maybe he was even a hero.

"My family," he asked of agent Farrell. "What about my family?"

"What about them?" Farrell inquired.

"They have been held hostage for months. It was Bancock. That bastard. I've been his prisoner here and my wife and daughter are prisoners. Lord knows where. He threatened me to perform at his will or my family would die."

"We'll get on it immediately," Farrell stated. "What exactly is it that has happened here? What is your project?"

Aldrich briefly explained how the DREAMS project was able to tap the mind of the selected victim and extract from the subconscious that person's darkest fears and transform them into a living nightmare, with Johnnie Limbo as the harbinger of death. And, ultimately, the fear of death was so real the victim goes into cardiac arrest while sleeping.

"Is such a thing possible?" Farrell demanded.

"Possible," Aldrich answered. "Yes. Not only possible. It is reality."

"And this hit man, Johnnie Limbo, where is he?"

"I don't know specifically. But I'd say he's got to be somewhere in the building."

# Chapter Thirty-Three

Johnnie Limbo was nowhere in the building. Like the vanishing shadow he had been all his life, he had simply disappeared. Federal law enforcement officers entered the small apartment to which he had been assigned and discovered nothing, not even a fingerprint.

Limbo had always been aware of the shortcomings of the life he lead. As a result, he traveled light. He left no traces. He had spent a lifetime training to be nothing more than a shadow.

He had established bank accounts and safe deposit boxes, both national and international, that he could tap into at a moment's notice. All were registered under aliases and code numbers. He had enough money tucked away to live out the rest of his life in some safe foreign country and not have to worry about repercussions from the feds.

Limbo was the product of a rough city street environment. Grew up in the South Bronx in New York City. Given over to an orphanage when he was barely in his teens. Ran away as soon as an opportunity presented itself.

Johnnie Limbo never knew his real name. All he knew, growing up in a rough New York City neighborhood, was that he had been dubbed "Limbo" by his peers, and the name stuck. He wasn't even sure of the surname John. His ethnicity could have been of any white European lineage; it was that difficult to trace his origins.

Johnnie lived on the streets, educating himself in the survival techniques and became part of a street gang in the Bronx. His group was known as *The Devils*. The gang was a racial mix; white, black, Hispanic. Johnnie fought his way into *The Devils*. He was a tough kid and proved his mettle in many street fights. The members sold drugs, committed numerous robberies, careful enough to break into homes only out of their territory. Their turf was sacrosanct in their beliefs.

He made a life as best he could on the streets. He was shrewd enough to survive on his own. There were times, during his teens, either in gang fights or individual muggings, when he had to make a quick and safe escape. Johnnie had learned to take flight during

231

the dark of night by escaping into the tunnels of the New York subways. He learned the byways of the tunnels and lost his persuers within minutes.

He easily escaped the adversaries above ground but found a new enemy in the myriad tentacles of the subway tunnels.

Rats! How he hated them.

Johnnie saw many rats in the dark tunnels. It had been estimated that there were more rats in the city of New York then there were people. Johnnie believed it. While escaping in the many miles of myriad tunnels Johnnie had seen more of the bastards in one night than most city people see in a lifetime; all sizes; some as big as cats.

Damn frightening sons of bitches. And you never knew where they were. Could be all around you, just waiting for you to let down your guard. He often thought that if he had gotten struck by a passing subway train and lay unconscious the rats would have devoured him as a meal. The bastards would eat anything.

God damn! The thought scared the crap out of him!

And now, here he was, in those tunnels once again, running for his life.

Was he wide-awake? Was this reality? What the hell was he doing here? Escaping. From what? His plan was to get out of the country. Overseas. Somewhere far from New York. Why would he elect to come down here in the subway tunnel? For old times sake? A last hurrah? It didn't make sense. Got to get out of here right away, he thought, whatever the reason.

He was deep into the tunnel. There was only the dim glow of light as far as he could see in either direction. Between stations, he thought. That's where I am.

He would never come here to escape; like he had in his youth. Had his subconscious mind decided to come here?

Never like this! It must be a dream, he thought. It has to be a dream. I'll wake up and leave this memory behind. That's all there is to it. It's just a dream.

Try as he might, he could not break out of the dream. He convinced himself he would find his way out of the dark into the light of a station. None was seen in any direction. But there ahead of him in the dim glow of tunnel light a dark shape appeared. It glided toward him as if floated a foot off the ground. Above the rats. It was a man.

Yet, not a man...

It was Elymas. He knew instantly.

"What the fuck is going on?" Limbo shouted.

"Why John, my boy," Elymas answered softly with a lilt of sarcasm. "It's time to say goodbye. That is all."

"What are you talking about?" Limbo said. "I'm getting out. My way. Take my money and run."

"Not quite, John boy. You have been invited into *my* dream, specially prepared for you. Just the way you like it. As the walrus said, 'The time has come.' *I* am running, John. You are not."

And Elymas was gone. Snap! Just like that. Gone.

In his place came a swarm of huge hungry...RATS!

Rats, as far as the eye could see, racing towards him like an unstoppable wave.

Not so fast, Johnnie Limbo thought. He had his Glock pistol with a full clip. He would shoot his way out. He could fire one shot and they would scatter in fear. The noise alone would scatter them. Give him enough time to learn his surroundings and make his escape. There were enough rounds in the pistol to clear the way to an exit.

The rats were coming in dense droves that he had never witnessed before; rolling waves of death, their sharp teeth seeking food to devour. He raised the pistol, aimed down at the horde and pulled the trigger.

Click! Nothing but a click. Again. Nothing.

What was happening? He fired again. Click.

And then they were on him. Covering him. Nothing could stop them now.

The little monsters ripped at his hands, his face, all flesh that was revealed. They ripped his clothing from him in shreds. He had no defense against the onslaught. He fell to the ground and was covered in an instant by the swarming sea of ravenous flesh devouring monsters.

Johnnie Limbo died in his bed of a heart attack and would not be discovered for a week after his demise.

\* \* \*

Jenni Butler had moved back into her apartment and settled into the future she must face. She hoped only for resolution to the trauma that had lately engulfed her life.

Her own fault, she believed. She realized that she alone had created the circumstances that had challenged her well-being. In playing with the reality of creative dreaming she had tapped into situations far beyond the realm of normalcy. What, she wondered, was the end game to this madness...this imaginary world that had become reality.

The phone rang. It was Carl Spendler.

"How are you holding up?" he asked.

"I'm okay. No problems so far," was the answer.

"Can I see you again?" Spendler asked.

"You want to see me?" she responded. "I should be asking you. I'm the patient, remember."

Spendler chuckled. "All right, then. I'd like to ask you to have dinner with me."

She was silent for a moment. "Certainly," she responded. "What's the occasion?"

"Nothing in particular. I'd just like to see you. Talk."

Jenni smiled. What was happening, she wondered gleefully. Was there more here than met the eye?

"Certainly," she replied. "I'd enjoy that."

Later, the couple had dinner at a restaurant near Lincoln Center. The conversation concentrated on Jenni's immediate plight and accidentally drifted into a discussion of philosophical opinion.

"Do you think we've seen the last of DREAMS? And that murderer who had been pursuing me?" Jenni asked.

"I hope so," Spendler answered. "It seems from what I've learned that the FBI and local authorities have shut down the operation. I'm so sorry this happened. I had never dreamed that organization had become something so evil."

"It's done now," Jenni said. "Just hope this is the end."

Spendler thought a moment about Elymas, his longtime adversary, with whom he had vowed to settle the score. The murder of his two closest friends had not been resolved. How to settle the issue remained an open wound.

The time to strike back was upon him and Spendler knew it. He must move before Elymas decided to make the first move against him.

*Dreams*

"About your book," Jenni said. "I read most of it. I'm not finished yet."

"My book," Spendler said. " So you're that one sale. What about it?"

"I really am interested. I'd like to hear more about the concept of the essence of evil you mentioned in it."

But Spendler wasn't sure if Jenni was serious or merely patronizing him to make conversation.

"Hell," Spendler said, "I don't want to dominate our dinner with my gibberish. I'm involved in this piece I'm writing now. It relates to one chapter in the book on the connection of good and evil in mankind as a natural phenomenon."

"I really am interested," Jenni said.

Spendler smiled, thinking what the hell. She certainly is a cut above the average. Not all physical like Jillian. This was a person with a brain.

"All right," he said. "Imagine this. What if evil is a natural behavior in all humanity? Assume it is a tangible force that exists from the beginning of time and is as strong and as equal as the supposed element of goodness. Assume that all humanity is composed of an equal balance of intrinsic good and evil."

"That's an interesting concept," Jenni said, her interest piqued.

Spendler continued, "Supposing humankind is not fundamentally good, but is equally balanced by an evil side. And let us suppose that evil side of humanity is suppressed mainly by rules laid down by society. Let's assume humanity is twofold in nature. The secular faction sets laws to control the evil nature while standards of morality come from the spiritual side."

"Are you talking about the stain of original sin?" Jenni asked, whose Catholic upbringing came to the fore.

"Could be," said Spendler, mildly impressed. "I don't necessarily believe in creationism, but this opinion could transcend religion. According to the religious aspect, the evil nature of man emerged with the fallen angel followed by Cain and Abel as stated in the Bible. Doesn't it follow then that God is therefore the creator of both good and evil."

"That's a hell of a difficult theory to push," said Jenni. "People think of God only as goodness."

"Yeah, it is difficult to maintain my belief. But think about it. If

235

God created all, then everything comes from Him...as first cause."

"Then God alone is not only goodness but is also the purveyor of evil as well," Jenni offered.

"Now, on the other hand, for the sake of argument," Spendler continued, "let's presume metaphysically that evolution is the route in which mankind developed. Let's say that there is no God; that the universe did not come from a divine source that has dominance over it all. Supposing the nature of man has always been evil from the time of The Big Bang; that goodness has to be learned and enforced. Would that not mean that we are all capable of committing unspeakable crimes if not for those laws society has laid down? In either case, religious or secular, does it not hold that man is basically evil?"

"I suppose that's possible," Jenni answered, her voice faltering.

"Jenni," Spendler said, wondering if the creases in her brow indicated her unwillingness to participate because her personal problems rose to the fore. "Are you sure you want to hear all of this?" Do I sound condescending, he thought.

"Certainly," Jenni responded, smiling.

"Well then," he continued. "Here is what I'm driving at. Imagine that evil exists as a tangible reality; as a physical substance emanating from God or The Big Bang, whatever, and has the ability to manifest itself into human form."

"And?"

"...And evil walks among us physically...corrupts mankind, proliferates evil, encourages corruption, brings it to the fore in all of mankind."

"What physical form would it take?"

"Human. A man."

"Are you talking Heaven, Hell...the devil? Satan? A fallen angel?"

"Possibly. Not necessarily the devil. Perhaps an emissary of either Satan...or God, for that matter. To test mankind. Not just one demon, but many. There might be demons in society who have been with us forever to balance good and evil. They bring us war, pestilence, crime, devastation. They manifest in such forms as Hitler, Der Veis Engele, Attila, Ghengis Khan, Tojo, Stalin, the terrorists we know now. It goes on."

"Are you saying that God created these evil people on

purpose?" Jenni asked. "To...maybe test us?"

"Good and evil both emanate from God. Yes. I have heard this belief before. Not as a theory but from someone who claims it as truth," Spendler said, thinking of Elymas, the evil one, who murdered his two closest friends, Roger Evans and the priest, Father Gerry Stuart. "His name is Elymas, a monster, who claims his allegiance was to God not to Satan?"

"Who is this...Elymas?" Jenni said.

"He is the purveyor of evil," Spendler answered. "And I truly believe he was the driving force behind DREAMS."

"DREAMS?" Jenni said. "You are referring to the institute on the river?"

"Yes. The man dressed in black you described. Who was standing with the killer from your dreams. That one."

"Yes. All in black."

"His name is Elymas. He is an emissary of evil."

"Carl," she said. 'Are you telling me that particular man is not human?"

"That is exactly what I believe."

Jenni rested her chin on her head and said, "Do you believe this, Carl?" She was, by now, addressing him by his first name.

"Absolutely. I've seen it manifested in this one person," Spendler stated. "This monster had caused the deaths of two close friends. I hope we never see him again."

\* \* \*

Every human being fears death. The unknown heightens that fear, not knowing how or when death will come. To die a horrible death is the ultimate terror. Each mind contains its own personal nightmare, created by some incident in life that seemed impossible to face.

Jenni's nightmare was that the blond man would kill her.

Edna Rothmann's was the fear of rape by a brutal man.

Johnnie Limbo was the fear of rats.

Carl Spendler's was about to unfold...

In his dream he was suddenly placed in the violent ward of an insane asylum. It was evening. There were no lights turned on yet. Grim shadows streaked the walls. Spendler was alone in the center of a long, straight corridor that housed the many rooms of the inmates. At the other end was a closed door with bars on the small window. Spendler immediately recognized his own nightmare. Must he live through it again? Was this yet reality or was he dreaming?

He knew what was going to happen and he was powerless to prevent it. He shuffled to the door, his feet dragging as if they were leaden weights. This, of course, was a dream, was it not? The door was locked as it always was. He struggled to open it. Outside was freedom. Here, inside the corridor, lurked only doom. He realized he was trapped in the violent ward of an asylum.

He knew what to expect. He had lived it before. The cell doors along the corridor walls opened one after the other and dark, subhuman shapes came from them. They slithered towards him, bunching together and sealing off any escape. Slowly, surely, they advanced towards him. Their eyes revealed a message of doom; their mouths drooled from their madness. They stretched out their ragged arms to him, to maim, to kill.

Fear raged through his body. His mind was ready to explode from fright. These people were all mad, psychopaths who kill without remorse, who knew no guilt. He was at their mercy.

They were closing in on him.

But surely he would wake up before they got to him. Always, as the fear peaked, he was awakened by his own terror and panic.

*No one ever dies in a dream.*

The gliding shapes surrounded him. Their claw-like fingers clutched at him, ripping at his face and throat with broken, ragged nails. They punched his body, pulled at him, dragging him to the cold, hard floor. When he was down they kicked him. Blood streaked his shattered face, his eyes completely closed. He threw his arms across his face to protect himself and screamed. They kicked in his ribs, driving shattered bone into his lungs.

This time he felt the physical pain along with the psychological terror. He was literally being brutalized and murdered!

Get hold of yourself, his mind screamed. This is Elymas at work.

His thoughts, as he fought eternal darkness were ... what had happened ... how had he gotten here? Where is the light? Force yourself to find the light. This was a dream! A nightmare fashioned by Elymas.

Spendler concentrated, staggered to his feet, laughed and shouted, "Fuck you, Elymas!"

His mind screamed. "Saint Paul outwitted you. He proved it has been done. And you know it. Like Paul, Jenni Butler is 'the thorn in my side.' Damn you to the hell God condemned you to. You are only what I allow you to be. You prey on the weak"

Spendler stood tall out of the madness, raised both arms to the sky and cried out, "God be my source. Rid the earth of this monster, this Elymas bastard whom you and you alone created. He is your creature. Return him to where he belongs."

And Spendler woke up in his own bed. Unharmed.

He rolled over and his left arm encountered the gentle touch of a female hand. Jenni Butler lay next to him in bed. She was awake.

"Are you okay?" she asked. "Your sleep seemed disturbed."

Spendler clasped her hand in his. "Just a nightmare," he said. "Nothing I couldn't handle."

Spendler and Jenni Butler had become lovers. It didn't take long for them to discover each other. They found more than just a common bond. On each level...Jenni found in Spendler the solid substance of a man who related to her in many ways...while Spendler discovered in Jenni both the physical and intellectual platforms to which he aspired.

They bonded sexually this morning as the phone rang.

Spendler reached over and lifted the receiver to his ear.

"It's Laura Whitney here," came the familiar voice.

"Laura," Spendler responded, his mind conjuring images of Laura Whitney's paintings in his subconscious. "How are you? How is the work going?"

"Fine. But here's why I called, Carl. You remember we thought we had seen Elymas himself when we had lunch?"

"Yes," Spendler answered.

"Well I'm sure of it now," Laura said. "At my book signing I saw him sitting in the audience."

"Are you sure?" Spendler gasped.

"Absolutely. And then he was gone in an instant. You know how he pulls that disappearing business. Presents a figure he is not in reality and then vanishes. He did it at the meeting."

"Laura," Spendler said. "I believe you. I didn't at first. But now there's no doubt. He was involved in a diabolical plot through

239

dreams to assassinate specific people in power."

"Through dreams?" Laura questioned. "How serious is it?

"It's damned serious. A long story. We'll sit down and discuss it."

A pause. Then Laura said, "We have got to do something about this situation. Especially in light of what you're saying. Assassination. My God, this is staggering in implication."

A pause, then Spendler said, "Laura, you must have had something in mind. Why did you call?"

"Remember what happened at the séance we conducted in Maine to summon Vera Lancaster, the medium?"

"How could I forget?" Spendler answered.

"Well, I want us to conduct another séance...again. Here in New York City. I want to summon her spirit once more. She seems to be the only power he fears. And remember, I am carrying her eyes. It might be easy for us this time."

"What could we hope to accomplish?" Spendler asked.

"We might rid ourselves of the demon once and for all," came the immediate answer.

* * *

The séance was scheduled to take place at Carl Spendler's house in the parlor. The participants were Jenni Butler, Carl Spendler and Laura Whitney. Spendler and Laura Whitney were major participants in the first séance conducted in Maine that conjured the demon, Elymas, into reality.

The members knew the end game was a challenge to trap the demon Elymas and eliminate his reign on Earth. They decided the only way was to summon the spirit of Vera Lancaster, the medium who had once brought Elymas into reality. She could be the catalyst needed to destroy the demon.

A white cloth was laid over a round table. Around the room the group placed white candles in brass candlesticks. Only the candlelight saved the room from total darkness.

They were ready to begin.

The three locked hands. Spendler joined with Laura, she with Jenni Butler. Jenni completed the circle by clasping Spendler's free hand.

## Dreams

Laura Whitney repeated, over and over, words that the deceased medium, Vera Lancaster, had scripted in her journal. Laura implored Vera Lancaster to make her presence known. She intoned the name of God, Christ the Savior, and the spirit of Vera Lancaster in that order, in the name of all that is holy and sacred.

After a seemingly suspended period of time, Laura's hand suddenly broke from Jenni's. Laura moved sharply, knocking her chair backwards with a clatter. She broke free of the hands holding her and pointed to wall near the windows. She stood up, fully erect, her arms outstretched. Something adverse was taking place within her own body. She groaned and squirmed, as if in agony. She clutched her head with both hands to crush the sudden pain and end the unwelcome occurrence.

Jenni and Spendler recoiled in wonder. Their hands parted and both stood gaping at the apparition appearing before their eyes where Laura Whitney pointed. A cloud of white spectral mist formed and swirled in a corkscrew gyration, swiftly becoming substance. Hovering in the air, it took human shape; a woman, her hands outstretched before her, the palms upturned, beckoning.

And Laura knew...it was the spirit of Vera Lancaster.

The spirit of the deceased medium appeared in full form. The face became defined. The ghost was angelic, dazzling in the light. Her countenance was unmistakable. A piercing, radiant light shone from the two hollowed-out cavities where once her eyes had been. The heavenly form moved swiftly. Her arms reached forward and enclosed Laura Whitney in embrace. The immaculate spirit flowed around Laura. Within seconds it dissolved and assimilated into her body, leaving behind, for a brief instant, a brilliant glow that lit the room.

Laura experienced a surge of energy flow through her arms and into her body. She was astonished. It was like an electric jolt. It had the sensation of a magnificent rapture that flooded her entire being, a concentrated center, an overall tingling of nerves. And then she felt it in her brain—a potent eruption of power that seized and took control of her movements. She was subjugated to the dominating force now within her.

This had happened to her once before at the séance conducted at Vera Lancaster's house in Maine. Laura was once again blessed with the spirit of Vera Lancaster's soul. As the power of Vera

Lancaster's spirit fully engulfed her body, Laura seemed elevated off the floor. She radiated a glow that seemed ethereal and in the instant it came, it was gone.

Laura reached out and clutched Vera Lancaster's journal in her hands and tucked it under her arm.

In the room, the distinctive, ethereal mist that was the spirit of Vera Lancaster floated in the air. Her vaporous substance swirled into an angelic female shape and rose out of the room. It glided upward, holding out both arms to the three astonised spectators and vanished as mysteriously as it had come.

"It is settled," Laura Whitney said with assurance. "She will see to it."

\* \* \*

Elymas, the clandestine demon in black, was proud of the DREAMS organization he had assembled in less than three years. As an emissary of evil, he appeared as a human many times over the two thousand years of his on-and-off earthly existences. While endowed with unearthly powers, each new life was extremely favorable to Elymas for he retained memories from life to life.

Over the eons of time Elymas had accumulated uncountable wealth. He had grown accustomed to the cherished earthly lifestyle in which he lived. And he loved the human body that this planet Earth provided. The pleasures associated with a body that did not age, the sensual and palpable favors that untold wealth could buy, the abridged powers over corporeal factors, all combined to convince him that life on earth was his preference...forever. No other life form, in all the planets he had been subjected to habitat, compared to the human body here on Earth. The life form was very efficient and provided all the sensations he thrived; not like some of the ridiculous living forms he had to accept in so many other planets. What good were three or four arms, when you only needed two? And two eyes were so much better than the one huge one in the center of an oversized head. And the wonderful women of earth, their soft, silky efficient bodies, so much more precious than some of the lumpy, spiny, two-headed monsters that existed in the universe.

He came to Earth to spread evil through the ravages of war,

pestilence, hatred, murder; all the grand schemes of The Master Himself. He delighted in corrupting humanity. What a thrilling way to exist.

In his grand penthouse on the Upper West Side of Manhattan, Elymas sat before his large-screen TV and watched Charlie Washburn on CNN. Throughout his speech he chortled at the senator's ludicrous phraseology and, by the time he finished, the demon emitted a stifled laugh. He poured a full glass of champagne, walked to the wraparound floor-to-ceiling windows facing west and, his black form silhouetted against the blazing setting sun, he laughed aloud.

He glanced down at the throng of pedestrians in the streets far below, like so many insects moving through the paved paths.

"Lenin was right," he muttered. "They *are* useful fools."

He reached his outstretched arms to the flaming sky as the unimpeded sun slowly withdrew from his part of the earth.

"A sign," he pleaded to *whatever gods may be*. "Give me a sign, Great Father. Is the time now?"

And suddenly, as he spoke, from out of the canopy of fire-filled clouds, a moving shape appeared in the distance, miniscule and dark at first. Breaking swiftly in small circles, it gathered substance as it dived downward. Larger. Larger. Now it took form. The shape became distinctive. It was an horrendous demonic bird. Its huge glowing wings swept outward, spreading from the body with each motion like exploding bursts of fire. From the legs there protruded two sets of giant claws, monstrous scimitars that clutched a delicate human form.

The giant bird loomed above the great deck of the penthouse directly over Elymas. It threw back its gargantuan head, spread its black beak and screeched. Its hollow flaming eyes, showing no pupils, appeared transparent as the fiery sky showed through them.

It gently deposited a human figure on the deck and hovered above the form in the air. Elymas glanced at the kneeling body facing him. It was a female.

The great bird opened its giant wings wide and engulfed the entire deck area, a gesture to protect its precious cargo. In an instant it released a blood red liquid that encompassed the exterior of the penthouse and flowed down over the windows. The monstrous bird became blood red. In moments the flowing liquid drained clear and nothing of its presence remained. The giant creature hovered protectively over the royal female.

The crouching figure slowly rose and revealed herself to him. She was a sign from infinity.

It was Vera Lancaster, the blind medium, who reached out one hand to Elymas, while a blinding light glowed from her naked hollow eyes.

"It is dreamtime," she said softly to Elymas. "Your time has come, my dear."

The tremendous bird suddenly snapped its gigantic head forward, the monstrous beak open wide. In an instant the demon bird devoured Elymas in one swift, horrendous gulp.

POOF! and he was gone, nothing more than fodder before the Gods.

The giant bird then gently engulfed his esteemed female passenger within its great wings and vaulted away into the setting sun. Gone, and with it, both good and evil.

And the sun had set, taking with it only the awareness that another day on Earth had passed. Nothing more.

# The End

www.ingramcontent.com/pod-product-compliance
Lightning Source LLC
Chambersburg PA
CBHW060423180626
46817CB00007B/2636